THE
KILLING
SHOT

D0958364

THE KILLING SHOT

JOHNNY D. BOGGS

PINNACLE BOOKS
Kensington Publishing Corp.
www.kensingtonbooks.com

PINNACLE BOOKS are published by

Kensington Publishing Corp.
119 West 40th Street
New York, NY 10018

All Kensington titles, imprints, and distributed lines are
available at special quantity discounts for bulk purchases
for sales promotions, premiums, fund-raising, educational, or
institutional use. Special book excerpts or customized print-
ings can also be created to fit specific needs. For details,
write or phone the office of the Kensington special sales man-
ager: Kensington Publishing Corp., 119 West 40th Street,
New York, NY 10018, attn: Special Sales Department; phone:
1-800-221-2647.

PINNACLE BOOKS and the Pinnacle logo are Reg. U.S. Pat.
& TM Off.

ISBN-13: 978-0-7860-2275-5
ISBN-10: 0-7860-2275-2

First printing: October 2010

10 9 8 7 6 5 4 3 2 1

Printed in the United States of America

For Verna, Vic, Cody, and Ma

CHAPTER ONE

That morning found him bleeding more than usual.

"You gotta keep your head back, Jimmy," Three-Fingers Lacy coaxed him in her nasal, whiskey-rotted drawl. "Keep your head back, honey, till the bleedin' stops."

"I keep looking into that sun," he told her, "I'll go blind."

"Close your eyes, sweetie," she said, and pressed the dirty, blood-soaked handkerchief tighter against his nose. "Close 'em tight."

Reluctantly, Jim Pardo obeyed, but it didn't help. Ten in the morning, and the sun blasted like a furnace. Of course, she could have suggested that they turn around, so they weren't facing the sun, but Lacy didn't have the brains to figure that out. It didn't matter. His neck hurt. Keep this up, and he'd get a crick. Blind, with a bent neck, and a bitch of a nosebleed. Wouldn't Wade Chaucer and the other members of his gang love that? He'd be deader than dirt.

"I'm gonna need another rag or somethin'," Three-Fingers Lacy said. "This one's soaked through." She pulled the handkerchief away. Her tone changed.

"I'm worried about you, Jimmy. It ain't never bled this much before."

She reached for him, but he shoved her arm away and slid off the boulder.

"Jimmy—"

"Shut up," he told her. "Where's Ma?"

He pinched his nose, looked at the blood on his fingertips, then wiped them on his vest. Three-Fingers Lacy dropped the bloody rag onto the dirt. The ants would love that. He scratched the palm of his hand against the hammer of his holstered Colt, looked around, tasting the blood as it dripped over his lips. He cursed his nose, loosened his bandana, and saw how his words had hurt Lacy.

Hell of a thing, he thought, softening, and gave her a reassuring grin. "Don't fret over me, Lacy," he told her. "Nosebleed ain't going to bury Bloody Jim Pardo. Thanks for looking after me."

"It wasn't nothin', Jimmy. Ain't that what wives is supposed to do?"

His smile turned crooked. Wife. Concubine. Whore. Whatever she was. He rolled up the bandana and placed it under his nose, holding it there with his left hand, keeping his right near the Colt.

"Where's Ma?" he asked again.

"Up yonder with The Greek." She pointed.

He had to tilt his head back again, but the flow of blood seemed to be slowing. It wasn't fair. Pardo never knew when his nose would start acting up. He had stopped six or seven bullets, plus a load of buckshot. He didn't recollect how many men he had killed, and there were prices on his head here in Arizona Territory, plus in New Mexico Territory, Texas, Missouri, Kansas, even California. He led a gang of the toughest black-hearts he had ever known. Seven men, plus his mother and Lacy, not including Bloody Jim Pardo himself. But his nose, and those cursed weak veins, could stop him cold, damned near put him under.

He checked his watch.

"Running late," he said, and swore.

"What if it don't come?" Lacy asked. "What if there was some accident?"

"It'll come," he said. "The accident won't happen." With a wry chuckle, he pointed. "Till right there."

"But Jimmy—"

"Why don't you pour yourself a bracer?"

"It's nine in the morn, Jimmy. That ain't proper."

The smile and friendliness vanished. "What the hell do you know about proper?" He walked down the hill toward the Southern Pacific tracks.

They had never tried robbing a train. Banks, stagecoaches, mines, Army paymasters, regular citizens, and wagon caravans, sure—so many times, Pardo had lost count—but never a locomotive, yet Ritcher had told Pardo about the payload, even suggested the place to pull off the robbery, and the Army major had never led them astray yet. Number 18 would be hauling passengers and an express car loaded with greenbacks for the soldier boys stationed at Bowie, Lowell, Huachuca, and every other post that stank of Yankee fools in the Sonoran Desert.

She would come charging around that blind curve, and the boys would jerk the rail loose, sending the locomotive and her cars crashing down the embankment, likely killing everyone on board, and thus making it easy for Ma and the boys to collect the strongboxes full of money. They could take anything of value off the dead passengers and be back in their hideout in the Dragoons before the blue-bellies knew they wouldn't be collecting their fifteen dollars that month and those fools waiting at the Tucson depot realized their loved ones were feeding buzzards.

With dead eyes, Wade Chaucer watched Pardo slide down the hill. Despite the heat, Chaucer wore a coat of black wool, a fine silk shirt, and red necktie accented with a fancy diamond stickpin. The coat remained unbuttoned, and the slim fingers of his right hand drummed a tune on the holster he kept below his stomach. His left hand emptied a cup of coffee by his black boots, and slowly pushed back his wide-brimmed gray hat.

"How's your nose, Pardo?" he said easily.

Smiling, Pardo slung the bloodstained bandana over his neck, but didn't bother to tie the ends into a knot. That would take two hands, and Pardo wasn't foolish enough to give Chaucer any notions, or chances.

"I'll live," he said.

Chaucer grinned back. "For how long?"

"Longer than you."

With a shrug and a bow, Chaucer said in Spanish, *"Vamos a ver."*

They were opposites, and Pardo hated Chaucer for it. Wade Chaucer was tall, handsome, knew about good wines and champagne, wore a nickel-plated Remington, and could speak, when he wanted to, like an educated man. Pardo had even heard him talk in some fancy language. Latin, Chaucer had told him. Ma had never got around to teaching Jim Pardo how to read, probably because she couldn't read or write herself, though she often pretended to.

Pardo couldn't make five-foot-four with two-inch heels on his boots, and he dressed like some saddle tramp with an old Colt that was beaten and scarred, but well-used. So Chaucer and Pardo despised each other but needed each other.

At least, for now.

Pardo pointed a short finger at the small fire a few yards away underneath a outcropping of rock, a blackened coffeepot on the coals. "Your idea?"

Chaucer's reply came as a shrug, but the gangly man with the rough beard squatting next to the fire answered for him. "We rode hard, boss man. Ain't et nothin' since day 'fore yesterday. We figured coffee would put somethin' in our guts."

Pardo's right hand gripped the Colt, and he glared. "I'll put something in your gut right now, Duke, if you don't put that fire out. If that engineer spots our smoke . . ."

"The fire's small, boss man, and we built it under—"

Pardo drew the Colt, but Duke started furiously kicking sand over the fire, spraying the pot and cups while he pleaded with Pardo that he was doing it, he was doing it, the fire was out, no harm had been done.

Glancing back at Chaucer, Pardo kept the Colt level. The black-clad gunman merely smiled and rose easily.

"Train isn't here, Pardo."

"It'll be here. Major Ritcher said—"

"What if it doesn't come?"

"Then you can help Duke build another fire and make another pot of coffee."

"Where's Lacy?" Chaucer looked up the hill.

Pardo shoved the short-barreled .44-40 into the holster. "That's Missus Pardo to you, pal."

"So you keep reminding me."

The flash of white light caught his eye, and Pardo was moving past Chaucer and Duke, stepping up a series of rocks. He saw the sunlight reflecting off his mother's Winchester.

"Train's coming, boys," Pardo said, his smile widening again, and he whipped off his sweat-stained hat, and waved it at the lookouts, turning, moving quickly.

"Duke, you sure those ropes are tied good?"

"Yes, boss man!"

"They'd better be. Soledad!"

Two wiry Mexicans in buckskins, appearing out of nowhere, suddenly slid down the hill.

"You and your brother know what to do, *amigo*?" Pardo asked.

"*Sí,*" the older one, with the salt-and-pepper mustache and goatee, answered.

"Then do it. Come on, Chaucer."

Running now, sniffing, Pardo climbed back up the hill, kicking dust and gravel at Chaucer, who was coming up right behind him. Three-Fingers Lacy had found a bottle where he had left her, but she quickly corked it and dropped the rye in the brush beside her.

"The train?" she managed.

"Get to the horses," Pardo barked. "When that train goes over, it's going to sound like the world's coming to an end, and if those horses spook, leave us afoot, we're all dead. But you'll be the first to reach hell, girl. Phil?"

"It's done, Jim." *Good old Phil,* Pardo thought. Phil had been riding with Pardo since Missouri during the War. He was the only man out here Pardo could trust, though not enough to turn his back on him.

He spotted the dust, sifting off to the southwest on the other side of the butte, and heard the hoofbeats as

Ma whipped the bay gelding. *That old woman must have been born in a saddle,* Pardo marveled, as she reached the bottom and never slowed, leaping over the Southern Pacific rails, then swinging from the saddle and handing the reins to Duke. Winchester in her left hand, she scurried up the hill and slid to a stop.

"How you feeling, Jim?"

"I'm fine now, Ma," Pardo answered. "Finer than frog hair cut eight ways. Where's The Greek?"

"Up yonder. With his Sharps. Just like you wanted."

"Good. How far away's the train?"

"It'll be here in a few minutes. Then it'll be in hell."

He laughed. There was nothing to do but wait.

The Greek, that sharpshooting son of a bitch, would keep them covered with his .45-70 in case anything went wrong. Three-Fingers Lacy and Phil would hold the horses. Soledad and Duke had mounted up and dallied the ends of their lariats around the saddle horns. As soon as they heard the train roaring around that curve, they'd spur their mounts and pull out the rail they had loosened last night. Soledad's brother, Rafael, stood closer to the tracks, his hands gripping a double-barreled Parker ten-gauge.

Pardo, Ma, Chaucer, and Harrah, who had just come out of the brush after nature's call, stood on the ledge, hands on their guns, sweating, hearts pounding, excited.

Black smoke drifted into the pale sky. That was all for several minutes. Then they could make out the chugging engine. Pardo wet his lips. At least his nose had stopped bleeding. He scratched the palm of his hand on the .44-40's hammer. The chugging turned into a roar, almost deafening it seemed, but Pardo figured that had to be his imagination. Smoke, thicker now, blackened the sky as the 4-4-0 Baldwin rounded the curve and came into view.

Immediately, the air brakes screamed, and the giant wheels bit into the rails—even before Soledad and Duke spurred the horses and jerked the rail off the track. That engineer was savvy, Pardo conceded, had a pair of eyes on him a falcon might envy. Must have spotted the ropes tied on the loose rail, hit the brakes, and tried to reverse the engine. But that old 4-4-0 was going too fast. Trying to make up time. Damned shame. Pardo laughed.

One man leaped from the cab. The fireman, Pardo figured, and then Pardo saw nothing but dust, steam, black smoke, and black metal. The 4-4-0 leaped off the rails and slammed down the embankment, the tender toppling over and crashing down on the locomotive as it smashed a boulder and toppled onto its side, followed by a violent explosion that knocked Pardo off his feet and started his nosebleed again.

His ears rang, and the dust blinded him. Pardo swore, trying to find his Colt, but he had lost it. He shook his head, felt strong fingers on his shoulders, and he fought them off, but couldn't, felt the fingers biting into him, shaking him. Then he heard the words:

"Son. Jim! Jim! It's me. It's your mother! Son! Are you all right?"

Another explosion.

He shook his head. Tried to answer his mother. Tell her he was fine.

Metal smashing metal, the splintering of wood, savage blasts, and that damned ringing in his ears. Pardo tasted blood again. He spit. Cursed. Felt his mother putting the Colt in his right hand, and he saw her old, weather-beaten face, those cold blue eyes, felt himself being helped to his feet. His hat, somehow, remained on his head. He pulled it off, waved at the dust, seemed to tell his mother he hadn't been hurt, and wiped the blood from his nose with the back of his left hand.

The hellish noise ceased, as did the ringing in his ears, and he walked to the edge and looked down upon his handiwork.

Beside him, heavy sarcasm laced Wade Chaucer's laugh.

"Is that the way Jesse James used to do it, Pardo?" Chaucer asked.

A piercing scream sounded below. Ignoring Chaucer, Pardo looked at the tracks. The bay gelding his mother had given Duke was a gory mess, but Duke seemed to be all right. So was Soledad. He couldn't say the same about Soledad's brother, who lay writhing on the ground like a dying snake. Soledad tried to hold him down. Duke stared, gagging, at Rafael's bloody body.

Pardo spit and looked down at carnage that had once been a Southern Pacific train.

The tender, smashed to pieces, lay atop the locomotive, which had been turned into nothing more than a pile of twisted black metal that looked as if it had been blown apart by ten howitzers. The express car and two passenger cars had slid off the rails and fallen onto their sides before the caboose had flown over the rails, splintering the last coach.

"Which one's got the money, Cap'n?" Harrah asked.

"Express car." Chaucer answered for Pardo. "The one that's burning like hell."

Pardo's eyes smarted. Damned car was going up like a tinderbox. Wood crackled, and Rafael screamed for mercy.

"The money," Harrah said. "The Army money. It's burning—"

"Check on Lacy and the horses, Ma." Pardo's voice was soft. He wet his lips, shoved the Colt bitterly into the holster. "Tell Phil we won't have need of the buckboard."

Chaucer snorted again.

"One more snigger, and I'll bury you here, too." Pardo spit again, before turning to Harrah. "All right, boys. Might as well go check out the passenger coaches before they go up in smoke, too. Salvage something out of this mess."

He slid down the hill and made a beeline for Soledad, Duke, and what once had been Rafael. When the engine's boiler blew, it had sprayed slivers of wood and steel like grapeshot. The bay gelding had caught most of the blast. Rafael had gotten an unhealthy chunk. Only something short of a miracle had protected Duke, Soledad, and the other horse, not to mention Pardo, his mother, and those watching from the hilltop.

Blood poured from both corners of Rafael's mouth, his nose, and what looked like a thousand holes in his body. His left arm was gone at the elbow, and a piece of metal three inches wide and two feet long stuck out of his groin like a saber. Pardo knelt beside him and slowly lifted his head to find Soledad.

Tears streamed down the tall Mexican's face. He crossed himself, and made himself look at Pardo. He mouthed something in Spanish. Pardo didn't know what he had said for sure, but he knew what he had to do.

Slowly, he drew the Colt, thumbed back the hammer, and shot Rafael in the head.

"Sorry, *amigo*," he told Soledad, as he stood, shoving the revolver into the holster.

"*Gracias*." Soledad wiped his eyes with a gloved hand. "With your permission, I will take my brother back to the home of my blessed mother."

"Take your time." That was proper. He liked the Mexican for that, for thinking of his mother. Family was important. The most important thing, maybe, next to money and dead Yankees. "We'll see you in the Dragoons."

Pardo was moving again. Seemed like he was always moving. He saw the fireman, half-buried in debris, his neck broken, and wondered if he'd find the engineer somewhere beneath the rubble, probably his hands still pulling on the brake. The engineer had died game, which is more than he could say about the fireman. Or Rafael. Or Ma's bay gelding.

He slid down with an avalanche of stones, dirt, and pieces from the train, feeling the heat from the roaring fire, put his hand on the smashed wood of the second passenger coach, or maybe it was the caboose. Hard to tell amid all this ruin. A fire had started licking its way down the smashed wood. Behind him, The Greek was riding his dun horse down the butte, letting the horse pick its own path downhill, keeping his Sharps cradled across his saddle. Harrah and Chaucer were checking the first passenger coach. Mostly Harrah. Chaucer had kept his distance from the wreck. Now Duke ran over to help.

Pardo swallowed and looked into what once had been a window of the second coach. He saw a dead man's face, and walked on, then stopped, frozen.

Harrah had climbed out of the ruins of the first coach, stopping to mop sweat off his face with a calico bandana. Behind him rose a small arm, so white, so stained with blood. The scene completely mesmerized Pardo.

The fingers stretched out, fell on Harrah's shoulder, and Harrah screamed.

CHAPTER TWO

Charleston's whores came out that morning to serenade the Kraft brothers.

A couple of strumpets, Deputy U.S. Marshal Reilly McGivern decided, could actually sing, so well that he found himself humming a few bars of "When Johnny Comes Marching Home" when deputies Gus Henderson and Frank Denton led L.J. and W.W. Kraft, arms and legs chained, out of the jail and toward the black-barred prison wagon waiting for them at the corner of Stove and Second streets. Deputy Slim Chisum, who was the definition of the word *cautious*, climbed into the wagon's driver's box and thumbed back the hammers of his sawed-off twelve-gauge.

Reilly pulled open the door at the back of the wagon and waited.

Next, the whores started "Oh, My Darling, Clementine," which everyone seemed to be singing that year. Reilly hated that stupid song and tried to hum "Lorena" instead, but he couldn't keep it up because of the whores, who crowded Charleston's streets while other residents, the kinds usually seen on the streets in the daylight, gathered along the boardwalks—

keeping a respectable distance, naturally, from the whores—to watch the show.

It had turned hot that morning, and the air stank of the smoke pouring out of the stamp mills along the river. Reilly shot a glance at the rooftops, spotting the sheriff's deputies and town marshal's men in position, rifles ready, and made himself relax. K.C. Kraft wouldn't try anything today. Not here. The only threat out in Charleston, he thought with a grin, was a case of the clap.

He kept his left hand on the door.

Marshal Zan Tidball had spent a lot of money on this prison wagon, and Reilly had decided it would pay for itself once he got the Kraft brothers to Yuma. If he got there. It was a black wagon—except for the freshly painted yellow wheels, and silver words, U.S. MARSHAL, ARIZONA TY., on the left side—with a wood bottom, housing an iron jail on the bed that would soak up the Arizona heat like the sand swallowed water. The iron bars allowed a breeze, at least, and they could chain the brothers to the floor if needed.

Marshal Ken Cobb, who typically oversaw the district that covered Cochise and Pima counties, had instructed Reilly to transport the prisoners in the wagon along the San Pedro River north to Contention City, where they would board the train to Benson, then catch the Southern Pacific all the way to Yuma, where they would deliver the two Krafts to the warden at the territorial pen.

Simple enough.

Except everybody in Arizona Territory knew about it, including K.C. Kraft, the third, and meanest, brother, who hadn't been captured or killed. So Reilly had thought of something better, although he hadn't gotten around to telling Cobb or Marshal Tidball, or anyone else. Hell, Reilly never had been good at following orders.

"All right, ladies," he said easily. "Let's make room for the gentlemen."

He wore blue trousers tucked inside black, $15 stovepipe boots inlaid with green, four-leaf clovers; a mustard and brown-checked collarless shirt; faded blue bandana; and a wide-brimmed, flat-crowned hat the color of wet adobe. A six-point star hung from the lapel of his gray vest, and a long-barrel Merwin, Hulbert & Co. .44 fit snugly on his right hip, six shells for easy access on the tooled leather holster. He turned so that the Krafts couldn't reach the revolver, and let the whores keep singing.

L.J. Kraft climbed into the wagon without a word, but W.W. stopped to hold out his manacled hands.

"How about taking these bracelets off, Mac?" W.W. showed his yellow, crooked teeth.

Reilly stared.

"Hell," W.W. said, "I just want to feel Matilda's titties before I take my leave, and don't want to hurt her none with this iron."

Somewhere in the crowd, Matilda giggled.

"That iron," Reilly said, "stays on till you get to Yuma."

"You ain't Cupid," W.W. said, and climbed into the wagon with his older brother. Reilly slammed the door, locked it, and tossed the keys to Frank Denton.

"Gus," Reilly told the young, pockmarked deputy, "get up there with Chisum. Frank, fetch our horses." He looked at the rooftops again. A sheriff's deputy nodded that everything looked fine. Reilly let out a breath.

"All this for just us two poor, misguided souls." W.W. Kraft laughed. "We can't be *that* dangerous."

No, Reilly thought. K.C. was the dangerous one. The free one. That's what worried him.

The whores started singing "Rock of Ages."

Stepping back, Reilly wiped the beads of sweat peppering his forehead.

"Why don't you shut them the hell up, McGivern?" Slim Chisum grumbled from the driver's box. He hadn't lowered the hammers of the scattergun.

Reilly shrugged. "Maybe I'm Cupid after all," he said, but not loud enough to be heard, and walked across the street toward Denton, the horses, and, most importantly, Reilly's .44 Evans Sporting Rifle in the saddle scabbard. Taking the reins from Denton, Reilly started to swing onto the buckskin gelding. That's when he saw her, moving through the crowd down the boardwalk, past Wilbur's Tonsorial Parlor, and into the sea of whores.

He almost didn't recognize her, not wearing that French sateen skirt with the ruffled bottom and the silk ottoman wrap. Then again, he tried to think of how many times he had seen her with her clothes on. Not that many. At least, never for long.

"Oh, hell," he said, and tossed the reins back to Denton.

She was moving fast, reaching into her purse.

The whores had started singing "Ar fin y don," a Welsh tune he'd often heard Gwendolyn sing. That'd be ironic, he thought, shoving one strumpet aside.

One flailing arm knocked his hat off.

He kept moving.

She was standing in front of the bars now, right hand coming out of the purse. No, the purse was falling into the dust. No one noticed her. Not Matilda. Not the other whores. Not Slim Chisum, Gus Henderson, or any of the guards on the flat roofs. Not

W.W. Kraft, whose hands gripped two iron bars, as he leaned forward and kissed a whore whose name wasn't Matilda. Not L.J. Kraft, who sat in the shade, working on a mouthful of chewing tobacco.

She pulled out the sawed-down Colt, cocked it, and aimed the .36 at W.W. Kraft's chest. Finally, one of the whores spotted her and screamed. W.W. Kraft pulled away from his lover. His mouth fell open. His brother spit between the bars.

Gwendolyn Morgan pulled the trigger.

The hammer caught Reilly's left hand as it came down on the Colt, biting into the meaty flesh between his pinky finger and wrist. Blood spurted. It hurt like hell. He shoved Gwendolyn aside, felt the hideaway gun fall into the dust, and he kicked it underneath the wagon.

"What the hell?" Slim Chisum called out.

"She tried to kill W.W.," a whore cried.

"Bitch!" Matilda snapped.

Reilly put his right hand to keep Gwendolyn back. He saw her now, the ugly bruise that blackened the left side of her face, down which tears streamed. Her eye remained almost swollen shut. Her lips trembled.

Blood dripped down Reilly's fingers into the dust.

W.W. Kraft giggled. "Gwen, ol' gal, are you still mad at me?"

His brother shifted the plug of tobacco to the other cheek. "She come from Contention to see you off."

"Hell, Gwen, you didn't need to do that. We's going to Contention City. I could have given you some good loving there."

"Shut up!" Reilly snapped, and W.W.'s face froze. He pulled Gwendolyn away from the wagon, steered her across the street. "Gus, get that belly-gun from under the wagon. Now!" One of those whores would likely pick it up, slip it to one of the Krafts.

She was sobbing, shaking with rage, when they reached the boardwalk. Her head fell on his shoulder, and he let her cry.

Cupid, he thought, and cursed silently.

Slim Chisum had had enough. He braced the shotgun on his left thigh, and let one barrel sing. "I've heard enough music today!" he bellowed. "You strumpets, get gone. Everybody get gone. This wagon's leaving for Contention, and if I sees anybody—wench, baker, miner, or parson's wife—anywhere on the street in the next two minutes, I'll blow him or her apart." Pellets from the first load rained onto the roofs of nearby buildings.

The concert was over.

"Reilly?"

She had pulled away from him. He tried to smile.

"I'm sorry, Reilly. I hurt you."

"I'll be fine," he told her, but she had lifted his left hand, found a handkerchief, and wrapped it around the torn flesh.

"You need a doctor."

"It's nothing," he told her again.

She looked past him, at the prison wagon. "I want him dead."

"I don't blame you. But Judge Spicer gave him and L.J. fifteen years."

"Not for what he did to me."

Reilly put his right hand under her chin, turned her face toward him. "He'll get his, Gwendolyn. Fifteen years in Yuma . . ."

"If he gets there."

He frowned.

"Can you get back to Contention?" he asked.

"I made it here."

"You best go. Matilda's girls can be meaner than guttersnipes."

"I can take care of myself. Maybe I should have waited till you brought him to Contention." She smiled at him. She had quite the smile, even with her face disfigured by that bastard W.W. Kraft. "Can I see you in Contention, Reilly? I won't try to kill that peckerwood. I promise."

He started to say something, stopped himself, then decided to tell her. "We're not going to Contention."

"What the hell?" The words came from Gus Henderson, who stood at Reilly's side, stupidly holding Gwendolyn's Colt and purse.

"Be quiet, Gus," Reilly said. He cursed his own stupidity. Should have kept his big mouth shut.

"Gwendolyn, you get back to Contention. Pretend that you're waiting for us. Anybody asks you, I told you that I'd see you in Contention before the train left. That'll buy us some time. Do this for me?"

"Sure, Reilly."

She took the purse and reached for the belly-gun, but Gus pulled it back, eyeing Reilly.

"Give it to her," Reilly said. "It's some rough miles to Contention."

She took the gun, dropped it into her purse, and hurried down the boardwalk, rounded a corner, and was gone.

"We're supposed to catch the train in Contention," Gus said.

"We're not," Reilly told him, and looked across the saddle at Frank Denton.

"Everybody knows we're going to Contention." Reilly spoke in a hoarse whisper. His left hand throbbed. "Including K.C. Kraft."

"It's about three hundred miles to Yuma," Denton told him. "Across the desert."

"I know." Reilly wet his lips. "K.C.'s not going to let his brothers reach Yuma, not without making a play. He'll be waiting for us in Contention, maybe Benson, maybe Tucson, or somewhere on the road, somewhere on the rails. When we don't show at Contention, he'll start wondering, fretting."

"And looking," Denton said.

"And looking," Reilly agreed. "But looking west of here. We're crossing the San Pedro and riding northeast. Skirt around Tombstone, through the Chiricahuas, and to Fort Bowie."

"That's the opposite way of prison," Gus told him.

"But I know an Army officer at Bowie." Reilly ran his fingers through his unruly brown hair. He realized his hat was gone, saw it in the dust on the street. "He's agreed to let us tag along with a company he's leading to California."

"The Krafts aren't a military matter," Gus said. "Why would he do that?"

"Because I asked him." Reilly was losing his patience. He hadn't planned on telling them this until they crossed the river. "And the Army doesn't like the Krafts any more than we do. We ride with them. It'll take longer, but I don't think even K.C. would attack a company of cavalry."

"Does Cobb know about this?" Denton asked.

"'Course not."

Denton chuckled. "You got style, Mac. I like it."

"I don't," Gus said, pleading. "I just got back from Dos Cabezas, Reilly. My wife'll worry sick if we don't get to Contention. She's bringing me fried chicken for the train. You got to let me go tell her, Reilly. Before she leaves. Before we leave. Please, Reilly, *please*!"

Underneath his breath, Reilly McGivern muttered, "Cupid." He shook his head, but sighed. "All right. Go tell her. But tell her not to breathe a word of this to anybody. *Nobody*. If she wants you alive. If K.C. Kraft finds out, we're dead. Savvy?"

"Thanks, Reilly." Gus dashed down the boardwalk.

Frank Denton led his dun toward the prison wagon. A bandolier full of the large .44 shells for the Evans rifle dangled from the saddle horn of Reilly's buckskin. Reilly slipped the canvas over his shoulder, grabbed the buckskin's reins, and followed Denton, picking up and dusting off his hat on the way.

A vast emptiness, the Sulphur Spring Valley could hide hell. Seemed like a body could see forever, only there was nothing much to see among the Dragoons, Chiricahuas, and other brown, mostly barren mountains that tried miserably hard to make the country look somewhat hospitable.

For the past hour, a dust storm had choked and scalded the lawmen and their prisoners, but finally the winds had abated, and Reilly McGivern pulled down the bandana that had been covering his nose and mouth and sucked in a lungful of air that didn't taste of dirt and smell of acrid creosote. His face felt heavy with dirt and grime, and he reached for the canteen secured around his saddle horn. He took a long pull.

"How about some *agua* for me and my brother?" W.W. Kraft asked.

After swallowing, Reilly nudged his mount close to the prison wagon and stuck the canteen between two hot, black bars.

"Not too much," Reilly warned. "That's got to last us to Bowie."

"If I poured it out, you'd be in a fix." W.W. grinned.

"Nope. But you'd be."

The slim gunman laughed. "You got sand, Marshal, and savvy. Me and my brothers respect that, even in a law dog. Especially K.C." He wiped his mouth, and tossed the canteen to his brother. "We'll regret killing you. Well, not really."

L.J. Kraft drank little water before returning the canteen to his brother, who took another long pull. The iron bracelets sang a metallic tune as they scraped the iron bars when W.W. Kraft handed Reilly the water.

"Much obliged," Kraft said. "How much farther was it you said before we hit Fort Bowie?"

"I didn't say." Reilly made sure the canteen's cork was firm, then wrapped the rawhide sling around the saddle horn.

W.W. Kraft held up his hands and let the chain and cuffs rattle. "How about giving my wrists a break?"

"You heard me back in Charleston."

"Yeah. *The iron stays on till . . .* you don't trust me, do you?"

The prison wagon lurched over brush and sand.

"The newspaper over in Tucson once wrote that Mrs. and Mr. Kraft couldn't spell, and that's how come us brothers got only letters for our names." The dust storm had forced W.W. Kraft to keep quiet. Now, he was making up for it. "But they stand for something. W.W. stands for Wily, because I'm mighty smart. L.J. stands for Loco, because my big brother is slightly tetched in his noggin. You know what K.C. stands for, Marshal McGivern?"

Reilly tried to ignore him.

"Crafty. Best keep that in mind, pard."

The Chiricahua Mountains looked closer, but not close enough. They'd keep climbing in altitude, cut through Apache Pass, and they'd be safe. Well, safer. They'd still have maybe 375 miles across Arizona Territory to Yuma. Reilly started questioning his plan. He didn't care much for what W.W. Kraft had to say, but he knew the outlaw was right about one thing. The middle brother, K.C., was crafty.

And cold-blooded.

"McGivern," Chisum called from the wagon as he tugged on the reins and set the brake.

Reilly and Frank Denton stopped their horses. "I got to piss," Chisum called, and leaped from the box, carrying his shotgun as he walked a few rods and began unbuttoning his trousers.

After pushing back his hat, Reilly looked up at Gus Henderson. The boy wasn't yet twenty-two years old, and his face was pale. Not from the heat, either, Reilly figured. Kid was nervous. Had been fretting since they'd left Charleston. Maybe that's how you acted when you were married.

"Still worried, Gus?" Reilly walked the horse closer to the wagon. He had to ask again before the boy heard.

"Huh?" Gus's Adam's apple bobbed.

Reilly wet his lips. He doubted himself again, muttered an oath underneath his breath.

"Reilly," the kid said, tears welling in his eyes. "I . . . I . . . oh, God . . ."

That's when Reilly knew for certain, but it was too late, because the first bullet sang across the valley's desolate floor.

CHAPTER THREE

Screamed like some damned petticoat. *That's the kind of men I get these days*, Jim Pardo thought with disgust. Yet the shriek had snapped Pardo out of his inability to move, and now he watched as Harrah turned around, clawing for his Smith & Wesson. The small, bloodstained hand dropped from his shoulder, fell on the wooden wreck.

"Don't shoot!" Pardo yelled. He made a beeline for Harrah, the white arm, and the ruins of the passenger coach.

Harrah was still breathing heavily when Pardo reached him, the big-caliber .44 Russian at his side. The white hand gripped the cracked door frame, followed by another small hand, and a small head appeared. Blond hair, matted with blood, sweat. Next came the face, also small, also white, bloody, with brilliant green eyes.

"Hell," Harrah said, and laughed a silly laugh. "It's just a little girl."

"Just like you," Pardo said. "Put that damned gun away."

The girl's mouth moved. *Help*, she pleaded voicelessly.

"What is it?" asked Duke, standing near the inferno of the express car.

"A girl." Harrah's voice giggled with nervous excitement. "Scared the hell out of me, she did."

The Greek had ridden over, still mounted, cradling the heavy Sharps, watching. Wade Chaucer kept his distance, as well, those dead eyes taking in the scene.

"Help me," the girl croaked.

Only Pardo moved. "Easy," he said, like he was approaching a green bronc, holding out his hands, trying to smile. "Easy, girl." He put his hands under her armpits. She grimaced. "I'm sorry," Pardo said. He could feel heat from the flames sweeping across the coach. He pulled. The girl screamed. Her blouse caught on a splinter of wood, ripped. Next came duck trousers, and dirty brogans. *Pants?* Pardo wondered. *Pants on a girl?* He laid her on the ground at Harrah's boots, and her eyes fluttered open. She couldn't be older than twelve. Likely a whole lot younger, but Pardo didn't know much about kids.

She tried to rise, but Pardo, kneeling over her, pushed her down, as gently as he could. "Stay put," he said.

"Bull!"

Pardo pulled back as if he had been struck by a diamondback, blinked away his amazement. She shoved his hand away, scrambled to her feet, grunting, gasping, and headed back to the burning wreckage. Pardo followed, angry, shocked by the kid's language, but she was fast. He barely caught her before she disappeared into the twisted metal and thickening smoke, had to pull the girl away, kicking, screaming, trying to claw his eyes out.

Somewhere, Wade Chaucer laughed.

"My mother!" the girl screamed when Pardo dropped

her on the dirt again. "My mother's in there, you damned fool!"

Her yells stabbed at his heart. He wasn't aware he was moving until he heard Duke's shouts, warning him not to go, that he'd burn to death, but Pardo was already climbing into the scorching destruction. Coughing, gagging, blinded, he felt his way, cut his left hand on something, saw the red dress, the disheveled blond hair—just like the girl's—and tossed a stovepipe off her leg.

He felt a presence, tried to blink away the tears welling in his eyes. It was Phil. Good old Phil.

"Help me get her out of here," Pardo said, choking on the smoke. He could feel hell at his back.

Pardo took the arms of the unconscious, maybe dead, woman. Phil gripped her feet. They moved, coughing; then Phil was staggering into the daylight. Someone came to help, and Pardo cleared the smoke, leaped off the coach.

His mother beamed as they carried the woman away from the burning mess.

"Plunder's gettin' better," Duke said.

They laid her on the ground, and Pardo backed away, rubbing his eyes. His mother came to him. "You all right, Jim?"

He coughed again, slightly waved off her concern. "Be fine. Let me catch my breath."

"That was a brave thing you done, son."

"It was nothing, Ma."

"Get me some water," the girl demanded.

Harrah spit at the unconscious woman's head. "There," he said.

Pardo took a step past his mother, watched the girl manage to stand and face Harrah. "My mother needs water," she said, her voice cold, firm.

"You got balls, girl, but I ain't wasting precious water on no woman who'll be dead in ten minutes," Harrah said.

Pardo saw the little Sharps in her waistband, saw her pull it, long before Harrah did, and grinned at the girl's spunk. It was a four-barreled .32 Triumph, and the kid jammed it into Harrah's crotch.

"You don't get some water, you'll not have any balls to speak of," she told him, and thumbed back the tiny hammer.

The Greek laughed.

"What the hell's the matter with you people?" Pardo snapped. "That's a lady lying there, and she needs water." He went to Harrah and the girl, jerked the .32 from her hand, and gave Harrah a savage shove. "Fetch a canteen. Phil, I reckon we'll need the buckboard after all."

"We're takin' 'em with us, boss man?" Duke asked.

"Yes. Of course we are. Ain't that right, Ma?"

"Whatever you say, Jim."

Chaucer shook his head. "This whole thing has been a bust."

"You think so, Wade?" Pardo dropped to a knee, put the back of his left hand against the woman's cheek. If not for the blood, the busted nose, she'd probably be a fine-looking woman, and her breasts put Three-Fingers Lacy's to shame. He grinned. Lacy would be almighty pissed to have this woman tagging along with them. She might strangle the woman in her sleep.

Harrah handed him a canteen, and he wet down his bandana, put it on the woman's forehead. She stirred slightly, shivered, and went still again. Pardo bit his lip until he detected her chest rising and falling.

"I don't think it was a bust, Wade," he said again, washing the blood off her pale face. "Not at all."

"We didn't get that money," Duke reminded him.

"And the Army ain't, neither. Blue-bellies can't spend ashes, and that's all that'll be left of that damned Yankee payroll." He looked up at Harrah. "What'd you collect off the people inside?"

"Not much," Harrah said timidly.

"What?" Pardo demanded.

"A couple of watches and a money belt. And a broach."

"Too busy looting the dead to notice a kid and her ma, I reckon."

"You told us to—" Harrah stopped himself.

"Give your plunder to Phil. Have him put it in the wagon. We'll split it up when we get back to the Dragoons. Like we always do." He handed Harrah the canteen, checked the woman's ribs, her arms, her legs. "I don't think she broke anything except the nose and some ribs," he told the girl. "And I can fix the nose." He winked at the kid. "I'm right experienced with busted noses."

The kid lifted her mother's head, and let Harrah give her a sip from the canteen. Most of it ran down her face and into the dust.

"She might be bleeding inside," the girl said.

"Can't do nothing about that," Pardo said, "except bury her when the time comes."

Somewhere from the bowels of the wreckage, a scream suddenly sliced through the morning air. The whippersnapper of a girl went rigid, and Harrah dropped the canteen.

"Careful with that water, you damned fool," Pardo barked.

Another scream. Then nothing but the roar of the inferno.

"Poor bastard," Pardo muttered. He looked at the girl again. "What's your name, kid?"

She glared at him. "I don't have to tell you damned bushwhackers anything."

He backhanded her and stuck a finger under her trembling lip. "And I can throw you and your ma back inside that coach, and you can burn like that poor, dumb, screaming bastard just did. I like grit, kid, but just a little of it for flavor. What's your name?"

Her lips still quavered. But she was too damned stubborn to cry. "Blanche," she answered at last.

"How old are you?"

"Ten."

Ten, and a mouth like that. He stared at the unconscious woman. That would make the woman thirty, perhaps younger. Didn't look much older, even with her face and body all beat to hell.

"And your ma? What's her name?"

"Dagmar."

"Dagmar what?"

"Dagmar Wilhelm."

"All right, Blanche Wilhelm, we're going—"

"I'm not Wilhelm. My name's Blanche Gottschalk."

Pardo blinked.

"My father died," the girl had to explain. "My mother remarried."

"Gottschalk. Wilhelm. I don't know which name's ornerier on the tongue."

"Gottschalk," Chaucer said. "It means 'God's servant.'"

"I wouldn't know nothing about that," the kid said, which got a laugh out of Chaucer.

"Where were you bound?" Pardo asked.

"Tucson," she said.

"That where your pa, your new pa, lives?" Pardo asked. He was thinking that a husband might pay a handsome reward for a woman like this, maybe a few bucks for the spitfire of a stepdaughter, too. It was something, he figured. Something to keep a lid on the tempers of the boys, because, no matter what he could claim about burning Army money, Chaucer had been right. This damned robbery was a bust.

"Sigmund Wilhelm," the girl said, "was probably that poor, dumb, screaming bastard we just heard." She turned away, dropped her head, and whispered, "He was a poor, dumb bastard, too."

"That ain't right, girl," Pardo roared, his finger back in Blanche's face. "You don't speak like that of your pa, stepfather, no kin. You don't speak of them like that." But he was thinking: *My pa was the same, kid. Just a poor, dumb bastard.*

He rode in the wagon with Ma, the kid, and the woman. Wouldn't trust any of his men with such a fine-looking lady. He also rode with the watches—one with the glass busted, no longer running, but the gold would bring enough for a whiskey—broach, money belt, and other items Harrah hadn't bothered to mention, their loot for their first, and last, train robbery. Pardo decided he'd stick to other ventures such as stagecoaches, banks, and the like.

They had left the burning wreckage, camped that night in an arroyo, and crossed Alkali Flat the following morning. Most of the boys wanted to stop at Dos Cabezas, but Pardo and his mother knew better than that. Yankees weren't fools. Nor were the Southern Pacific brass and Cochise County's law. Probably, a posse was already raising dust from the bend in the tracks, moving south, heading for Bloody Jim Pardo and his gang.

He bathed the woman's face again with a wet bandana. Her eyes fluttered, opened, and darted from Pardo to the sky, to quiet little Blanche, who firmly held her mother's hand. The woman might live after all, Pardo thought. Thanks to his doctoring. He'd even set her busted nose. Swollen, purple, but it would look almost normal in a week or two. So would Dagmar Wilhelm.

"Ma'am," Pardo said, but the kid's voice drowned him out.

"Mama!"

Dagmar Wilhelm wet her lips, tested her voice, forced a smile. Then her face changed. "Where's . . ." Barely audible. "Sigmund?"

Blanche didn't answer. The woman's eyes locked on Pardo.

"She's awake, Ma," Pardo said happily. He couldn't look away from the woman. Green eyes. Just like her kid.

"That's fine, Jim." Ma showed no interest in the woman, but she had never liked any woman, especially not Three-Fingers Lacy. "Just fine."

"What happened?" Dagmar tried again.

The kid cleared her throat. "These bastards derailed the train. Killed every—" She stopped herself.

Pardo smiled. "James B. Pardo, ma'am. At your service." He tipped his hat. "I pulled you out of the pits of perdition, Miss Dagmar. Saved your girl's hide, too."

Her eyes squinted. "Par-do?"

"Call me, Jim, ma'am. I'd be honored."

He put his hand on her shoulder, felt her entire

body tense. Closing her eyes, she mouthed the words:
Bloody . . . Jim . . . Pardo . . .

With a sigh, Pardo shot Blanche an angry look, then felt the buckboard stopping. He turned toward the driver's box, saw his mother setting the brake, reaching for her Winchester. The boys had reined in their mounts, too, atop a ridge.

As Pardo rose, drawing his Colt in the same motion, he saw the turkey vultures circling overhead, and the black wagon and dead horses, mules, and men down below.

CHAPTER FOUR

The buckskin's front legs buckled as Reilly swung his left leg over the saddle, trying to pull the Evans rifle from the scabbard, yelling something at Denton and Chisum, looking for the powder smoke to find the location of the bushwhackers, watching Gus Henderson dive for cover into the driver's box, searching for something that might resemble cover, all in one motion, in a matter of seconds.

A bullet sang past his nose. Another ripped the horn off the saddle. The buckskin dipped forward, then fell away from the wagon, landed hard on its side, shuddered, and went still. Reilly managed to free the Evans, leap clear of the tumbling dead animal. A slug carved a furrow across his neck. Blood and sweat dampened his shirt, his bandana. He cocked the rifle with his right hand, drew his revolver with his left, pressed back against the dead horse.

He tried to breathe.

Bullets slammed into the buckskin, kicked up dust around him. The mules pulling the prison wagon lay dead in their traces. Beneath the wagon, he could see Denton's dead horse, but not the deputy. Nor could he spot Slim Chisum, but he knew they were dead, knew he should be shouting at the devil himself.

Above him, around the driver's box, Gus Henderson showed his head. Reilly fired the Merwin with his left hand, and the traitorous deputy's face disappeared. The shot had gone wild, the kick of the big .44 almost breaking Reilly's wrist. He had never been much of a shot with his left hand.

Another cannonade of fire pounded into the dead buckskin. Then laughter. Reilly looked up to see W.W. Kraft's face behind the iron bars.

"Told you my brother was crafty," W.W. said. "Told you you'd never get me to Yuma."

Reilly lifted the barrel of the Evans, and W.W. screamed, "You can't—"

Reilly pulled the trigger as the outlaw dived. Sparks flew off the iron bar as the chunk of lead ricocheted and thudded somewhere in the wagon's bed.

"Jesus, McGivern!" Kraft yelled. "We're unarmed!"

Reilly shot again, then sank deeper as K.C. Kraft and his men cut loose with several more volleys.

Tilting the barrel downward, he levered another round into the .44, and rolled over, testing his neck. Just a crease. Wetting his lips. Sizing up his chances.

Chances? He tried to laugh but couldn't manage anything more than a silent sigh. None. Livestock all dead. Denton and Chisum dead. That left him alone with two unarmed men in the prison wagon and Gus Henderson, that son of a bitch, cowering in the driver's box with a Winchester and Colt.

The sun was a blistering white orb, high in the sky. A long time till sundown. He wouldn't live that long. The dead horse gave him some cover, but Kraft had at least five or six men with him. One of the rifles sounded like a Sharps, so K.C. would send his best sharpshooter around to a new position. Before long, the man with the Sharps would begin taking a few shots, find his range, and Reilly McGivern would be dead.

He loosened his bandana, tied it across the wound in his neck. He could run. But where could he go? They'd cut him down before he got thirty yards. He could toss away his weapons, give up, let them shoot him dead when he rose.

"L.J.," said a voice Reilly recognized.

"Yeah, K.C.," the middle Kraft brother called from his hiding place on the floor of the prison wagon.

"You and W.W. all right?"

"For now."

"Hey, lawman!" K.C. Kraft shouted. "You hear me?"

Reilly stared at the prison wagon.

"It's McGivern!" W.W. cried out. "Reilly McGivern, K.C. That bastard took a shot at me."

"Just keep your damned head down, little brother, and shut up. Reilly! You want to stay alive?"

Silence.

"You're alone, Reilly. I can sweat you out. I can ride you down. Or, you toss away your guns, I can let you walk out. Walk out of here. Walk and live. Name your pleasure."

Nothing.

"It was a good plan, Reilly. You almost got away with it. But let's consider where you are now. The law don't know where you are. It's too far from Dos Cabezas or Fort Bowie to expect help from there. You're alone. There's nothing to do, Reilly, but surrender. While you still can."

Reilly eased up the barrel of the Evans slightly. Wet his lips. Pulled the trigger.

Thirty grains of exploding gunpowder rifled a

220-grain centerfire bullet through the wagon's black wooden side, blowing out a chunk of wood, and whined off the iron frame.

"Christ almighty!" W.W. Kraft yelled. "We're unarmed. You can't shoot us—"

"Can't I?" Reilly's voice was hoarse, but he made sure all of the Krafts, and that coward Gus Henderson, could hear him. He jacked another shell into the rifle and slid over a few feet, while K.C. started talking.

"Don't you fret, boys. Reilly, your bullets won't go through iron. You can't get a clear shot from where you're lying down, and if you stand up or move, you're dead. You're making a fool's play."

The Evans boomed. The bullet slammed into the iron wall behind the driver's box, put a dent in Marshal Tidball's prized possession, cut down, and whined off the floor somewhere out of his view. L. J. and W.W. cried out in terror.

"Bullets don't have to go through iron," Reilly said. "Ever seen how bad a ricochet can tear a body up, K.C.?"

"Reilly!" K.C. yelled. "Reilly, that's murder!"

"I don't give a damn."

Silence.

"Odds are against you, Reilly," K.C. Kraft tried again, but he no longer sounded so sure of himself. "Hitting one of my brothers—"

He shot again, jacked the lever, fired again, and again, and again. Let the smoke cleared, then shot twice more, listening to the bullets whine, and the Kraft brothers scream. His bandana was soaked with sweat and blood, so he unloosened it to wipe down and cool off the rifle barrel. As far as Reilly knew, he was the only man in Arizona Territory with an Evans rifle. Marshal Cobb called the weapon a pain in the arse, and sometimes Reilly would agree with him. He had to go to Tucson to get the ammunition, and even that was getting harder to come by since the Evans Repeating Rifle Company had gone out of business three or four years back, and the big rifle was damned heavy and cumbersome, but Reilly loved it. Especially right now.

"K.C., you stupid ass!" L.J. shouted when the din faded into the desert heat. "You ain't the one stuck in here. Bastard just nicked my left earlobe."

"I'm hit, too!" W.W. whimpered. "He blew off my damned boot heel."

Reilly shot again, pushed out cartridges from his bandolier, and began reloading the rifle.

"He'll be out of bullets soon," K.C. said.

"Like hell," W.W. argued. "That rifle of his holds more rounds than an armory."

Reilly almost smiled. W.W. was right. Designed by, of all people, a Maine dentist, and featuring a rotary magazine in the walnut stock, the Evans had a 30-inch octagonal barrel that could chamber twenty-eight .44 cartridges—earlier models could hold more than thirty shells—and Reilly had filled every loop on the bandolier with a cartridge before leaving Charleston.

He wouldn't die for a lack of ammunition.

Out of the corner of his eye, he caught the flash of light, and rolled, pulled himself closer to the dead horse, already drawing flies. Off to the northeast, maybe three hundred yards, among a couple of spindly ocotillo cactus that were probably in a dry wash. That would be the man with the Sharps. At least, that's where Reilly would have gone.

Reilly wiped sweat off his brow, rested the barrel against the buckskin's stiffening forelegs, adjusted the tang sight he had a Tombstone gunsmith add two years back, and waited.

"Reilly!" K.C. yelled. "Looks like we're at a standoff. I don't want my brothers dead, especially not shot without a chance. And you don't want you dead. Let's work out a deal. A deal that'll leave everybody alive."

"Everybody?" Reilly said, never taking his eyes off those ocotillo. "What about Denton and Chisum?"

The wind kicked up.

He drew a breath. Waiting. Exhaled.

He made out the figure, or what he guessed to be the man with the Sharps, adjusted his aim for the wind, and squeezed the trigger. The Evans roared, but he detected something behind him and rolled, working the lever, cursing, seeing that Gus Henderson had found his courage, was leaping from the driver's box, swinging up the Winchester.

Reilly's lever jammed. If the Evans had one flaw, it was its tendency to jam. That's one reason the company had gone out of the rifle business. Reilly swore again, pitched the .44 aside, reached for the revolver. Henderson's shot spit sand into Reilly's face and kicked away the Merwin. Reilly grabbed for the pistol again, Henderson's shot almost tore off a finger or two, and the deputy was pleading: "Don't, Reilly. Please don't."

He made another play for the revolver. Had to. This time, the Winchester's slug spanged off the pistol, and Reilly let out an exasperated sigh. Slowly, he rolled away from the revolver, knowing it was over, that Gus Henderson wouldn't give him another chance, that the Merwin was ruined, that his rifle was useless.

That he was as good as dead.

"I got him, Mister Kraft," Gus Henderson shouted, smiling. "I got him covered."

K.C. Kraft smoothed the handlebars of his reddish brown mustache. Except for those big ears of his, most people considered him a good-looking man: cowlick that gave a little height to his hair and forehead, a firm jaw, angular nose. He wore a brocaded vest, and, satisfied with his mustache, removed his wide-brimmed straw hat, and began running his fingers around the sweatband. Waiting. Studying Reilly with his brilliant hazel eyes while W.W. exchanged boots with the dead Slim Chisum and other men rolled smokes or reloaded their weapons.

One man rode up from the ocotillo-dotted arroyo, but didn't bother to dismount.

"Carter's dead," the man said. "Gut shot. Bled out mighty quick."

K.C.'s eyes twinkled, as he set the straw hat back on his head. From his vest pocket, he found a cigar, and nodded at Reilly. "You that good?"

"Scratch shot," Reilly admitted.

"I'm reckon Carter'll appreciate knowing that." Still looking at Reilly, he said, "You about done, W.W.?"

"Just about."

They had stripped the dead of money and watches, gone through the weapons—tossing Reilly's jammed Evans, bandolier, and busted revolver atop the dead buckskin—and tied a silk rag tightly over L.J.'s bloodied ear. One of the riders had taken his gunbelt and shoved Frank Denton's weapon into the holster. Another was pulling coin and scrip out of Reilly's pouch.

"You probably could have held us off," K.C. said, "if it hadn't been for Judas here."

Gus Henderson's head dropped.

Reilly spit. "No. You would have killed me."

"Maybe. But you probably would have shot one, or both, of my brothers to pieces."

He jutted his jaw at the Evans. "Jammed. That ended it."

"Would have been interesting, though," K.C. said, "if not for Judas."

Gus Henderson choked back something, and toed the sand with his right boot.

K.C. Kraft struck a lucifer against the butt of his holstered Colt and fired up the cigar. He took a long pull, removed the cigar, and asked, "You want a smoke, Reilly?"

He shook his head.

"What about you, Henderson?"

The deputy looked up.

"Don't give me that look, boy. So you sold out your pards. You had good reason. Woman in the family way. You making hardly no money to speak of, risking your life for Arizona's finest citizens. Reilly don't blame you none, do you, Reilly?"

If Reilly had planned to answer, he never got the chance. Heavy iron slammed into the back of his head, and the next thing he saw was sand. His head throbbed. Blood matted his hair. He felt himself being jerked up, and he tried to shake away the pain, blink back the tears.

Heavy iron, hot from the sun, fell against his right wrist, and he felt the manacles tighten. Laughing, W.W. Kraft squeezed the other cuff until it bit deep into his left wrist, then held the key in front of

Reilly's face, and dropped it in the dirt beside the dead buckskin.

"That iron stays on," W.W. said, "till you get to Yuma." Even L.J. laughed with his brother, and Reilly felt rough hands jerk him back, shove him. The heavy door opened. After they threw him inside, he heard the door clang shut. And more laughter.

With iron-cuffed hands, he gripped the hot bars, pulled himself to his knees. The Krafts mounted their horses, and W.W. tipped back his hat with the scattergun—Slim Chisum's twelve-gauge—he held in his right hand. "Don't look like you're going to get to Yuma no time soon, Mac. That's too bad."

K.C. jerked the cigar from his mouth, as if it suddenly had turned bitter, and threw it in the dust.

"He'll die here." Gus Henderson's voice trembled.

"Look around, boy," L.J. Kraft said. "You helped send two other lawmen to their demise. *Now*, you're getting soft?"

The young deputy stared at his dirty boots and walked toward a ground-reined bay horse without shooting Reilly another glance. Sighing, maybe even crying, he grabbed the reins and mounted. Immediately, W.W. Kraft jammed the shotgun's buttstock against his shoulder, and cut loose with both barrels, blowing Henderson out of the saddle. The bay bolted toward distant buttes, and other horses danced nervously from the deafening roar, the fresh scent of blood.

Eyes and mouth open, Henderson lay faceup, spread-eagled on the ground, his chest blown apart by buckshot at close range.

"Damn you, boy," K.C. said, trying to control his big dun mare, "why'd you do that? I gave that kid my word."

"Your word? To a law dog?"

"My word, you jackass." He pulled the reins tight, and the horse stopped twisting, though, snorting, it fought the bit, eyes wide.

"He sold out his own men," L.J. Kraft said. "Sold them out for money. A Judas."

"That's right. A turncoat," W.W. said.

K.C. turned his horse around, waved a hand at Reilly, and coughed out a mirthless chuckle. "Reilly," he said, turning. "My idiot brothers have short memories, don't they?"

"Appears," Reilly said.

"If not for Henderson," K.C. said, turning back at this brothers, "you two would be dead. Reilly would have seen to that. That Judas saved your lives. I wasn't about to forget that. The money I promised him, well, that'll be going to his woman. And it'll be coming out of your share."

The brothers said nothing, although W.W. looked like he wanted to. L.J. tugged at the bandage covering his bloody ear.

"Look at him," K.C. said. "That's murder. Next time you go up in front of a judge, it ain't going to be fifteen years you're looking at. It'll be a hangman's rope. Same as me. Now ride out of here, boys. All of you. Ride hard. I'll catch up."

The younger Krafts, and the five other riders spurred their mounts. For a long minute, K.C. watched the dust, and eased his mount toward the wagon. Turkey buzzards already circled in that dead sky. He found his canteen, offered Reilly a last swallow of water. Reilly took a long pull before returning the canteen.

"This ain't my doing, Reilly," K.C. said softly. "I want you to know that."

"I know it."

"I would have killed you quick."

"I know that, too."

"But this had to be left up to my brothers."

"Makes sense. I arrested them. I was taking them to prison."

"Yeah." K.C. looked through the bars, past Reilly, at the rising dust. "You got family, Reilly?"

He shook his head.

"Lucky," K.C. said absently, and galloped after his brothers.

CHAPTER FIVE

You could smell the stench all the way up the ridge.

Below, coyotes pulled noses and fangs away from one of the bloated mules, spotted the riders, and took off running toward an arroyo. Above, buzzards kept circling in black-winged silence.

Pardo climbed out of the wagon, dropped to a knee, and studied the valley.

"That's a prison wagon," Harrah said. "I seen one just like it in Prescott."

"I got a better look at one over in Yuma," Duke said. "Got a real good look. From the inside." He laughed and mopped the sweat off his neck.

"Shut the hell up," Pardo told them. His eyes went over every rock, every cactus, every hole.

Nothing stirred except dust and coyotes. Four mules had been pulling the wagon. Two horses, one close to the black wagon, the other off a few rods on the far side, equally still. Pardo could make out a body near the bloated mules, and something, or someone, lay inside the jail-on-wheels. Nothing else.

Leather creaked, and Pardo looked up to find Wade Chaucer pulling a spyglass out of his saddlebags.

Pardo hated Chaucer for that, too. The gunman slid open the telescope and looked—slowly, carefully—then shook his head.

"Nothing's moving down there."

"I can see that," Pardo said. "Without no fancy glass."

The telescope slid shut with a snap.

"We could ride around this," Three-Fingers Lacy whined. "I don't like it. Let's ride around, pretend we never seen nothing."

"Bloody Jim Pardo don't ride around nothing," he told her angrily. "But he don't ride into nothing, either."

"We can't wait here all day," Chaucer said, "not with that posse likely on our trail."

"Something's in that wash," The Greek said. "I don't know what."

Pardo turned quickly, and Chaucer jerked the telescope back to his face. They stared. "The Greek's right," Chaucer said. "Looks like a man in that ocotillo. But he's not moving. I think he's dead. Everyone down there's dead."

"Greek." Pardo stood. "Make your way down that way." He directed with his finger. "Into the arroyo, come on up alongside those cactus. See about the man there. If he's dead, good. If he ain't, kill him." He let out a mild chuckle, and walked to the edge of the wagon, holding out his arms toward Blanche whatever-the-hell-her-name-was. "Come here, little darling," he told her. "Uncle Jimmy's got a chore for you."

The girl didn't move.

"Come here, you damned little wench, or I'll rip the veins out of your throat."

She leaped over the buckboard's side, avoiding

Pardo's hands. The kid's mother tried to rise, said something in protest, but sank back onto the rough bed they'd made for her. He shoved Blanche forward, and pointed at the wagon and animals. "You're going down there, kid. Just walk down this hill, make sure that ain't no ambush."

The girl took in the scene quickly, and shot Pardo a hard look. "There's not a damned thing down there but dead animals and deader men." White-faced she was, but gamer than many of Pardo's men. He liked that about the girl, but didn't let that show.

"You don't get a move on, Blanche, and there will be a dead ten-year-old girl down there, too. *Vamanos.*"

A weak cry rose out of the buckboard. "Shut up, you hussy," Ruby Pardo told the kid's mother, and reached for the can of snuff she kept at her boots. "Ain't nothing going to happen to your girl."

Pardo took the Winchester from his mother's hand, squatted again by the team of mules, and watched.

"There's another body," Chaucer said, still looking through his telescope. "Pinned underneath that horse on the other side. I don't think this is any ambush, Pardo. Was an ambush, yes. But not now."

"Likely you're right, Chaucer," Pardo said easily. "But you don't mind if I play this hand my way, do you, pal? I'm cautious by nature when it comes to my hide." He shot a glance behind him, saw that The Greek had made his into the arroyo, and looked back at Blanche. The kid was halfway down the ridge.

Her knees buckled and she fell. She tried to stop the rising bile in her throat, but gagged and vomited all over her dirty brogans. She wanted to turn, run back up the hill, but knew better. *You're tough, girl*, she told herself. *There's nothing down here that can hurt you. What can hurt you is up that ridge.*

After wiping her mouth with the back of her hand, she staggered to her feet, and went forward, keeping her hand over her nose and mouth. Her eyes burned from sweat, from the stink. So hard to breathe. A gust of wind pushed a black cloud of flies off the dead mules, and she came to the dead man.

His shirt, once white, was blackened by blood. His face had . . . She looked away, and wretched again, falling, putting out her hands, catching the hot iron bars to keep from sinking.

When she forced her eyes open, she found another body, manacled hands reaching out toward the locked door, the wind blowing through his curly hair that wasn't pasted with dried blood.

Blanche let out a sigh. She wasn't as tough as she tried to make others believe.

She stepped from the wagon, read the words on the top of the iron cage.

U.S. MARSHAL, ARIZONA TY.

Something moved off to her right, and she jumped, stared, mouth dropping open. A man. A man was rising out of that wash, amid the ocotillo, and she tumbled backward, almost falling on the bullet-riddled carcass of what once had been a beautiful buckskin horse. Then, the dead man, the man in the wagon, rolled over, and she whirled but had the sense, the will, not to scream. His face looked leathery, but the dark eyes flashed open, and the cracked lips parted.

Blanche looked away. Back toward the cactus.

Her heart skipped, and she realized it was The Greek, raising his big rifle over his head, signaling the others. She turned, faced the ridge, saw Bloody Jim Pardo tossing his mother the rifle and climbing back into the wagon bed with Blanche's mother. The older man, the one called Phil, eased his horse down the slope, and others followed.

She spun around, focused on the man in the wagon. His eyes had closed. He was probably dead. His hands were manacled, but something wasn't right. Her eyes locked on the six-pointed star pinned on the vest's lapel, and she moved back to the wagon, stuck a trembling hand through the iron bars. She looked back at the dead man on the ground. He was wearing a badge, too. Deputy U.S. Marshal. So what was this one doing locked inside a jail-on-wheels, wearing handcuffs?

The dark eyes opened, and the lips tried to form a word.

Water.

"You a real lawman?" she asked.

"Yes." Barely a whisper. And again: "Water." But she couldn't hear him, just read his lips. The eyes closed.

She reached for the badge. He jerked back into consciousness, the manacles grating as he dragged his arms across the iron floor, toward her hand, tried to stop her, but he was too weak.

"Mister," she said, "I don't know who you are, but I'm guessing you don't belong locked up in this box. You damned well better be a lawman. If you ain't dead yet, listen to me." She pulled off the badge, surprisingly heavy, secured the pin in its clasp, and slid the piece of nickel into the pocket of her trousers. "My ma and me are prisoners of Bloody Jim Pardo, and him and his gang are coming down to fetch me.

And maybe you. Though they might kill you." She felt the bile rising again, knew she was about to throw up, if she had anything left in her gut, knew she had to finish quickly. "Don't tell them you're a lawman. That's your . . . *our* . . . only . . ."

"This one's dead, too," Duke called out well beyond the prison wagon, and followed that with a laugh. "Some son of a bitch stole his boots. Don't that beat all? He was a lawman till the end. No boots, but he's still got his badge, by golly."

The Greek pointed the barrel of his Sharps toward the arroyo. "The one there had no badge, just a bullet hole. . . ." He stuck his thumb right underneath his rib cage. "Right here."

Blanche let out a weary sigh. "That one's still alive, I tell you!"

Pardo ran his hand across the beard stubble on his face. The girl started again, pointing at the still body on the floor of the wagon. "Harrah, check on the one locked up."

"I don't see no key."

"You need a key for everything?" Pardo said wearily.

Harrah's gun roared. He pulled the door open and went inside, while Pardo found his canteen and drank greedily. Three lawmen, all deputy U.S. marshals, dead in the desert. Another man over in the ocotillo, maybe one of them, maybe one of the gang that shot them to pieces, dead with a hole in his brisket. Dead mules. Stinking horses, and plenty of tracks heading south.

"How long you reckon, Ma?" Pardo asked.

Ruby Pardo sent a stream of tobacco juice between

the mules pulling the buckboard. "No more'n two days. Likely the day we was wrecking the S.P."

"Hell," Harrah said softly, then louder. "Hell! That girl's right. This fellow . . . he ain't dead!"

Pardo moved back to the black iron cage, past the ten-year-old, as Wade Chaucer, the lazy bastard, nudged his horse toward the wagon and drew the nickel-plated Remington with his left hand, handing it, butt forward, toward Harrah. "Here," Chaucer said, "put him out of his misery."

"Leather that gun," Pardo said, and stared through the bars at the tall man. "We ain't killing nobody. Yet." He lifted his gaze at Harrah. "How bad is he?"

"Man ought to be dead," Harrah said. "Been baking in this oven for a day or two. Looks like he caught a bullet across his neck. Back of his head, hair's matted with dried blood, too. He taken a pounding it'd take me or you a month of Sundays to get over."

"You maybe," Pardo said. "Not me."

"Well, sure, yeah."

"Get him some damned water!" the girl barked. "What kind of men are you?"

"Shut up," Pardo told her, but he nodded at Phil, who removed the canteen from his saddle horn and headed for the wagon.

"Somebody wanted this hombre dead," Pardo said, nodding at his deduction. He pointed at the bullet scars denting the black wall at the front of the wagon. "That's for sure. And wanted him to hurt before he went under."

"That the way you figure it, son?" his mother asked.

"Yeah. I think so." To the men in the wagon: "You recognize him?"

Harrah shook his head, lifted the unconscious man's head as, uncorking the canteen, Phil said,

"Nope," splashed a little water in his free hand, and wet the man's lips. The man stirred, and Phil gave him a little more water.

"Three lawmen guarding one man. Maybe four lawmen." Pardo's head bobbed again. "If that one in the arroyo was with them. Either way, that's impressive. Mighty impressive."

"What's so impressive about that?" Chaucer asked.

"Jimmy," Three-Fingers Lacy whined from her horse. "This place smells bad. I'm about to get sick."

"It makes me wonder," Pardo answered Chaucer. "That's all. Get the bracelets off that gent, boys. Put him in the back of the wagon with the petticoat. If he lives, I'd like to talk to him."

Chaucer snorted. "Maybe next time we'll bring an ambulance with us instead of a buckboard."

"Maybe next time, you'll need an ambulance," Pardo said. "Or a hearse."

The gunman frowned. "All right, Pardo. Since you've figured everything out, you tell me something. Where were they hauling your impressive prisoner?"

"Yuma," Duke answered bravely. "They haul prisoners to that hellhole in this contraption."

"Wagon's not pointed toward Yuma," Chaucer countered.

"Fort Bowie," Pardo said. "Could be this gent was bound for Fort Bowie. Maybe from there, they'd send him to Leavenworth. I'll see what the major knows, next time we have us a palaver."

"Jimmy!" Three-Fingers Lacy cried again. "I'm getting sicker."

While Harrah and Phil carried the unconscious man from the marshal's wagon to the buckboard, Duke almost tripped over a rifle, covered with dust, leaning against the bloated remains of the buckskin horse. "I ain't never seen no long gun like this," he muttered, and picked up the weapon. He tried the lever, tried harder, then swore, spit tobacco juice, and started to bust the rifle against a wagon wheel.

"Give me that thing, you damned fool," Ruby Pardo said from the buckboard, and Duke quickly obeyed.

"It's jammed, Miz Ruby," Duke told her. "Lever won't work no more."

"I can see that." She hefted the rifle. "This is an Evans forty-four. Ain't seen one in five-six years." She braced the stock against her shoulder, took aim at the ocotillo, squeezed a trigger that wouldn't move. "Hell of a gun."

"Can you fix it, Ma?" Pardo asked.

"It's a gun, ain't it?" His mother laughed, and she slid the rifle onto the floor at her feet. She spit, and looked up the ridge. "We'd best skedaddle, son," she said. "Make for the Dragoons."

"Ma's right, boys," Pardo said, and he helped Blanche into the back of the wagon, then climbed up beside his mother. *Odd*, he thought, watching the kid as they pulled away from the massacre site. That little hellion was doting on the man they had pulled out of the prison wagon, bathing his forehead, his wounds, letting a few drops of water fall into his mouth. Kid practically ignored her mother.

Well, it made sense, in a way. Pardo was pretty sure the girl's mother would live. He wouldn't bet on the man's chances.

CHAPTER SIX

The first thing he saw was a face. Sunburned. Blond hair, dirty and unkempt. Green eyes. Thin lips. A hard face. A girl's face. A kid's face.

"My name's Blanche," the face said.

"I'll do the talking, kid," came another voice, followed by another face. A man, needing a shave, wearing a battered hat. Wild, angry eyes. "Who are you?"

"Mac," was all he could manage before plunging back into that cold, midnight void.

A blacksmith's sledge pounded an anvil inside his head, the top of which felt as if someone had poured steaming water over it. With a groan, Reilly forced his eyelids open and saw the girl's face again. Her bright eyes darted before landing back on his, and she whispered, "You remember what I told you?"

He remembered nothing but the girl's face. His confusion must have showed. The girl's lips moved. It looked like she said "Damn," but Reilly didn't think little girls spoke like that. He smelled piñon wood burning, coffee boiling. He tried to move his head, but that hurt. He tried to remember.

"Listen to me," the girl started, only to be cut off by that second voice he vaguely recalled.

"I told you to holler when he woke up, kid. I talk to this hombre first."

Spurs jingled, and the other face, the man with the crazy eyes, reappeared as he shoved the girl aside.

"All right, Mac," the man said. "You got some questions to answer, and they'd better satisfy me."

A ton of sand coated Reilly's throat. "Water," he said softly.

"Later." A short-barreled Colt sprung into the man's hand. The cylinder rotated a huge bullet as the revolver cocked. The man pressed the barrel under Reilly's nose.

"What happened down in the valley?" the man asked.

"Ambush," Reilly said, and he started to remember. Gus Henderson. Poor Frank Denton and Slim Chisum shot dead, Slim while he was taking a piss. And Frank, as good a lawman as Reilly had ever known. But this man with the bulldog's face and the madman's eyes, he hadn't been part of K.C. Kraft's gang. More memories came. K.C., riding south. W.W., slapping those manacles on Reilly's wrists. And . . . the girl, the kid. He could picture her lips moving, her hands reaching through the bars of the prison wagon. Reilly looked down, saw his hands were freed. He reached up, fingered over his bandaged neck, felt his chest.

"My patience," the man with the gun said, "is about to end."

"Give him some water," the girl's voice said. "He can't talk."

"Shut up." His finger tightened on the trigger. "Ambush, you said. I ain't blind. I could see you was ambushed. Don't play me for—"

"Give him some damned water!" the girl barked.

"I'm going to give him a hole between his nostrils and his mouth. Then I'm going to wash out your mouth with soap."

Another voice, from off in the shadows. "Give him some water, Pardo."

"Why don't you introduce all of us to this hombre, Chaucer?" the man said, glancing over his shoulder. He looked again at Reilly. "Start talking. Or start dying."

Reilly's fingers ran down his vest. His badge. His badge was gone. His eyes found the girl. The name bounced around in his weary head. *Pardo . . . Pardo . . . Pardo . . .* He saw the girl's face again, remembering, heard her saying something, felt her small hands on his chest, taking off his badge, heard that voice, that warning.

The man with the Colt wet his lips. He swallowed, thinking, and grinned. "One sentence, Mac. One sentence, but make it a good one. Then I'll give you some water. Or a chunk of lead."

He tried to swallow, couldn't. "They were," he tried, wondering if anyone could really hear him, "hauling my ass . . . to . . . prison."

He closed his eyes. He didn't expect Pardo to believe him. He expected to feel a bullet tear into his brain, and he wouldn't have minded it one bit.

The water revived him. The girl smiled at him, and even Pardo grinned. He still held the Colt, and the pistol remained cocked, but it was on Pardo's lap now, not pressed against Reilly's nose.

Reilly wanted to drink forever, but the girl pulled the canteen away. "Not too much," she said. "We'll get you some broth in a minute."

"Feel better?" the man with the gun, the man named Pardo, said easily.

"Not really," Reilly answered honestly.

"Hauling you to prison, eh?" Pardo said. "Yuma, I take it?"

Reilly started to nod, but there was something about Pardo's tone. He tried to savor the taste of water, the wetness on his cracked lips. The girl had dipped a bandana in a bowl of water, wrung it out, placed it on his forehead. The coolness almost put him back to sleep, but the man's voice called out, sharper.

"Why were they taking you to Yuma?"

Reilly swallowed. He had been taking W.W. and L.J. Kraft to Fort Bowie, to meet up with Lieutenant Jeremiah Talley. The man named Pardo was lifting the revolver.

"Not Yuma," Reilly said, and the gun lowered. "Huntsville."

"Huntsville?" Pardo's eyebrows arched. "Huntsville?"

"Texas," Reilly said. It seemed far enough away.

"You're in Arizona Territory," Pardo reminded him.

"Thought it was far enough from Texas," Reilly said. "It wasn't."

The girl let him have more water. Another woman, lean, harder, reeking of mescal, squatted beside him with a bowl of something that smelled a lot better than she did.

"Want me to give him this, Jimmy?" the woman asked.

"Leave it," Pardo told her, his eyes boring into Reilly. "All right, Mac. What were three deputy marshals in Arizona taking you to Texas for?"

Reilly looked at the bowl the stringy woman had left at his side. His stomach pleaded for the broth. He had never known broth could smell so good. He looked back at Pardo. Pardo. The name, the face. Bloody Jim Pardo. Everybody in Arizona Territory knew about Jim Pardo. So did the people in Texas. Maybe he shouldn't have tried lying about Texas, but it was too late now.

"Fort McKavett," Reilly said.

"Where's that?"

"Texas." His pal Talley had been stationed there before being transferred west to Bowie. "San Saba country."

"What about it?"

Reilly tried to grin. "Soldiers there don't like me much."

Explosively, Pardo laughed. "They don't like Jim Pardo, neither." He lowered the hammer on the revolver, and shoved the Colt into his holster, reached over, and lifted the bowl and spoon. The spoon moved in Pardo's hand to Reilly's mouth. Reilly's lips parted. The broth went in, warming him as it made its way down his throat. Pardo brought the spoon back to the bowl, filled it, and moved it back to Reilly's mouth.

"What do you think, son?" Ruby Pardo spit into the fire, the tobacco juice sizzling against a stone.

He shrugged. If Mac had told him they were taking

him to Yuma, he would have killed him then and there. 'Course, they could have been headed to Yuma, could have turned the wagon around when they were ambushed, could have turned back because of some other problem, but Texas made sense. *Extradition*, Wade Chaucer had mentioned. Some big word like that.

"If he robbed the Yankees at McKavett or killed one of them, he might be all right," Pardo said.

"You trust him, then?" His mother put a screwdriver to the Evans.

Reilly filled a cup with black coffee. "You know me better than that, Ma. Man still has some questions to answer. Like how come he wasn't killed? Like who ambushed them? Like what exactly is he wanted for in Texas?"

"Maybe Apaches done it," Ruby said.

"No, Ma. Apaches wouldn't have left him to bake to death in that wagon. They would have had their fun with him."

"What are you going to do?"

"Wait. I'll see the major before long. Major Ritcher would know something about this guy."

Ruby set the rifle and screwdriver aside. "That's smart, son. Real smart. Don't trust nobody, and keep your eye on that Wade Chaucer."

"I always do, Ma."

"Smart. You're smart, and brave. You pa's proud of you, Jim. Real proud."

Pardo rubbed his nose and frowned. Pa. If only his father could tell him that, to his face, but he had been shot down like a mangy dog during the war. Kansas redlegs had burned down his home, turned Pardo and his ma into outlaws. Well, a lot of bluecoats had paid for what they'd done to his family, and Pardo hadn't finished collecting.

"I'm proud of you, too, Jim," his mother said. That meant more to Pardo than anything. He sat a little straighter.

"And what about the woman and her kid?" Ruby asked. "The woman's fit as a fiddle now."

"We'll see about them, too." The coffee tasted as bitter as his mother's voice had turned when she spoke of Dagmar Wilhelm.

The girl's face had changed. A slim hand lifted a spoon, but pulled away.

"You are staring at me," she said. A trace of a German accent.

Reilly tested his voice. "Either I've slept as long as Rip Van Winkle . . ."

She tried to laugh, but couldn't. Tears welled in her eyes, but she fought them down. "I'm Blanche's mother," she said. "I'm Mrs. Wilhelm."

She was tall and slender, her clothes torn, stained with blood; face, hands, and arms purpled with bruises, cuts; her eyes filled with a pain caused by something other than those injuries. He could see her in the kid named Blanche, but this one wasn't so tough, and her lips were full, round, not the thin, frowning, hard lines of her daughter. Mrs. Wilhelm had fashioned a bandana into a bonnet, and grimaced when she lifted the spoon again.

"I'm . . ." He stopped. Who could he trust in this camp? The kid had said she and her mother had been taken by Pardo. The kid had saved his life. But . . . still . . .

"Call me Mac," he said. He slid up, and took the

spoon from her shaking hand. She seemed grateful, and quickly lowered her arm, pressing it slightly against her side. *Ribs*, Reilly thought. She had busted a rib or two. He wondered, *How long have I been here?*

"I can feed myself, ma'am," he told her.

When he had finished eating, he tried to stand, but needed Mrs. Wilhelm and Blanche to help him to his feet. He leaned against a tree, aware of every eye in camp trained on him.

They were far from the sagebrush and desert, higher, much cooler. He felt the trunk of the tree supporting him, looked up at the giant limbs, and shade. A massive oak. Piñon and sycamores also hemmed them in, stretching toward a blue sky, climbing through boulders and brush, and beyond them, almost blocked out by the trees, rose towering spires of granite.

The Dragoon Mountains, Reilly guessed. No, it wasn't a guess. He knew. More than a decade ago, the Dragoons had been the stronghold of the great Apache Cochise, and he could see why an Apache, or a man like Jim Pardo, would choose this spot as his hideout. It had to be damned near impregnable, with plenty of shade, and, more important, water. He forced himself to the clear spring in the boulders, heard the rhythmic dripping of the water, squatted with cupped hands, and drank.

It hurt to pull himself up, but he managed, leaned back against the hard rock, and looked at the camp-fire.

An older woman, thin but mean, worked on a rifle. Reilly blinked. His Evans! She spit into the fire, not giving Reilly a moment's thought. That would be Ruby Pardo, Jim's mother. He had read one account, in a newspaper, or maybe it had been in a dime novel, that said Ruby Pardo tied the scalps of the men she had killed on her pants legs, but she didn't wear pants. She wore a filthy riding skirt that maybe once had been a brilliant red, and, anyway, he didn't see any scalps.

Away from the fire, a man stood in front of a Sibley tent, half of his face lathered, an ivory-handled razor in his left hand. Shirtless, with black pants, and still wearing a gun while he shaved. Wade Chaucer, Reilly guessed.

The other men's names he didn't recollect, but he wouldn't forget their faces. A sorry-looking bunch, who sat around the fire, trying to focus on the poker game they were playing, but staring at him. One tossed his cards on the deadwood, unsheathed a giant Bowie knife, and began running the blade against a whetstone. He seemed older than the rest.

Reilly remembered the dark-haired woman who smelled of mescal. He didn't see her, but there were other tents, a cabin halfway built, two lean-tos, and a corral. This had been a camp for quite a while. He went back to the fire. Three men. Plus the man shaving. And Pardo, wherever he was. But there had to be more. Jim Pardo would have at least one man on sentry duty.

When his head started swimming, he decided he'd better head back to his bedroll, before somebody had to carry him there.

For supper, the girl brought in a plate of beans, two burned tortillas, and a cup of coffee. Reilly was sitting up, rubbing his wrists, watching the men and women at the fire. The graybeard was gone, but a swarthy gent had replaced him. Likely trading off guard duty.

"Where's Pardo?" he asked, taking the plate from the girl's hand.

"I ain't his keeper," she said, kneeling.

"Somebody's going to slap that smart mouth of yours shut," Reilly said. "And it might be me."

Handing him the coffee, she eyed him with a measure of respect.

"He rode off this morning."

"How many men does he have?"

"Five. That's all I seen. But I hear them talk that one of them got killed when they wrecked the train, and his brother took him home to get planted. I don't know when he'll come back."

"They wrecked a train?"

"Yeah. Killed my stepfather. Don't give me that look. He was a louse."

Reilly tested the coffee. It was terrible, but it was coffee. "You best get back, look after your mother. They don't want us talking much."

"Back in the desert, you said you were a real lawman," she said softly.

"I am."

"What you plan on doing?"

He didn't really have an answer. "Try to keep you, your mother, and me alive," he said as she walked away. A thought struck him, and he called out, "Blanche?"

She turned.

"Where's my badge?" he whispered.

Her fingers began dribbling the pocket of her pants.

"Bury it," he said.

CHAPTER SEVEN

"See, the boys been betting on when my cussedness would get the better of me, and I'd kill you," Pardo said. "You're walking around pretty good now. Amazing what a few days of rest, grub, and good coffee'll do for a fellow."

"*Good* coffee?" the tall man from the prison wagon said, and Pardo cackled, but the mirth ended a second later. Pardo tested the Colt in his holster, just letting this hombre called Mac know that he still might die. Today. In the next minute.

"Where you from?" You didn't ask a man where he hailed from, didn't even ask his name, you just let him tell you if he had a mind to, but nobody had ever accused Bloody Jim Pardo of being polite.

"Grew up on a farm in Johnson County," he answered easily as he lifted the blackened coffeepot off the fire and filled his cup.

Pardo took his hand away from his revolver. "Hell, Mac, we was neighbors." He found a tin cup on the ground, held it out for the stranger to fill. "I growed up on a Cass County farm myself."

The man didn't seem nervous. Just topped Pardo's

cup with miserably bad coffee—making it was never one of Three-Fingers Lacy's strongest talents—then sat across the fire on a boulder, sipping casually. Like they were in some café in Tucson, talking about the weather or the parson's sermon last Sunday.

"You fight in the war?" Pardo asked.

He shook his head. "Too young."

"How old are you?"

"Thirty-four."

"Look older. Well, maybe not older, but experienced."

"I've done some traveling."

"Me too." Pardo laughed. "'Course, me, I'm four years older than you. I fought in the war."

"Everybody knows that about Jim Pardo. You rode with Quantrill."

He set the cup down. "You got a problem with that?"

The man had a disarming smile. "Not at all. My mother used to sing praises of Captain Quantrill, said he was saving us all from damned Yankee tyrants. Too bad how it all had to end."

Pardo frowned. He remained silent for a long time, staring at the small fire, then spit on a coal, and watched it bubble and disappear. "Yeah. 'Course I rode with some boys as young as you would have been then. I reckon your mother wouldn't allow you to fight those invaders."

"My brother fought. Somebody had to work the farm. That was me."

Pardo started scratching the palm of his right hand against the Colt's hammer. "Who'd your brother ride with?"

"First Missouri."

He spit again. "Some real outfit, eh, not irregulars like me and Quantrill. Not bushwhackers. Not murderers."

"I don't know about that. My brother was killed somewhere down in Tennessee. Ask my mother, and me, the war was being fought in Missouri."

"And your ma? Where's she now?"

"Dead. When Paul, that was my brother, died, it pretty much killed her, too. I buried her the next fall."

"What about your pa?"

"I never knew him. Lightning strike got him when I was a baby."

"No family, eh?"

He shook his head.

"That's too bad, Mac. Me? Kansas redlegs, gutless bastards, got my pa killed. All I got now is Ma. Had me a kid brother, but he died of fever when he was just a tot. Would have been about your age now, I reckon." Pardo's eyes became slits. "So, Mac, let me guess. You grow up, hating Yankees, go down to Texas, get into trouble at Fort Concho, and light a shuck to Arizona. That's your story as I remember."

"McKavett. Not Concho." The man smiled. Smart fellow, this Mac. He knew Pardo was trying to trap him.

"What did you do?"

"Robbed the paymaster. Killed a guard."

Laughing, Pardo reached for the cup, took another sip. "Yankees don't care much for that. I guaran-damn-tee you that. How much money did you get?"

"I don't know. I lost the strongbox crossing the Pecos. Kept riding, but Texicans and the Army have a long memory, and a longer reach."

"Yankees get their money back?"

"I don't think so. They were asking me about it when they caught up with me in Bisbee."

"That's good. That they didn't get that money, not that they arrested you. Me, I had me a little plan. Robbed us a train. That's how come I got the kid and that handsome woman with us. Derailed that son of a bitch, but everything went to hell. Boiler blew in the engine, express car and everything else went up in flames. The boys didn't care much for it, but I say, at least the Yankees didn't get their pay." He clinked his mug against the cup in Mac's hand in a rebel toast.

"So they caught you," Pardo continued. "They started hauling you back to Texas. Who ambushed you in the valley?"

"Apaches."

"That's too bad." Pardo emptied the coffee into the fire, watching the ash bubble and boil, and pitched the cup aside.

"Would have been," the man said, "if you hadn't happened along."

Pardo rose. "Let's take a ride, Mac. Don't give me that look. Man's strong enough to walk, he's able to ride, I say. Saddle us up a couple of horses. I'll ride that roan. Saddle the sorrel mare for yourself."

The man kept frowning. Hell, Pardo didn't blame him for that. Suspicious. Maybe a little scared—he ought to be—but it didn't show in his face.

"No offense," he said softly, looking at the corral, "but that sorrel's not much of a horse."

"Don't matter. We ain't going for much of a ride. That's my saddle yonder. You take the McClellan."

"McClellan?" The man frowned. "That's a Yankee saddle."

"Makes you feel better, I took it off a dead Yank. Get to it, Mac. I need to talk to Ma and the boys before we light out."

* * *

Ruby Pardo drowned an ant with a waterfall of brown juice when Pardo walked up to her. Working the lever of the Evans rifle, she grinned, and tossed the weapon to Pardo, saying, "Good as new." He caught it but didn't return his mother's smile, and butted the stock in the dirt.

"Something's the matter," she said.

"Yeah." He bowed his head. "I wanted to like Mac, Ma. Wanted to trust him. Says he hails from Johnson County."

"Johnson County ain't Cass County, son," his mother said bitterly. "Damned Yankees didn't force Southern folks from their homes over there. That was us good people in Cass, Jackson, and Bates counties. A few families down in Vernon County. You remember Order Number Eleven."

He made himself meet his mother's hard stare. "I remember, Ma."

She hooked the dip of snuff out of her mouth—a few flakes still stuck in her teeth—and shot a quick glance at the corral. "I never trusted him. You'd be better off killing him, plus that woman and her kid with a mouth like a privy."

"He says Apaches jumped him."

She squinted. "Apaches, eh? But you said—"

"I know what I said." He hefted the rifle, tried to change the subject. "Heavy, ain't it?"

"It's loaded," she said. "Where you taking him?"

"Down below."

"Be careful."

"I always am."

"I'm sorry he didn't work out, son."

"It's all right. He ain't family. And like you said,

Johnson County ain't Cass County. I got to go talk to The Greek."

Carrying and studying the Evans, he stopped where the boys were playing poker in front of the Sibley tent. Wade Chaucer didn't bother to look up, but Harrah, Duke, and The Greek did.

"Got a chore for you, Greek," Pardo said.

Silently, The Greek waited.

"You and your Sharps."

Now, the swarthy man smiled, and looked at the corral. "Him?"

Pardo nodded. "Wait till we leave camp, then follow us. We'll ride down in the valley a bit. Stay in range. Might not have to do nothing, but I want you to back my play."

"I always do," The Greek said.

"You're gonna kill him, boss man?" Duke blurted out, a little louder than he should have, but likely not loud enough to be heard over in the corral.

"You got the brains God gave a cactus, Duke. Shut up." Back to The Greek: "*I* want to kill him. But if something happens . . ."

The Greek tossed his cards into the dust. He reached for the Sharps. "I never miss, Pardo. If you don't get him, I will. There's a science into making that killing shot, and I'm a scientist. It's all—"

"I don't give a damn. Just do your job."

With that, Pardo strode over to the corral.

The game was over, not that it had been much of a poker game. Not playing against fools like Harrah and Duke, Wade Chaucer thought, although The

Greek had some skill. They watched Pardo and the man known only as Mac ride slowly out of camp.

"I should go." Slowly, The Greek finished wiping the brass telescope on his Sharps, stuck the rag in his vest pocket, and started to rise.

"It would be a shame," Chaucer said absently.

The Greek shouldered the heavy rifle. He said nothing.

Duke, stupid Duke, had to ask the question. "What would be a shame, Wade?"

With a grin, Chaucer shrugged. "Why . . . if The Greek happened to miss, just once."

The silence kicked like that big .45-70 rifle The Greek held. Chaucer looked across the camp. Ruby Pardo had retired to her tent. Phil was on guard duty. The woman and her kid sat quietly in a corner, and Three-Fingers Lacy was somewhere sleeping off a drunk.

"You're talking dangerous," The Greek said.

Chaucer shrugged again. "I'm just thinking out loud. Thinking about how tragic it would be if somehow Pardo got himself killed. Accidentally, I'm thinking. Thinking of how nice things might be were things to change."

"You'd best watch it, Wade," Harrah said.

"I've been watching." He couldn't keep the bitterness out of his voice. "I watched that Army payroll go up in flames because Jim Pardo is an idiot. How much money have we seen in the past eight months? I told you how we should have robbed that train."

"I need to get moving," The Greek said, but his boots remained planted.

"We could have gone to Dos Cabezas, too," Chaucer said, "instead of coming back here. That posse, any posse, would have given up long before then."

"I wanted to," Duke said. "They's women in Dos Cabezas."

"There's women . . . a woman, at least . . . here, too." Chaucer stared at Dagmar Wilhelm. "A fine-looking woman. And Lacy, well, she has certain charms, too."

"You heard what Pardo said about that woman," Harrah said dryly. "And if you try something with Lacy . . ."

"I've heard what Jim Pardo has said about lots of things," Chaucer said. He found a cigar. "Mind you, I'm just thinking out loud."

"I'd better go." This time, The Greek moved.

"Good luck, Greek," Chaucer called out. "But, yes, sir, it sure would be a shame. . . ."

When The Greek disappeared, Chaucer's laugh frightened off Harrah and Duke. Chaucer started to light the cigar, thought better of it, and decided to walk across camp, see if Three-Fingers Lacy had awakened from her little nap.

They were being followed.

Reilly knew that much, and he knew Pardo was aware of it, too. He also knew Pardo planned to make this Reilly's last ride. It had taken them more than three hours to pick their way down the mountains, through the forests and creek beds, riding in silence, but finally they had moved into the clear desert.

"Where are we going?" Reilly asked.

"Nowhere in particular," Pardo said, but he jutted his jaw southeast toward a spartan wasteland of rock. Reilly looked at him, frowning at the Evans rifle in Pardo's scabbard. He nudged the sorrel forward.

Down here, it was murderously hot. They should

have stopped, rested, watered their horses, but Pardo went like a mad dog, moving, moving, moving. Reilly wet his lips, trying to figure out where he had gone wrong, what he had said. He had been born in Johnson County. His answer had been a slip, but he had, or thought he had, gotten away with it. Johnson County, Indiana, but Pardo thought he had meant Missouri. The rest of the lies weren't really lies. Paul McGivern had taken a rebel ball through both lungs at Pittsburg Landing, Tennessee, but he had been campaigning with 11th Indiana—Slim Chisum had served in the First Missouri, seldom shut up about "seeing the elephant" at what the Rebels called Shiloh—and when Reilly's mother had learned of Paul's death, she gave up any effort at living. The next fall, Reilly had buried her on the farm beside Reilly's father, who had been struck and killed by lightning when Reilly was only twenty-one months old.

He was barely in his teens when his mother had died. He'd been on his own since.

What had he said to Pardo?

No, it didn't matter. What mattered was staying alive. But how?

Pardo pulled back on the reins, letting Reilly move in front of him. Reilly looked for an arroyo, some boulders, something he could use for cover. Also, he listened, for the creak of leather, the click of a gunmetal. Instead, he heard Pardo's voice behind him.

"Rein up, Mac. And turn around."

Reilly pulled the reins, turned in the saddle, saw Pardo slowly drawing the Evans from the scabbard. He said nothing, just looked. "I need to test out this here rifle." Pardo grinned.

"On me," Reilly said.

"That's right. You ain't surprised?"

Reilly said nothing.

"You said it was Apaches," Pardo jacked a cartridge into the Evans.

"It was Apaches."

"That's a damned lie. Apaches been no trouble of late."

"They jumped the reservation."

"Why?"

"Ever been to San Carlos?"

Pardo shook his head.

"I have."

"Then you know Apaches, Mac. Problem is, I know them, some. And I can read sign. Whoever waylaid you, they was on shod horses. Injuns don't ride shod ponies."

"Apaches ride what they can steal."

"Them dead marshals wasn't scalped."

Reilly tried to match Pardo's grin. "You know Apaches. You know they don't take scalps."

"But they wouldn't have left you alive, Mac. Not no Apache. They would have had their fun on you, my friend."

Now, Reilly chuckled. "I don't speak Apache," he said, "but from what I heard, those Apaches seemed to think they were having some fun. Leaving me in that can to bake."

Lying had always come pretty easy to Reilly. It helped him win more than he lost when he sat down to play poker, and it had gotten him a deputy's job when he had told Marshal Tidball that he had never spent time in jail.

"Nice story, Mac." Pardo raised the rifle to his shoulder. "But Major Ritcher would have told me if Apaches was on the prod."

Reilly dived off the horse just before a shot left

his ears ringing. He hit the ground, rolled, hearing another shot, and another, hearing the sickening wail of a dying horse, then Pardo's cursing. More gunfire. Even a man with an Evans couldn't shoot that fast. Horses running, wild yips like those of coyotes, only . . . Reilly looked up and found Pardo's leg pinned underneath the dead roan. Bullets kicked up dust around Pardo, the horse. Another tore off Reilly's hat. The sorrel was galloping due south, leaving nothing but a cloud of dust.

Across the desert floor charged a half-dozen Apache riders.

CHAPTER EIGHT

He stood, stepped, and dived, practically in one motion, feeling a bullet's tug on his bandana. As he landed beside Pardo and grabbed the Evans rifle, the thought struck Reilly: *Second time in a week I've found myself pinned behind a dead horse.* Quickly, he aimed, let out a breath, squeezed the trigger.

A horse went down, throwing a young brave into the dust. Reilly jacked the hammer.

Beside him, Pardo cursed, his leg stuck under the weight of the dead horse. The battered old Colt lay just beyond his reach. Reilly didn't have time to fetch it for him.

He swung the rifle around, found his mark, pulled the trigger, levered another shell into the Evans, swung back, fired. He hated killing the horses, but they were bigger targets than the riders. A bullet sliced his shirt, somehow missing his flesh but spoiling his next shot, yet he worked the Evans, felt the kick of the big rifle.

Before he could cock the Evans again, they were on them.

An Appaloosa and rider leaped over their makeshift redoubt, the hoofs of the big stallion barely missing Reilly's head. He started to turn, but the next Apache leaped from the saddle, slammed into Reilly and the Evans. Another shot, from where, Reilly couldn't tell, echoed, but the bullet must have gone wide. The Apache was on top of him, black, malevolent eyes unblinking, dirty hands gripping the Evans, trying to rip the gun from Reilly's hands.

He let the Apache lift the rifle off his chest, felt the freedom in his right leg, and kneed the young brave savagely in the groin. The black eyes closed in pain. The Apache's grip loosened, and that was all Reilly needed. He shoved the warrior aside, rose, spotted the Apache on the Appaloosa levering a cut-down Yellow Boy rifle, and ignored the Indian writhing near him. Another shot boomed behind him. Sharps, from the sound of it, but the rifleman missed whatever he was aiming at. Reilly had to fire from the hip. The stallion buckled, fell, throwing the mounted warrior to the ground.

Reilly spun, reversed his hold on the Evans, slammed the stock savagely, crushing the skull of the warrior he had kneed in the groin. Spinning while working the lever, Reilly fired again from the hip, missed. The Apache scrambled for the old Winchester he had dropped when he leaped clear of the dying Appaloosa. Reilly cocked the Evans, this time made sure of his aim, and shot the brave through the chest.

A scream came behind him, and Reilly spun. Another Apache came charging, armed with only a knife. Reilly brought the rifle to his shoulder. The Evans barked, and the running Apache staggered, dropped his knife, kept on running, weaving, and as Reilly chambered a fresh round into the Evans, he finally fell, started to rise, and sank, shuddering, into the dust.

At last, he filled his lungs and sank behind Pardo and the dead horse, scanning ahead of him, looking behind him. Three Apache horses lay still, two in front of them, plus the dead Appaloosa. The piebald gelding trotted about, surprisingly patient, easy, about ten rods behind them. Another horse, a blood bay Reilly had shot, stood over its motionless rider. None of the Apaches moved.

"Get me my damned pistol," Pardo said. "And get me from under this horse."

"Quiet," Reilly said, trying to catch his breath. "Keep your head down. There's somebody else out there. Somebody with a long gun. Sharps, from the sound."

"I know that, Mac. It's The Greek. Now give me a hand."

Reilly turned, his eyes steady, his voice controlled. "Give you a hand? A minute ago, you were about to shoot me."

"A minute ago, I didn't believe you about Apaches jumping the reservation. Now get me up, damn it."

He pondered his chances, thought about Dagmar Wilhelm and Blanche. He thought about how much he could use a shot of rye just about now. Softly, he lowered the hammer on the Evans, leaned the rifle against the dead roan, and helped pull out Pardo.

The first thing Pardo did was grab his gun and blow grit from the cylinder. After checking the barrel, he eared back the hammer. "I'll take that rifle, Mac." He aimed the Colt at Reilly.

"I just saved your hide, Pardo," Reilly told him.

"Put in for the Medal of Honor if you want. You saved your ass, too."

Reilly lifted the Evans, and tossed it to Pardo, who caught it in his free hand. The killer pitched the rifle behind him, removed his hat, and waved it over his head for several seconds, yelling, "Greek. Come on. It's over." Then, to Reilly: "Better make sure it is over." Limping slightly, Pardo moved to the Apache lying facedown near the Appaloosa, and shot him in the head.

Reilly stepped over the roan's legs, found his hat, stuck his finger through the hole in the crown, then slapped it against his thigh as he walked toward the other Apaches. A rider, The Greek, appeared from the rocks, started trotting easily toward them. Reilly knelt beside another Apache, and jumped as Pardo fired another coup de grâce into another Apache.

The fall from the horse Reilly had shot had killed this young brave. Slowly, Reilly reached over and closed the unseeing, dark eyes. He let out a snort, part laugh, part sigh, and shook his head. These Apaches, maybe, had saved his life, coming as they did, after jumping the San Carlos reservation. Saved his life, and he had killed them for it. Of course, they would have killed him.

He looked down, saw the pearl grip sticking out of the warrior's breechclout, and he reached down and withdrew the derringer. It was an over/under .41 Remington, nickel plated. He didn't have time to see if the hideaway gun was loaded, but quickly shoved it down into his left boot top, and stood. The Greek was about fifty yards away when he suddenly stopped, raising the big Sharps. Reilly wet his lips, thought the man planned to kill him, but The Greek was looking beyond Reilly.

Quickly, Reilly whirled. Pardo stood in front of one dead Apache, his back to another who was still alive, lifting his head, raising an old musket, aiming at Pardo's back.

The Greek waited.

The Apache cocked the rifle, started to squeeze the trigger.

The Sharps boomed, spitting dust a yard behind the Apache, who didn't flinch.

Reilly jerked the derringer from his boot, firing as Pardo whirled. The Apache rolled over, and Pardo emptied his Colt into the dead man's chest, then quickly reloaded while limping toward Reilly.

He stopped a few yards in front of Reilly and holstered the Colt. "Reckon you saved my life again, Mac."

Reilly lowered the smoking Remington. "Maybe I'll put in for another Medal of Honor."

Riding up to them, The Greek still carried the big Sharps with the telescope, but he looked scared as he reined up. "I am sorry, Jim," he said. "I missed."

"You missed quite a lot, Greek," Pardo said, but he kept looking at Reilly, sizing him up. "I thought you never missed."

"The first shots, I feared I would hit you. The last one, I just rushed."

"It's all right, Greek. We all have our bad days. Besides, Mac here came through. That's a damned good shot, Mac, with a derringer. Not to mention how you handled that rifle. Like you was born to shoot them. Where'd you learn to shoot like that?"

"I've had plenty of practice."

Pardo held out his left hand, palm up. "Still," he said, "I reckon I'll take that little peashooter."

"Still don't trust me?" Reilly handed him the Remington.

"I'm starting to, Mac," Pardo said, only now his eyes

drilled on The Greek. "But I tend to trust men who ain't heeled a lot more than I trust them that is. Catch up them horses, Greek. See if that bay's fit to ride. I'll scalp these bucks and we can sell them in Mexico next time we cross the border."

Pardo filled the mugs with whiskey and raised his own. "A toast," he said, "to Mac. God gave him a pair of eyes, and a steady hand. Wasn't for Mac, Bloody Jim Pardo would be burning in hell." He drank, and the others followed his example.

It was mescal, not rye, but Reilly liked the way the liquor burned his throat, even how it exploded in his stomach. They were all drinking that evening, all but Dagmar and Blanche, who remained in their little corner of the camp. Three-Fingers Lacy quickly held out her cup for a refill. Often Reilly had wondered how the leathery woman had gotten her name, for she sported all of her digits. *Three fingers?* Reilly thought. *More like four or five.* The woman could drink more whiskey than anyone Reilly had known.

Feeling generous, Pardo refilled the mugs, giving Three-Fingers Lacy a generous pour. Quickly, Pardo drained his mug, and tossed the cup aside.

"I can use a sharpshooter like you, Mac. We have need of a new man. If you're game enough to ride with me."

The Greek's swarthy face went ashen. "Pardo . . ." he began.

"Rest easy, Greek. We lost Rafael. Not sure when Soledad will get back. And I trust you, Greek." Pardo's face said he didn't trust The Greek at all. "Just don't let it happen again."

"I won't." With trembling hands, The Greek raised the cup to his mouth.

"You trust me," Reilly said, "enough to let me have a gun?"

Pardo laughed. "Don't rush me. In time. Now, you want to ride with me?"

"I'd be delighted." Reilly killed the mescal in his own cup.

"Glad to hear that, Mac. Ain't you, Ma?"

"Delighted," Ruby Pardo said, her voice mocking, her cold eyes flaming hatred in Reilly's direction. She trusted Reilly about as much as her son trusted The Greek. "How's your leg, son?"

"Bruised. But a bruised leg is better than being dead."

Reilly rose. "If you'll excuse me, it's been a hard day."

"A lot harder on those Apache bucks you killed, my friend." Pardo cackled. "But it was a profitable venture, or will be, when we get to Mexico. Mighty profitable." He was looking over Reilly's shoulder, at Dagmar Wilhelm.

"Let's eat," Pardo said, and began filling bowls with stew. Reilly picked up the first two filled.

"Thought you was turning in?" Pardo said.

He tilted his neck toward the captives. "I am. I'm a little off my feed." That wasn't a lie. He'd been sick most of the day. "This is for the woman and her kid."

"All right, Mac," Pardo said, his tone now wary.

Silence greeted him as he handed Dagmar and Blanche the steaming bowls. He didn't tell them it was horse-meat stew. Uninvited, he sat down anyway. Hell, he almost collapsed.

"You're the talk of camp," the kid said.

He let out a weary sigh.

"You saved his life." Blanche's voice was bitter. "*His* life. Some damned lawman you are."

Dagmar added, "Those men killed my husband, Blanche's father."

"He wasn't my pa." Blanche turned her wrath on her mother. "Just because you—"

"Listen to me." Reilly hooked a thumb toward the celebrating killers. "I saved my own hide, and feel like hell for doing it. But you two need to keep in mind that right now Jim Pardo's keeping us alive. If Wade Chaucer had his druthers . . ." He shuddered. Damn, but he was worn to a frazzle.

Blanche had heard enough. She kicked over her bowl and stormed into the night. Dagmar closed her eyes, let out a sigh, and looked at Reilly.

"I'm sorry," she said, tears welling.

"Don't be."

"I've lost my hold on her. Not that I ever had one." A tear escaped, but she quickly wiped it off her cheek. "I'm not as tough as Blanche."

"You're tougher," he said, and he meant it. "She's all bark. You've got grit." He meant that, too. It took a lot of grit to be a woman, a good-looking woman, with a daughter, and hold her own while a captive of a gang of black-hearts. "Don't worry about Blanche. She'll grow up, come around." He wasn't sure about that, though.

"Pardo was going to kill you today," she said.

He nodded.

"Good thing you knew about those Apaches."

He couldn't contain the laugh. "Would have been," he said, "had I known about it."

Her beautiful eyes widened. "You mean . . . ?"

"Luck," he said, and frowned, thinking about the dead Apaches and dead horses. The bay he shot had managed to get them into the Dragoons before it played out, and Pardo had slit its throat and ordered The Greek and Reilly to butcher it for their evening feed.

"Do you know what they're planning?"

He shook his head, though he had a good idea. Pardo had given him that much. At some point, they'd ride down to Mexico, turn in the Apache scalps for the bounty the Mexican government paid, and, likely, sell Dagmar to . . . he didn't want to think of that.

"Do you have a plan?" she asked.

He pictured Frank Denton dead, remembered W.W. Kraft pulling the boots off Slim Chisum's feet. "Last plan I had," he said in a dry whisper, "got two good men killed."

Her eyes widened, looking over his shoulder, and he heard the footsteps. Slowly, Reilly rose and turned, facing Jim Pardo.

"Thought you was all tuckered out," Pardo said icily.

"Just talking to the lady."

"Well, don't. I don't like nobody talking to Dagmar, except me. Maybe Ma. You'd best turn in, Mac. We got a busy day come first light. You and me is going for a ride."

Reilly straightened, tense. "Another ride?" He tried to make it sound like a joke.

"That's right." There was no humor in Pardo's reply.

CHAPTER NINE

Dos Cabezas lay a torturous forty-plus miles from Pardo's camp in the Dragoon Mountains. It took Reilly and Pardo better than two days to reach the bleak mining town shadowed to the east by two bald-topped peaks that gave Dos Cabezas its name, not to mention its life: from the water at Ewell Spring to the gold and silver mines on those rocky, rough ledges.

The clanging of a blacksmith's hammer greeted them as they rode past the National Mail and Transportation Company stagecoach station, the only building that didn't look worn down even though the town had only been around a few years. A few miners stood outside one saloon—too hot, maybe, inside—shaded by a palo verde tree as they passed around a bottle.

Silently, Pardo pointed at another saloon at the edge of town, and turned his horse toward it. When he reined up, he looked over his shoulder down main street.

"What do people do in Dos Cabezas?" he asked.

"They hide," Reilly told him.

Actually, they mined. Assayers said there were some

pretty rich claims in those hills. The town had a hotel, a stamp mill, and three saloons: one for the miners, one for the soldiers from Fort Bowie, and this one, an adobe square with a patched tin roof, one window, and one doorway without a door. Dos Cabezas also had no church, no telegraph, and no law.

"Let's cut the dust," Pardo suggested, and both men eased out of their saddles, and led their horses to the hitching rail.

It wasn't much of a saloon. A bald man with red sleeve garters and a white mustache stood behind a two-by-twelve plank nailed atop two barrels about fifteen feet apart. In a bucket of blood like this hellhole, Reilly doubted if he could get a clean glass, let alone a shot of Old Overholt. No fancy bottles were stacked on the back bar. There was no back bar. Just two more kegs, several brown clay jugs, and a clear jar filled with rattlesnake heads. Probably used to season the whiskey, Reilly figured. Without a word, the man handed Pardo a jug, spotted Reilly, and slid two glasses over the rough pine. He folded the newspaper he had been reading, left it on the bar, and began wiping glassware with a rag darker than wet adobe.

Pardo took the jug and glasses to the far, darkest corner, kicked a chair leaning against the table, and sat down hard, his back to the wall, with a good view of the door and window. He plopped the glasses and jug in front of him, drew the Colt, and placed it in front of him. Reilly dragged a chair to Pardo's left and sat.

Golden liquor filled both glasses. Pardo didn't bother stoppering the jug.

"To your health." Pardo lifted the glass and didn't wait. Reilly was still drinking his when Pardo refilled his own.

Reilly made no effort to refill his. Some might call it tequila, but Reilly wouldn't bet on its origins.

"What time is it?" Pardo asked.

"One of your boys took my watch," Reilly reminded him.

The glass emptied. Pardo refilled it again, and called out to the bartender for the time. A few minutes past noon, came the answer.

"Reckon everybody's taking hisself a *siesta*," Pardo said.

He drank again. And waited.

Two hours must have passed. Pardo had ordered some grub, and the taciturn barkeep had gone to fetch something. That had been an hour ago, and Reilly's stomach grumbled. Pardo didn't seem to care. A few minutes later, Pardo reached for the Colt on the table. Only then did Reilly hear the slow clopping of hoofs, followed by a horse's whinny, the creaking of leather, and footfalls on the dirt outside. A large shadow filled the doorway.

"It is me, Jim," a voice said. Hard. More German than Dagmar's.

"Come ahead, Major." Pardo kept his grip on the Colt.

He was a heavyset man in a dusty Army uniform, Second U.S. Cavalry, looked to be maybe fifty, with a Roman nose and thick eyebrows. He stopped when he saw Reilly, staring, wetting his lips.

"This is Mac," Pardo told him. "New man riding for me."

"*Guten tag*," the man said. He sat, hazel eyes locked on Reilly, trying to place his face. Reilly didn't like that at all. The Second Cavalry was his friend Jeremiah Talley's outfit.

"This is Ritcher," Pardo said, and slid the jug across the table. "Fetch a glass and have a drink."

Major Ritcher's eyes never left Reilly.

Slowly, Reilly rose, watching the major's stare follow him. "I'm not in the habit of drinking with blue-bellies," he said, trying to match the officer's stare. "I thought you were the same."

"Sit down, Mac," Pardo said testily. "The major's all right." He grinned. "For a damned Yankee."

Reilly found his seat.

"Your face is familiar to me," Ritcher said.

Reilly spit, brought the jug back, and refilled his glass. "It should be," he said. "You Yankees hounded me long enough."

Pardo laughed. "The Fort McKavett robbery," he explained to Ritcher. "Mac's the one who done it, the one being hauled back to Texas. Obviously, federal marshals didn't quite get that job done."

"Ah," Ritcher said, but Reilly knew the major had never heard of any Fort McKavett robbery. Reilly had made all of that up.

"Yankee bastards," Reilly said between clenched teeth.

The major sighed. "The var," he said, "has been over near twenty years. You should—"

Pardo's fist rocked the table, overturning his own glass, and knocking the jug onto the sod floor. "The war," he said, "ain't over, Ritcher. Not by . . ."

His nose started bleeding.

He took the bartender's rag away from his nose, started to throw it across the room, thought better of it, and dropped it by the Colt. Lucky, Pardo thought. Hadn't been much of a nosebleed. The major sat across from him, rigid. Mac leaned back against the wall, rocking his chair, not seeming to care about anything.

"Let's get to business," Pardo said. "Reckon my nose might cooperate now."

The major shrugged. "The desert. The dry air. It—"

"Don't doctor me, Major. I said let's get to business."

"Vat happened vith the train?" Ritcher asked carefully.

"Didn't go the way we'd figured things."

"The payroll?"

"Ashes to ashes, and dust to dust."

Ritcher's shoulders sagged, and the sigh came out of his mouth like a cannon shot.

"Twenty-three people vere killed on the train."

"Good day for the Tucson undertaker." Pardo downed another shot of tequila. "'Least, somebody got rich off it. Me and Ma sure didn't. The boys didn't." He refilled his glass. "And you didn't. Besides, we made a profit. Got us a woman and her kid. Nice-looking woman, too. Real nice."

"A voman?" Ritcher sat up, grinning all of a sudden. "I vould like to see—"

"You stay clear of that woman, Ritcher," Pardo spoke harshly. "I know about you and women. You stay clear of her, Major. Touch her, and I'll kill you."

Ritcher mumbled something in German. He studied Mac again, but only briefly, cleared his throat, and looked Pardo in the eye.

"I have more information."

"Figured."

"Dere is no money, no payroll, involved."

With a dry laugh, Pardo shook his head. "Then why in hell would I be interested?"

The major leaned forward. Mac stopped rocking his chair.

"Because, my dear comrade, you might be able to end dis var of yours against the Yankees, as you call us."

"I don't call *you* one. You're just a money-grabbing turncoat."

Ritcher sat up straight. "I vant ten thousand dollars."

Pardo laughed. "I told you that money burned up."

"You have robbed elsewhere. You are rich."

The tequila reached his mouth, but Pardo decided he had had enough. With a snort, he lowered the glass. "Yeah, that's why I hide in the mountains with a bunch of killers who'd gun me down in a second. Rich? In a pig's eye."

"Ten thousand dollars."

"I don't buy a horse without seeing her run, Major. Start talking."

He leaned back. "Did you know several Apaches escaped from San Carlos last week?"

Pardo's eyes twinkled as he looked at Mac. "We heard, didn't we, Mac?"

Mac's head slightly bobbed. His eyes remained on Ritcher.

"The colonel has requested additional weapons," Ritcher said. "Specifically, he asked for a dozen Gatling guns to be shipped to Fort Bowie." Ritcher's face briefly held a rare smile before he shrugged. "The colonel is overly cautious. But the Var Department granted him four forty-five-seventy-caliber Gatling guns. They are being shipped to Fort Bowie next month. By vagon train."

Pardo decided he'd have that drink after all, but he sipped it. "What am I supposed to do with four Gatling guns?"

This time, Ritcher held his smile longer. "Start a var?"

he suggested. "Avenge your precious Confederacy's defeat? Turn Arizona into a desert of blood?"

"You've been reading too many penny dreadfuls," Mac said, and went back to rocking.

The major's face flushed, but he regained control. "Four Gatling guns, and vagons of ammunition. Oh, and I failed to mention, dere is a howitzer, too."

"You must think I'm crazy," Pardo said. He killed the drink.

"If you don't vant the guns," Ritcher said, "they vould fetch a handsome price among the bandits— ah, I should say *revolutionaries*—in Mexico. Or the Mexican government?"

Pardo shook his head, and pinched his nose, then checked his thumb and forefinger. No blood. Good. "So, I just ride up to that Army train, and ask for them guns?"

"Do not play me for a fool, Herr Pardo." The major had gotten his dander up. "I know you are not one. It vill not be easy, but if any man can do this, it is Bloody Jim Pardo." The major found the jug and took a pull. He coughed, but he was game. After wiping his mouth with the sleeve of his blouse, he said, "And I trust you vill perform better than you did vith the Southern Pacific."

Pardo pointed the Colt at the major's chest. "Don't press your luck. Maybe Mac's right. Maybe you ain't nothing but a Yankee son of a bitch."

"Maybe."

"Which trail's the Army using?"

"That I vill have to find out. After I am paid my ten thousand dollars."

"Un-uh. Now you're playing me for a fool, Major. I'll give you a thousand when you give me the route. And four after we do the job."

"That does not equal ten thousand dollars, my friend."

"It don't equal a bullet in your belly, neither. Five thousand. Or a forty-four right now."

The major wet his lips. Finally, his head bobbed.

"I vill get vord to you later, Herr Pardo." He rose, bowed slightly to Mac, and walked outside.

On their way out of the saloon, Pardo grabbed the folded newspaper off the plank bar, stuck it in his saddlebag, and mounted.

They said little on the two-day ride back to the Dragoons, reaching camp shortly before sundown. There was a new man in camp, a Mexican with salt-and-pepper hair whom Pardo called Soledad. The Mexican tended to their horses, while Pardo strode to the campfire and knocked a whiskey bottle out of Three-Fingers Lacy's hand.

"That all you been doing since I been gone?" he asked savagely. "Or have you being enjoying some horizontal refreshments, too?"

"Jimmy," the girl began.

"Shut up. Get out of my sight."

"But Jimmy—"

He threatened her with a backhand, and she cringed, crying, and ran to her tent, stumbling. Pardo turned his wrath on Wade Chaucer.

"Who gave her the bottle, Chaucer?"

"Welcome home, Jimmy," Chaucer said. "How was the trip? The boys have missed you. Did you see that Soledad rejoined our lovely troupe?"

Pardo grabbed Lacy's bottle, killed it, and shattered the glass against the boulders behind him.

"Mac!"

"Yeah?"

"Bring me that newspaper." Reilly headed to the corral and heard Pardo call Dagmar to the campfire. He helped Soledad with Pardo's saddle, found the paper in the saddlebag, and walked back to the campfire. It was the *Arizona Daily Star*. He opened it up, still walking.

"Miss Dagmar," he heard Pardo saying. "I ain't much for letters, but a man like Bloody Jim Pardo needs to keep informed, so I'd be obliged if you'd read us this here newspaper."

"We sure do like to hear good stories," Duke muttered.

A headline at the bottom of the front page stopped Reilly cold.

Federal Lawmen Waylaid, Kraft Brothers Escape!

FOUR FOUND DEAD ON BOWIE TRAIL.

3 Deputy Marshals Savagely Slain!

MARSHAL MCGIVERN SOUGHT BY AUTHORITIES,
BELIEVED TO HAVE JOINED UP WITH NOTORIOUS OUTLAWS;
MASTERMINDED BLOODY ESCAPE FROM PRISON WAGON.

Tidball Offers $750 Reward!

"Hurry up, Mac," Pardo called.

Duke's gloved hand snatched the paper from Reilly's hand, and he thrust at Dagmar Wilhelm.

"Read it, ma'am," Pardo said. "You got such a nice voice. Read every damned word."

CHAPTER TEN

"What do you think?" Pardo asked when Dagmar Wilhelm folded the paper.

"You're right," Reilly answered. "She does have a nice voice."

Carefully, he reached up and took the newspaper from her trembling hands, thanking her with his eyes. Reilly didn't know how she had done it—must have been the look on his face—but she had skipped over the twelve-paragraph article on the *Arizona Daily Star*'s front page. She turned, started walking back to her daughter, and Reilly leaned closer to the fire, yet before he could drop the newspaper into the pit, Pardo stopped him.

"Don't burn that just yet, Mac," he said. "Let's see how your voice is. I want you to read me again that story."

"Which article?" He wondered if Pardo was teasing him, if Pardo could actually read and had seen the article about the ambush.

"The one about Swede Iverson."

Quickly, Reilly unfolded the paper, trying to find

the piece, turned to the third page, and saw the short note under the headline TERRITORIAL NEWS:

SWEDE IVERSON ARRESTED.

Reports confirm that the notorious killer Swede Iverson has been arrested and is confined in the jail in Wickenburg. The opprobrious dynamiter was captured without incident at a house of ill repute.

The hangman must be delighted at the opportunity to stretch this villain's neck.

After Reilly read the article, Pardo laughed. "Your voice ain't as pleasant as Dagmar's," he said, and topped off his cup with tequila. "Wickenburg," he said absently.

Reilly let the paper fall into the flames, watching it erupt and quickly turn into blackened ash. Taking a deep breath, he reached for the tequila.

Well, he thought, *you're in for it now. There's a price on your head. $750. Marshal Tidball, that idiot.*

No, Reilly couldn't blame the U.S. marshal. An Army patrol had discovered the abandoned prison wagon and three dead deputy marshals, plus one dead bandit. Reilly was gone, and so were the Kraft brothers. Nobody knew his plan, except Lieutenant Jeremiah Talley, and Jerry was off to California by now. Hell, he hadn't even told Jerry everything. Anyway, the law was the least of his concerns right now. Staying alive and keeping Dagmar and her daughter aboveground topped his priorities.

"Hey, Mac, I'm talking to you."

He killed the tequila and looked into Pardo's narrow eyes. "Yeah?" Reilly asked.

"You know this Swede Iverson?"

His head shook. "I know who he is. Can't say I know him."

"Dynamiter," Pardo said. "Paper called him oppo, oppro . . ."

"Opprobrious," Reilly said.

"Yeah, that's the word. What's that mean?"

"Scurrile," Wade Chaucer answered with a laugh.

Pardo glared. "All right, smart guy, what does that mean?"

"Contemptuous," Chaucer said. "Abusive. One mean bastard. You know, Pardo, the same things the newspapers call you."

Pardo turned away from Chaucer and stared at the fire, his mind working. A few minutes later, his head bobbing, the laughter back in his eyes, he looked up at Reilly. "What do you hear about this Iverson gent?"

Reilly shrugged. "He was working at a mine in Greaterville. Had a run-in with the Mexican boss, who fired him. Next morning, Iverson blew up the mine. The newspaper got the story a little bit wrong, though." Reilly remembered this fairly well. He had spent a week on a posse trying to find that bastard. "He didn't use dynamite. He used nitro."

"Nitro," Pardo said. "Nitroglycerine? That stuff's murder."

"That's what it was, all right. Iverson's explosion killed the boss, and three, four others. About two months back, he blew up a section of S.P. rails near Rillito with two sticks of dynamite. Just for spite, I guess, or maybe the Southern Pacific pissed him off. Nice guy."

"Man like him could come in handy." Pardo was staring again at the flames.

"How you mean, boss man?" Duke asked.

Pardo didn't answer. He just stared.

Reilly set his empty cup on a rock, stood, and left. He headed straight to Dagmar Wilhelm.

"So," she said softly, "your name's Reilly McGivern."

"Best keep it Mac for now, ma'am."

She smiled. "I skimmed the article."

"I burned the paper."

Silence. He broke it. "I didn't have a thing to do with that ambush."

"I know that . . . Mac. Else, we wouldn't have found you in the back of that transport, half-baked, half-dead. It'll make things . . . harder, though. I mean, for us, to get out of here. The law's looking for you."

"We'll be all right." He looked around. "Where's your daughter?"

"Sleeping."

He grinned. "I didn't think she slept."

She smiled back pleasantly, despite the strain etched into her face.

"I'd best get out of here. Pardo's jealous." He turned away, stopped, and looked back. "Thank you, ma'am."

"The name," she said, "is Dagmar."

Pardo looked at his mother, who spit a mouthful of snuff into the fire. They were alone. Everybody else must have turned in.

"I think I can use this Swede Iverson."

She wiped her mouth with the back of her hand. "I figured as much, son. You're thinking about trying for those Gatling guns."

With a grin, he reached over and patted her knee. "You know me pretty good, don't you, Ma?"

"Raised you. I reckon I know you."

He found the jug, lifted and shook it, sighing, then

brought it up and took in the last few drops of tequila. Afterward, he pitched the empty container onto the dirt. "Those guns could fetch us a handsome profit down in Mexico. And I might keep one of them for ourselves."

Her head shook. "They ain't so good. Jam, most of them will, like that Evans rifle I fixed. Gatlings, well, they make a lot of noise and smoke, but for killing . . ." She spit again, shaking her head.

"Well, first we got to get them. That's where this Swede Iverson could come in handy. Man knows how to use dynamite. And nitro. The way I see it, we could use a good man with explosives when we hit that Army wagon train. They ain't gonna just give us them Gatlings."

"So you're bound for Wickenburg?"

He nodded. "Reckon I'll take Mac."

Her eyes narrowed. "You trust him?"

"You know me better than that, Ma."

"I have suspicions about that fellow."

"That's why I love you, Ma. But—"

"No buts, Jimmy. I don't trust him at all. I trust him as much as I trust Wade Chaucer. And speaking of that son of a bitch, you watch him, Jimmy. You watch him good. Mind you, son, I can't prove nothing, but I think Chaucer done some talking, and that's how come The Greek got so careless with his shooting when those Apaches tried to put you under."

Pardo's grin flattened into a frown. "You hear them talking?"

"Nah, but I heard some such-and-such after it all happened. The Greek, he ain't prone to miss. Not as much as he missed on that day. It was Chaucer's doings."

"Well, I'll have to kill Wade Chaucer one of these days."

"Not if I kill him first."

Pardo moved, knees in the dirt, gripping his mother's arms, pulling her toward him. "Now, you listen to me, Ma." Panic was in his voice. "You stay away from Chaucer. I'll kill him, but only when it's time for me to kill him. You keep out of his way, especially whilst me and Mac's gone to fetch Swede Iverson out of that Wickenburg hoosegow. You hear me, Ma?"

She stared into his frightened eyes in silence.

"Ma?" he demanded.

"Nobody, and I mean nobody, tries to bushwhack my boy," she said at last.

"Ma." He gripped her bony arms tighter.

With a heavy sigh, she looked away. "Ain't like it was back in the war, son," she said, staring into the darkness. "Missouri men, they'd ride with you, side with you. Game, they was. They'd look after you. They was almost like family."

"I still got Phil."

She turned to face her son. "Phil? He ain't family. He's trash. Trash like all them other guttersnipes you got riding with you. And that Mac, he ain't one to trust."

"I told you I don't trust nobody. Now, you tell me. You promise me this. You stay out of Chaucer's way when I'm fetching this oppo, appro, this opprobra, ah, this contemptuous dynamiter back from Wickenburg."

Her nod was barely noticeable, and Pardo rose and kissed his mother lightly on the lips. She tasted of snuff, and it tasted good. He sat beside her and pulled her close.

"I ain't nothing without you, Ma," he told her, and then, as an afterthought, he added, "Reckon I'll bring The Greek with me, too. For a spell."

Sweat burned Reilly's eyes, blurred his vision until he had to rein up, remove his bandana, and mop his face.

For close to a week, Reilly, Pardo, and The Greek had been riding in a general north by northwest direction, keeping off the main trails and avoiding towns such as Tucson and Florence. Pardo hadn't said why they were bound for Wickenburg, just that they were going there, but Reilly figured it had to do with that murderous explosives man from the *Arizona Daily Star*.

With a frown, Pardo tugged on the reins and turned in the saddle. A moment later, he sighed and swung to the ground. "Might as well rest here," he said after he looked around.

Not that there was much to see. Just rocks and ridges peppered with towering saguaro, and a bleak expanse of desert that stretched into eternity in all directions.

"Thanks." Reilly dismounted, and The Greek eased from the saddle with his Sharps.

They were near the Gila River, somewhere west of Phoenix, maybe two, perhaps three days, from Wickenburg.

"What are we going to do in Wickenburg?" The Greek asked.

Pardo shrugged. "I got me a plan. It's a good one."

Reilly pulled the stopper out of his canteen, and took a small drink.

"Can you share it?" The Greek asked.

"Sure. I reckon I can do that, Greek. You see, if we're going to take those Gatlings from the Army, I think we might have need of the talents of Swede Iverson. So me and Mac here is going to break him out of the jail. I gots me a good plan." With his left hand, he reached inside his vest pocket and withdrew a deputy U.S. marshal's badge, which he pinned onto the lapel of his vest. "You can call me Marshal Smith from here on out, Mac. I'm taking you to jail."

Reilly stared at the badge. At first, he thought it was his, but now he recognized it as Slim Chisum's.

"They don't know me—my face, I mean—in Wickenburg. Ain't never been to that town, but I hope it's got a dram shop where I can cut the dust. So me, Marshal Smith I mean, brings in old Mac here, so as we got us a man inside that jail. Then I bust him and Swede Iverson out, and we light a shuck out for the Dragoons."

Reilly hung the canteen from the stock of the rifle in the scabbard. "Swede Iverson," he said, "naturally will want to join up with you, eh?"

"Well," Pardo said, grinning, "he'll certainly owe me something for saving him from a hangman, I reckon. Oh, no doubt he'll want some money, but I can arrange that. Anyway, I ain't got everything figured out yet, but that's my plan. What do you think of it, Greek?"

The Greek shrugged. "Sounds good to me. What do I do? Cover you from the hills?"

Pardo shook his head.

"What?"

"Nothing, Greek. You don't do nothing." Easily, Pardo drew his Colt and shot The Greek in the stomach.

The gunshot echoed across the hills and canyons,

and sent The Greek's horse into a gallop southeast. Reilly had to grab the reins to keep his own mount from running off. The Sharps clattered on the rocks, and The Greek, gripping his gut with both hands, sank into a seated position, mouth gaping, eyes slowly losing their light.

"You let Wade talk you into doing a bad, bad thing," Pardo said as he holstered his revolver. He knelt in front of the dying man. "Talked you into missing them shots. Didn't he?"

The Greek tried to swallow, couldn't, but nodded slightly.

"Well, don't worry, Greek. I'll fix Chaucer's flint after we do our business in Wickenburg."

He rose, shot a glance at Reilly, and nodded. "We best ride, Mac."

Silently, Reilly mounted. *Hell*, he thought, *if Pardo keeps killing off his own men, that'll narrow the odds of me getting out of here alive.*

"Don't . . . leave . . . me," The Greek pleaded, but Pardo had already mounted his horse. He started down the ridge, stopped, and turned back until he looked down at The Greek.

"It just struck me," he said, "you always talking about your killing shot. But mine's a killing shot, too. The question is: Will you still be alive when the wolves or buzzards start eating you? Ashes to ashes, and dust to dust. So long, Greek."

Turning with a savage laugh, Pardo kicked the horse into a trot.

CHAPTER ELEVEN

The mesquite was twisted and gnarled, a giant of a tree, perhaps seventy-five years old, with huge forks going every which way, some low to the ground, creeping like the legs of a tarantula, the main branch rising above the dust-coated adobe buildings of Wickenburg. Its branches and leaves, at least, shaded the four men chained to its limbs.

Pardo almost doubled over in the saddle, he laughed so hard, pointing, spitting out the words: "That's a jail?"

"It's a big tree," Reilly told him. "Best remember that."

"Getting out of here will be a piece of cake," Pardo said, and wiped the saliva off his chin.

"Piece of mesquite," Reilly corrected. He looked around for a guard, but saw none. The four men ignored the two men on horseback. One slept. Another tried to. A third rolled a smoke. The last one paced across the courtyard. Paced, that is, as far as he could with a ten-foot chain secured around his left ankle and the fork that branched off almost at the ground.

From the description Reilly recalled from the wanted posters, the pacing man would be Swede Iverson.

"Come on, Mac," Pardo said. "I'd best get you to the law dogs." He laughed again. "A tree for a jail. Piece of cake."

Men, miners mostly, but a few Mexican farmers, crowded Wickenburg's streets as Pardo and Reilly eased their way from the Jail Tree to the town marshal's office. Since leaving the dying Greek back in the desert, they had crossed the Gila River, drifted downstream a few miles, and turned northwest, following the Hassayampa River to Wickenburg. A few miles outside of town, Pardo had fastened handcuffs, which he apparently had taken from the prison wagon, on Reilly's wrists.

It was pretty country, Reilly observed, and a lively town, full of saguaro, shaded by the mountains to the north. Hot, but not the hellish heat from the desert south. He had never been to Wickenburg, didn't know the law here.

"Here." Pardo pointed to a small adobe shack on a corner, a warped plank sign hanging over an open doorway with the word MARSHAL branded into it. "Can't read, but I know what that spells. It says, 'This is the place for John Law.'"

They reined up and swung down, greeted by a mountain of a man who filled the doorway, a man with beard as red as his face. He eyed the deputy's badge on Pardo's vest and studied Reilly.

"Thought you might be bringin' in Luke Willett," the red-bearded man said.

"Who the hell's Luke Willett?" Pardo asked.

"Prisoner. Escaped."

Pardo grinned at Reilly, then shoved him toward

Red Beard. "Maybe you'd do better if you had a real jail, and not a tree."

"Tree's good enough for our little town, Deputy," Red Beard said. "Served us well for nigh a dozen years now. My posse's trackin' down Willett. Who's your prisoner?"

"Name of Mac," Pardo said. "I was hoping you'd be so kind as to lodge him at your Jail Tree."

"Be happy to accommodate you." Red Beard held out his hand. "I'm Thaddeus McCutcheon, town marshal."

"Jim Smith," Pardo said. "We rode by the Jail Tree on our way in. Who else you got chained to that mesquite?"

"Couple of Mexicans I'm lettin' sleep off their drunks. They'll be gone by evenin'. Gambler named Gene Peck who tried to supplement his income by robbing the stage. And Swede Iverson, the murderer. Waitin' for the law from Prescott to come down and fetch them latter two."

"When do you reckon that'll be?"

"Day after tomorrow, I warrant. Come on in, Deputy Smith. I was about to pour myself a bracer. We can have a snort or two; then I'll fetch a chain for your prisoner."

"Marshal McCutcheon," Pardo said eagerly, "you speak the language of my tribe."

"How did that Willett fellow escape?" Pardo asked after McCutcheon refreshed his tin mug with a splash of Scotch.

The marshal shrugged. "Oh, he got hold of a file, sawed through his chain last night, lit out toward the Vulture."

Pardo sipped the Scotch. "That happen often?"

McCutcheon shook his head. "Rare thing. Should have suspected it, though. Old Willett, he's got a passel of friends."

"What did he do?"

"Killed a man. We was to hang him yesterday."

"Didn't see no gallows."

"You seen our Jail Tree, though. It suffices."

Pardo killed his Scotch while McCutcheon laughed. Man laughed like a girl.

Forcing a grin, Pardo held out his empty mug, and the marshal started to pour from the bottle, but hoofbeats stopped him, and he slid the bottle across his desk, rose, joints popping, and made his way to the door. Pardo helped himself to the Scotch.

Reilly sat in a dark corner, silent.

"Well, boys," McCutcheon called out. "Where's Luke Willett?"

Someone answered in Spanish, and a moment later, McCutcheon and everyone outside were laughing. Pardo shot Reilly a glance, but Reilly only shrugged.

Still cackling, McCutcheon stepped back into the office, and in came an Indian in deerskin and a black hat, and another man, a gringo with a five-point star pinned to a collarless blue shirt, holding a grain sack, stained brown at the bottom.

"Deputy," McCutcheon said, eying Pardo, "this here is Henry Dunlap, my deputy. And this is our tracker. He's Yavapai. I call him Joe." McCutcheon stuck his head outside. "Boys, I'm right proud of you. You done good work. Ride over to Miguel's, and get good and drunk. Tell Miguel to bill the town council."

Cheers followed the red-bearded marshal back inside his office, and hoofs pounded the street. "Show Deputy Smith our escaped prisoner," McCutcheon instructed, and Dunlap reached inside the sack and pulled out Luke Willett's head.

He resembled, Reilly thought, Wade Chaucer, with shorter, blonder hair and a bullet hole in the center of his forehead. Flies buzzed around the grisly throat where the Yavapai had cut off Willett's head. At least, Reilly figured, the Yavapai had done it, using that machete sheathed on his belt. McCutcheon turned the dead man's face toward him, and clucked his tongue. "Well, Luke, looks like you cheated the hangman after all." He waved his hand at the flies, and told Dunlap to drop the head back into the sack.

"Let's nail his head to the post in front of Garland's Livery," the town marshal suggested, and grabbed a chain off the wall. "It's on our way to the Jail Tree, Deputy Smith. We can secure your prisoner, then join the boys for a round or two at Miguel's."

"Sounds like a fine plan, Marshal," Pardo said.

"Getting out of here will be a piece of cake," Reilly told Pardo when Dunlap and the Yavapai fastened one end of the chain around a giant limb, and the other to his left ankle.

Pardo's eyes danced. "It's a big tree. Best remember that." With that, he turned, and followed the marshal, his deputy, and the Indian out of the courtyard, around the little adobe wall, and across the street.

Reilly tugged on the chain, knowing it would be locked solid, and looked at his companions. The two Mexicans continued to sleep, the gambler had moved away from their snores and found a shady spot, and Swede Iverson continued pacing, dragging his chain across the gravel.

A barrel-chested, broad-shouldered man, Reilly

observed, with a lean, angular face, sandy-colored hair, and blue eyes. His fingers were long, hands too small for the rest of his body, for Swede Iverson towered over Reilly McGivern. Probably a good six-foot-three, maybe four. He wore faded jeans stuck inside well-worn black boots, and a blue cotton shirt dampened by sweat. Atop his head rested, at a rakish angle, a cap of gray herringbone.

Reilly wet his lips and walked over to the sleeping Mexicans, dropping beside the nearest, and cleared his throat.

Slowly, a dark hand left the muslin shirt and pushed a straw sombrero off his beard-stubbled face. Black eyes stared up at Reilly.

"Buenas tardes, señor," Reilly said. *"¿Cómo está usted?"*

The Mexican answered with a shrug.

"¿Habla usted inglés?"

The Mexican shook his head.

Reilly frowned. That might be a little difficult, for Reilly had practically used up the Spanish he knew. He pointed to the Mexican's still-snoring companion, his eyes forming a question.

The man shook his head.

He tapped his chest. *"Policía,"* he said.

With a grunt, the Mexican pushed himself up into a seated position.

"Es verdad," Reilly said, softly adding, "But it's a long story."

The Mexican pointed at the iron clamped across Reilly's boot. Reilly gave a mild shrug, and tried to smile. "That's an even longer story." He ran his tongue of his chapped lips. How could he warn Marshal McCutcheon of Pardo's plan?

"You having trouble talking to that greaser?" a voice sounded behind him.

Startled, Reilly turned, saw Swede Iverson rolling a cigarette. The big man licked the paper, smoothed it, and fished a box of matches from his jeans pocket.

The Mexican pulled the sombrero back over his eyes and slid back into a more comfortable position.

Reilly let Iverson fire up his smoke; then he reached over and took the cigarette from Iverson's lips. "Trying to get a smoke," he said. He took a long drag, held it, and exhaled.

Iverson smiled, and pulled the makings from his shirt pocket. "Tough guy, eh?"

"Some think so." Reilly had never been much of a smoker, but he liked the taste on his tongue, the way the smoke seemed to settle his nerves. He walked closer to the dynamite man. "You're Swede Iverson."

The killer's eyebrows arched. "You know me, but I don't recollect your face."

"Call me Mac," he said.

"All right, Mac. What did you mean when you told that greaser yonder, *'Policía'*?"

"You heard that?" Reilly said, trying to think up a lie, and think one up pronto.

"I got ears." He struck the match against the side of his jeans, and fired up the cigarette.

Reilly waved around the complex. "I don't see any guards. That's what I was asking the Mexican. Where are the guards?"

"You planning on escaping?"

"The thought struck me. You game?"

Iverson laughed, and squatted. "Nobody's busted out of this, ahem, jail, since 1863, Mac." He took a long drag, blew a smoke ring toward the branches over his head. "Well, unless Luke Willett got away. A drunken drummer brought him a file the other day.

He vamoosed." He looked at the branches overhead thoughtfully. "Maybe Luke made it."

"He didn't," Reilly said.

Iverson stared at him.

"Marshal McCutcheon nailed Willett's head to a post at the livery down that street." Pointing the way.

Iverson gave a shrug, put the cigarette back between his lips. At last, he said, "That Yavapai's pretty damned good."

"That why you didn't run out with Willett?"

His laugh was more snort. "Old Luke didn't share his file. Me and Gene begged him to share, but he took it with him and skedaddled. Ain't that right, Gene?"

"Bugger off," the gambler named Peck muttered.

Iverson laughed again. "Your smoke's gone out, Mac."

Reilly nodded. He had pinched it out. "Your makings are about played out. Figured I'd best save this one." He stuck it in his vest pocket. "Not likely to find a smoke for a long spell."

"Not the way I smoke," Iverson said. He studied Reilly long and hard. "You think you can get out of here?"

"What would you say if I told you that the deputy marshal who brought me in isn't really a lawman? That he brought me here to help break you out of this, ahem, jail? That he's really Bloody Jim Pardo, and he has needs of your, shall we say, expertise with explosives?"

Laughing, Iverson pulled hard on his cigarette, and shook his head. "I'd say you're loco."

Reilly grinned. "Well, Swede, you just watch for your chance. I don't know what Pardo has in mind, but I suspect we'll find out soon enough."

With that he turned, ducking underneath the mammoth branch of the mesquite, and found a spot on the ground. Swede Iverson's chains dragged across the gravel as he paced back and forth, back and forth. Slowly, Reilly reached inside his pocket and pulled out the cigarette. He ran a thumbnail over the paper, peeled it off, letting the tobacco fall onto his lap. He glanced over his shoulder, then drew a pencil from his vest pocket. Flattening the paper on his thigh, he wrote, carefully, legibly, trying not to tear the paper.

Dep Smith is Jim Pardo. Plans 2 break out Swede. Am Reilly McGivern. Wire Marshal Cobb, Tombstone.

He folded the cigarette paper and waited until he heard the two Mexicans awaken and rise. One, the one he hadn't spoken to, got up and headed for the slop bucket in the corner of the adobe wall. Reilly stood, moved underneath the branch, and came to the other Mexican. In the center of the yard, Swede Iverson was taking a piss.

Carefully, but quickly, Reilly pulled the paper from his pocket and thrust it into the Mexican's hands. "*So-corro,*" he said. "*Dar* McCutcheon, *por favor. Es muy importante.*"

The Mexican eyed the paper uncertainly, but at last said, "*Por supuesto,*" and stuck the folded paper into the mule ear pocket of his duck pants.

Shortly before sundown, Marshal McCutcheon and Deputy Dunlap brought sowbelly and beans in a bucket, and a blackened pot of coffee, to the prisoners for supper.

"Oh, no," the red-bearded lawman told the two Mexicans. "You boys don't get no meal. Not tonight. Henry, turn 'em loose."

Reilly watched, his heart pounding against his ribs, as Dunlap unlocked the manacles around the two Mexicans' ankles. The taller one fired out something in Spanish, too rapid, too hard, for Reilly to catch anything, and leaped over the wall. The second one reached into his trousers pocket, pulled out the cigarette paper, and walked timidly to McCutcheon. *"Abrala,"* he said, and turned, gathered his sombrero in his hand, and leaped over the small wall, hurrying to catch up with his friend.

"What the hell is this?" McCutcheon stared at the paper, but then Peck yelled for his supper, and the giant marshal pitched the paper into the dirt.

With a groan, Reilly closed his eyes. When they opened, his heart skipped a beat. Jim Pardo had walked into the prison yard, and was bending over, picking up the paper.

CHAPTER TWELVE

Her lungs burning, Blanche Gottschalk slid down the ridge, causing a small avalanche of gravel. Behind her came curses, shouts. She dived behind a boulder resting at the bottom just as a bullet slammed over her head, splintering off the sandstone, blinding her with dust.

"Damn!" she cried.

She couldn't believe they were actually shooting at her.

"Don't shoot her, for Christ's sake!" It was the old woman, the one who dipped snuff. "Jim wants her alive, you blasted idiot!"

Thank God for that, Blanche thought as she fiercely rubbed her eyes.

"I know that, Miz Ruby." One of Pardo's men. "I'm just tryin' to get her to stop a-footin' it."

A rifle roared again, kicking up a stone just an inch from her boot. Instantly, she drew up her feet, gripped her knees, and rocked back and forth.

She could see now, although tears blurred her vision. Her lungs weren't working so hard, but her heart pounded against her rib cage. She was in a valley of some kind, strewn with rocks and twisted juniper. She had no idea which way to run, but when she heard the gravel rolling down the ridge, she knew one or more of Pardo's men—maybe his damned mother—were on their way down. Blanche stopped rocking, shot to her feet, and cut a path away from her pursuers.

"Hell!" a man's voice said. "She's taken off ag'in."

A bullet clipped a juniper branch as she ducked below it; then she turned to her right, seeking the shelter of another granite sphere. Her lungs ached. Sweat plastered her bangs across her forehead. She knew she couldn't wait, not with those men right behind her. Biting her lower lip, she churned ahead, finding a lone pine and bracing her back against it. She listened for voices, for footfalls, but heard only her heart and heaving lungs.

It was a forlorn hope. She was starting to realize this. She had no chance of escape. Even if she got away from Pardo's minions, what could she hope for? Apaches? Other bandits? A rattlesnake bite? Or the slow, torturous death in the desert, dying of thirst, baking in the sun?

"Hey, girlie!" The man's voice. She recognized it now. The one called Duke. "If you don't quit this foolishness, your ma'll pay."

Blanche had thought about her mother when she lit out of camp. They wouldn't harm her. No, if they had any intention of molesting her mother, they would have done so long before now. Pardo had something else in mind for them.

"She'll pay dearly, kid."

His voice sounded close. Off to her right. She wondered if she could get his rifle, a pistol. She could shoot. She didn't need that lawman, wasn't sure she even trusted him, what with him off hobnobbing with Bloody Jim Pardo, riding off to Wickenburg with The Greek. Nope, Blanche Gottschalk trusted only Blanche Gottschalk.

A twig snapped. Then nothing.

"You see her, Duke?" Another man's voice. Farther back, off to her left.

"I don't see nothin'." Closer.

Blanche tried to still her heart. She braced herself against the pine. Waiting. She could hear him now, his heavy breathing, the chimes of his spurs, could practically picture him, not ten yards behind the tree.

"Kid?"

The voice almost caused her to jump, to cry out, it was so close. She heard his boot, felt his presence, saw the barrel of the Winchester inching its way beyond the tree. Heard Duke mutter an oath. Watched the barrel until she could see the walnut grip. Then, screaming like a wild demon, Blanche leaped, grabbing the Winchester with both hands, jerking as she dropped to the ground. The rifle roared, and Duke cried out, trying to keep his balance but being pulled downward. Blanche kicked out with her right foot, catching Duke full in the groin. His mouth fell open, tears welled in his eyes, and he gagged, releasing his hold on the rifle.

"Damn . . . you. . . ."

She was scrambling to her knees, working the lever, turning and firing a shot at the charging footsteps. A second later, she was on her feet, jacking another round into the chamber, catching a glimpse of Duke's long arm reaching for her. She kicked at him, lowered the barrel, pulled the trigger.

"Jesus!" Duke yelled as the bullet slammed into the dirt inches from his face.

Another bullet thudded into the pine. She turned, cocking the Winchester, running, ducking underneath a low branch.

"She's got my repeater!" Duke cried out.

"Hell," came a weary reply.

Her left foot twisted on a stone, sent her spilling, sent the Winchester clattering on the rocks. Blanche tried to stand, fell, grabbing the rifle, jamming the stock into the dirt, and pulling herself up. Her ankle ached. She glanced behind her, then looked ahead, saw another granite sphere. Lifting the Winchester, she limped toward it, took another quick look over her shoulder. No one. Not yet. She stepped around the rock, and a fist slugged her face.

The back of her head slammed into the rock, and she tasted blood as she slid to the ground. "Bitch," a voice said. Rough hands ripped the rifle from her grip, and pitched the Winchester behind him.

Her lips had been split. A knot was already beginning to rise on the back of her head. She looked up to see a black wool coat disappear around the rock tower.

"I got her, you lame assholes." A smooth hand shoved a nickel-plated Remington into a holster, and then two hands jerked her to her feet, shoved her against the granite, the forearm pressing against her throat.

"You try to run again, I'll kill you."

She fought the forearm, couldn't breathe, but the arm pressed tighter.

"Wade." Duke's voice. "Man, you're gonna choke her to death."

"Easy, Wade." Another voice. The one called Harrah. "Jim don't want her dead."

The forearm pulled away, and Blanche dropped to

her knees, breathing deeply, as if she couldn't get enough air. Blood dripped onto the ground.

"I don't give a tinker's damn what Pardo wants."

Blanche leaned against the rock, feeling her throat with one hand, wiping her lips with the other, staring up at the three men.

"Well . . ." Duke started, but fell silent.

"Pardo's going to get us all killed," Chaucer said. "You know what he plans on doing? You know why he went to Wickenburg?"

"I figure it had something to do with that dynamite man the woman and Mac read us about," Harrah said.

"Yeah. That's exactly. Lacy told me. He's going to break Swede Iverson out of jail, and use him to rob that Army wagon train."

"Well, that'll be a good thing," Duke said. "We could use a good man."

"An Army wagon train. For a bunch of Gatling guns." Chaucer shook his head. "We'll need more than Swede Iverson to pull off a job like that. There's no money in that train, no payroll, just a bunch of firepower."

"What's he want with Gatling guns?" Duke asked.

"Hell if I know. To start a war, rebuild his long-lost Confederacy. I'm sick of this whole thing."

"Then why don't you leave?" Harrah asked.

"Don't push me, Harrah. I might just do that. And take Lacy with me."

Duke cleared his throat. "Now, you best watch it, Wade. Lacy, she's the boss man's woman."

"She's anybody's woman." Chaucer spit.

"Better not let Pardo hear you say nothing like that," Harrah said. "Or Ruby."

Chaucer glanced down at Blanche, his face flushed.

"Now . . ." Again, Duke stopped.

"I've told you boys once, and I'll tell you again." Chaucer looked at both men. "Riding with Jim Pardo's a fool's play. You saw what happened at the train. All that money gone. Burned up. We haven't had any decent money in eight or nine months. Living up here in this hellhole. And now we've got Apaches to worry about. I'm for lighting a shuck out of here, heading over to Tucson, or Tombstone, someplace where there's money. Whiskey. Women."

Harrah cleared his throat. "You best watch it, Wade. Last time you started talking about such things, you almost got Pardo killed. Getting The Greek to miss them shots."

Suddenly, Chaucer chuckled. "Yeah, lot of good that did us. But I don't recollect you boys trying to talk The Greek out of it. Hell, it almost worked, but I'm glad it didn't. I want to kill Jim Pardo myself."

"Now that's foolish talk, Wade," Duke said.

"Might be foolish, but it's not as stupid as riding with Pardo. Anymore."

"I ain't comfortable listenin' to this kind of talk," Duke said. "Let's get this girl back to her ma, get back to camp. Let's wait and see what happens with the boss man, see what he says when he and The Greek and Mac come back."

Chaucer laughed again. "The Greek? He isn't coming back. Don't you boys realize that?"

Duke and Harrah gave him blank stares.

"He took The Greek into the desert to kill him. Payback for missing those shots. He knows why The Greek missed. So when he comes back, he'll be planning to kill me, too."

"Pardo wouldn't do that," Harrah said, but his voice trembled with uncertainty.

"Wait and see," Chaucer said. He patted the holstered Remington. "But he'll find me a little tougher to kill."

Duke shuffled his feet. "How you . . . how do you know that . . . that he was gonna kill The Greek?"

With a chuckle, Chaucer answered, "Lacy told me. Pardo told her."

When Harrah and Duke looked at each other, the discomfort apparent in their faces.

Chaucer laughed harder. "I told you, boys. Lacy's anybody's woman."

"You can get killed talking like that, Wade," Harrah said.

"You can get killed riding with Pardo. No, you *will* get killed riding with Pardo. Maybe not, if you were to ride with me."

The wind picked up, carrying the silence across the valley. Blanche just sat, silently, listening, bleeding, aching. Fear crept through her now. She recalled something the lawman—Reilly McGivern, her mother had told her was his real name—had told them: *You two need to keep in mind that right now Jim Pardo's keeping us alive. If Wade Chaucer had his druthers . . .*

"Well," Duke said, shifting his rifle from one hand to the other, "it might be nice, I mean, to be shun of these mountains, be in a town with some whores. Pardo, he drew on me, was gonna kill me back at the Southern Pacific tracks. He was gonna kill me for boilin' coffee. For nothin'."

"He's crazy," Chaucer said. "Crazy like his old man. Crazy like that bitch of a mother he has."

"Maybe you're the crazy one," Harrah said.

"Maybe I am."

A longer silence followed.

"What would you do," Duke said softly, "with her?"

His jaw jutted toward Blanche. He wet his lips. "And her ma?"

Blanche frowned. Her heart jumped into her throat. She was thinking, just maybe, since they had forgotten about her, she might be able to sneak around the other side of that tall rock sphere, start running, hightail it out of here. Now that chance had evaporated.

Chaucer jerked the Remington from its holster, and he thumbed back the hammer, the barrel just an inch from Blanche's head.

"I should kill her right now. Be done with her."

"You do that, Wade, and it'll be the last mistake you ever made." Blanche's eyes found Ruby Pardo a few rods away, aiming her Winchester from the hip. "Jimmy wants her alive. I reckon we'll keep her that way."

She could see pure hatred in Wade's eyes, see that Ruby's contempt of Chaucer in her own hardened face. Duke and Harrah stepped away, Duke going to fetch his rifle, Harrah just getting out of the way of any potential stray bullet.

Blanche breathed and bled.

Slowly, Chaucer lowered the revolver's hammer and shoved it violently into his holster. He turned. "I'm heading back to camp," he announced. "Then I'm going on a scout. Check things out in the valley." He tipped his hat at Ruby, adding, "Don't wait up, Miz Pardo," before disappearing around the rock tower. Ruby Pardo took a few steps back, keeping the Winchester ready, until she was satisfied Chaucer was no longer a threat. Only then did she spit and lower the rifle barrel. She nodded at Blanche. "Help the child up, Harrah," she ordered. "Let's get back to camp."

Duke reached over, roughly pulled Blanche off the ground, shoved her against the rock. "I ought to tan your hide, kickin' me in the nuts like you done, stealin' my rifle." He threatened her with a backhand, but Blanche knew he wouldn't strike her, knew that even before Ruby Pardo warned him not to touch the child.

He shoved her toward Ruby, and Blanche, still limping from her twisted ankle, walked toward the old woman, wondering how much of the conversation she had overheard.

CHAPTER THIRTEEN

Reilly hadn't time to think. Out of the corner of his eye, he spotted town Marshal Thaddeus McCutcheon stepping over the chain. Spinning quickly, he gripped the chain in his manacled hands and jerked upward. The metal lifted off the ground, catching McCutcheon full in the groin, and he pitched forward in agony, pulling against the chain, bringing Reilly to his knees. The pot McCutcheon was carrying went flying, spilling sowbelly and beans everywhere.

"Get that deputy!" Reilly bellowed while he scrambled to his feet, and raced toward the fallen lawman.

McCutcheon was no amateur. He knew what was happening, and, despite spitting out saliva, his left hand holding his balls, face contorted in pain, his right drew the Smith & Wesson. Reilly lashed out with the chain again, watching the metal slam into the marshal's hand, ripping the gun from his grip.

"Henry!" The lawman managed to spit out the words, a desperate plea to his deputy.

Reilly didn't have time to look. He hoped, prayed, Jim Pardo was taking care of Henry Dunlap.

* * *

"What the—" Pardo started. He saw Mac jerk the chain, then bolt toward the fallen marshal, screaming something.

He hadn't planned this. Hell's fire, he had been enjoying himself, pretending to be a lawman, drinking on the Wickenburg Town Council's budget, getting good and roostered. He hadn't given any thought to Mac or Swede Iverson. Damned near had forgotten about both of them until them two law dogs left Miguel's Saloon saying they'd best go see to their prisoners.

Mac's movement quickly sobered him up.

He looked toward the Jail Tree, finding the deputy, Henry Dunlap, who had been gathering the two chains that had held those two drunk Mexicans. Dunlap, pretty much in his cups like everyone else in that posse, was slow to comprehend. Suddenly, the town law called out, "Henry!" And Dunlap dropped the chains and went for his revolver.

This is no good, Pardo thought, and made three quick strides across the prison yard, pulling out his revolver. His first impulse was to shoot, but that would be no good. The shot would alert the town. Quickly, he spun the gun on his finger, grabbed the barrel, and swung the walnut grip at Deputy Dunlap's head. Dunlap looked confused as Pardo swung. Then he looked stunned as the butt smashed his head, knocking off his hat. The deputy dropped like a felled pine.

Turning, reversing the pistol, Pardo looked across the yard at Mac and the town marshal.

* * *

Reilly leaped onto McCutcheon, whose right hand went to his shoulder holster. The breath went out of McCutcheon's lungs when Reilly landed on his chest, but the lawman remained game, recovered quickly, frantic, and jerked an American Bulldog .44. The barrel was coming up, and Reilly's handcuffs slammed down, catching McCutcheon's forehead, cutting an ugly line just below his scalp, jarring his head into the rocky ground.

With a soft whimper, McCutcheon dropped the .44 and went still.

"What the hell are you doing?" Pardo bellowed.

Chest heaving, face dampened by sweat, Reilly rolled off the unconscious lawman, spotted Pardo standing above Dunlap's supine body. Barely, Reilly lifted his hands, tried to speak, but his lungs wouldn't let him just yet, and pointed at the ring of keys the deputy had dropped by the mesquite.

Pardo shot a glance up and down the streets, but they remained empty.

"This ain't what I had planned," Pardo said.

"Keys," Reilly managed. Still pointing. He craned his neck, saw Swede Iverson just standing and staring. Looked on the other side of the tree to find the stage-coach bandit named Peck doing the same.

Pardo shoved the Colt into the holster, dropped to a knee, and picked up the key ring, then hurried over to Reilly. He found a small key, and tried it in the leg iron. "You best hope this works," he said.

It didn't.

The next one, however, did, and the iron bracelet unclasped, and dropped off Reilly's boot. Reilly held up his chained hands, and Pardo let the key ring fall, and fished out the key to the handcuffs from his vest pocket. When those fell free, Reilly turned, pried the .44 Bulldog from McCutcheon's right hand, and shoved it into his waistband before staggering to his feet.

Pardo had grabbed the keys, and strode over to Swede Iverson.

"Your name Iverson? Swede Iverson?" he asked.

The dynamite man's head bobbed just slightly.

"I'm Bloody Jim Pardo." Iverson's eyes widened, and he sought out Reilly for confirmation.

"Don't look at him, damn it. You look at me." Iverson's eyes fell back on Pardo. "You want out of here?"

"Yes," he croaked.

"Good, we got business to discuss."

As Pardo went to work on Iverson's leg irons, Reilly locked the ankle bracelet on Thaddeus McCutcheon's left ankle, then moved over to Henry Dunlap, and secured his ankle to a chain, which he then affixed to the mesquite's lowest limb. He looked across the ground, saw the cigarette paper where Pardo had dropped it, still folded, unread. He wondered if he could get to it, somehow stick it into McCutcheon's hands, but Pardo was bringing Swede Iverson across the ground.

"All right, Mac," Pardo demanded. "Now we got you and this galoot free, how the hell do we get out of town?"

"Miguel's Saloon," Reilly said, straightening. "The posse's horses are out in front of it, I imagine."

Pardo snorted, and spit. "A dozen men are right inside that place. Armed to the teeth."

"And drunker than sin."

Pardo's eyes brightened. "Yeah, I reckon they is, at that." He ran his tongue across his lips. "Be risky, though."

"You got a better idea?"

Before Pardo could answer, Gene Peck cried out, "Hey, don't leave me here! I don't want to get sent to Yuma."

Pardo looked Peck over, considering him, scratched the palm of his right hand on the Colt's hammer, then let out a sigh, and walked back to fetch the key ring he had left by the end of the chain that had held Iverson. Reilly's eyes sought out the cigarette paper.

"You wasn't fooling," Swede Iverson said. "That's Bloody Jim Pardo."

"Yeah." Reilly knew he'd have to leave the paper where it was, pray that McCutcheon or Dunlap found it. Not that it would do anyone any good now. He realized his hat was gone, and he found it by Mc-Cutcheon's body. By the time he had it settled back on his head, Pardo had freed Peck and stood between the stagecoach robber and the dynamite man.

"Where's Miguel's Saloon?" Reilly asked.

Pardo jerked a thumb to the south.

Reilly started, but hurried over to Dunlap.

"Now what are you doing?" Pardo cried out.

Reilly didn't answer. He unloosened the bandana around Dunlap's neck, rolled it up, and used it to gag the unconscious deputy. He saw the Smith & Wesson beside the tree, and snatched it up, shoved it into his waistband, too.

"I rattled his brains long enough that he'll be sleeping through September," Pardo said with irritation. "Come on, Mac, we'd best light a shuck."

Ignoring him, Reilly removed his bandana, and tied the deputy's hands behind his back, then dashed over to McCutcheon. He snapped the manacles on the marshal's wrists, and gagged him with his own bandana. Then, Reilly laughed, thinking, *Yeah, they'll really believe that note on that cigarette paper now.*

Shaking his head, he hurried over to the three outlaws waiting for him.

"Let's vamoose," Pardo said, and led the way.

The clawing of an out-of-tune banjo, accompanied by an equally wretched fiddle, rose above the din of voices and the clinking of glasses inside Miguel's Saloon. Darkness was coming fast, and the glow of light seeping through the glass looked inviting. But not as inviting as the dozen or more horses crowding the hitching posts in front of the single-story adobe structure bookended by an assayer's office and a vacant building with a FOR RENT sign nailed to the door.

A man in duck trousers and a muslin shirt stood in front of the doors to Miguel's place, discussing with a raven-haired woman in a frilly dress, when not fondling her, the cost of a trip to the woman's crib behind the saloon. From the corner of a café, Pardo and Reilly watched, growing impatient, until finally, the woman, giggling, grabbed the man's hand and led him to the alley that separated the saloon from the assayer's office.

Reilly studied the streets. He found another saloon six or seven doors down, heard piano music coming from that one, but saw no one on the streets or boardwalks. A door opened and closed, and a man in a black broadcloth suit stood down the street. He locked the door, strode off northward, turned a corner, and was gone.

Laughter exploded out of Miguel's Saloon.

Reilly looked at the horses.

"I see my mount next to yours," Reilly said in a dry whisper.

"Didn't have time to find the livery," Pardo explained.

"You want to keep them?"

"Hell, no. I'm going for that blood bay on the far end."

Reilly's gaze fell on Pardo's roan, or rather, the Evans repeater sheathed in the saddle scabbard.

"Reckon I'll take yours, then," he said.

Pardo giggled. "I must like you, Mac, letting you steal my horse."

Reilly turned, nodding at Swede Iverson. "You think you can sneak up with us, grab the reins to that dun mare on the far side yonder, and lead it down the street till we reach this corner?"

The nod Swede Iverson gave didn't suggest complete confidence.

"Muzzle her while you walk," Reilly said. He looked at Gene Peck. "You take the bay next to the dun. Keep him quiet."

Peck gave a nervous nod.

The banjo and fiddle music stopped. An empty bottle flew out of the door, amid more laughter.

"I'd hate to be the county treasurer when he gets Miguel's bill," Reilly whispered.

Pardo grinned. "I'd hate to be you or me when we sneak up to steal them horses." He almost doubled over laughing, and when he straightened, he stared at Reilly and said, "Because I ain't told you something that's mighty important."

Frowning, Reilly asked, his voice strained, "What's that?"

"The scout of that posse, Yavapai Joe, he's in that saloon, too. Was, anyway, when them law dogs and me took our leave."

"Yeah."

"Well, he ain't the drinking kind." Pardo chuckled. "He was in that saloon, next to that window yonder, sipping coffee and eating mutton. I wonder how our heads will look next to Luke Willett's nailed to a corral post by that livery."

Wiping his clammy hands on his dusty pants, Reilly started for Pardo's roan, whispering, "Let's find out."

He realized his mistake when Pardo took off to his left and Peck and Iverson went to his right. Pardo's roan was tethered right in front of the open doorway, yet Reilly kept moving. Briefly, he wondered if he could draw the Smith & Wesson or Bulldog and cut down Pardo. But what good would that do? The posse would come out, and drunk as they were, they'd start shooting. And what of Dagmar and Blanche, back in camp in the Dragoon Mountains? No, Reilly realized, he would need to think of something better, something that wouldn't likely get him killed.

Pardo, making a beeline, reached the dun first and was already leading it down the street when Reilly eased to the roan's side. Rubbing its side gently, muttering a few soothing sounds, Reilly slipped between the roan and a bay mare. He could see Iverson and Peck loosening the reins to their horses. He looked at the window, but the table where the Yavapai tracker had been sitting, according to Pardo, looked empty. Reilly had worked his way to the roan's neck, continued to rub it with his left hand, and reached for the reins wrapped around the rail.

The batwing doors pounded open, and a man staggered outside, trying to light a pipe. His eyes detected Reilly, and he practically fell onto the hitching rail, catching himself with both hands, pushing himself back up, grinning.

"*¿Hombre, qué pasa?*" he asked. He wasn't Mexican, but an American with a thick mustache and beard. His breath reeked of tequila. He didn't seem aware that he'd dropped both match and pipe. Reilly looked over his shoulders into the saloon. No one seemed to notice, or hear. They were too busy watching a woman dance across the bar.

"Did you hear, hombre, that we caught Luke Willett? The Yavapai." He guffawed, and slapped Reilly's shoulder. "He cut off old Luke's head, he did. I seen him. With my own eyes." He nodded for emphasis. "Shot the son of a bitch, too. That injun's mean. Meaner than . . ." He struggled to find a word.

Reilly smiled at the drunk, and looked into the window. The table remained vacant. Maybe the Yavapai was in front of the bar with everybody else, watching a fat-legged woman do the cancan.

"Marshal M-M-Mc—the marshal," the drunk said, "he nailed it to a corral post in front of Garland's Livery. Want to see it, hombre? The flies shouldn't be so bad, not this time a night."

A horse snorted. The drunk weaved, then fell against the bay mare, which shied away, snorted, and kicked. Slowly the drunk righted himself, as his eyes focused on three men leading three horses down the street.

"Damnation," the man said, "what the hell is that squirt doing with Zeke's mount?"

Reilly jerked the Smith & Wesson and clubbed the drunk's head, caught him at the shoulders, and eased him onto the ground. He shot a look inside, gathered the reins, and pulled the roan out.

"Hey, Carl!" a voice called from inside the saloon. "What the hell's keeping you?"

He didn't know if Carl was the man he'd just buffaloed, didn't care. Instead of leading the roan down the street, Reilly grabbed the horn and swung into the saddle, keeping the Smith & Wesson in his right hand. He heard footsteps, heard the squeaking of the batwing doors, heard a voice call out, "What the hell's going on?"

Ahead of him, Pardo had mounted the dun, and Gene and Iverson were climbing into their saddles. Reilly touched the spurs to the roan's sides and felt the powerful horse explode into a gallop. He was chasing the dust raised by Pardo, Iverson, and Peck when a bullet sliced his left rein.

CHAPTER FOURTEEN

Once he had rounded the corner, Reilly jerked on the one rein he still held, pulling the powerful roan to a stop. Instantly, he swung off the saddle, shoved the Smith & Wesson into his waistband, and drew the Evans from the scabbard. He let the rein fall to the ground, knowing, or, rather, hoping, that Jim Pardo had trained this horse not to run during a gun battle. A quick look down the darkened street revealed nothing. Pardo and the two men he, Reilly McGivern, had helped free, were long gone.

Levering a round into the chamber, he ejected a .44 shell—Pardo had kept a live round under the hammer—and caught it, sticking it into his vest pocket. He ducked underneath a hitching rail, stepped onto the boardwalk, and peered around the corner. The light from the saloon gave him plenty of targets as men wandered out of the doorway. A few drunkenly attempted to mount their horses.

Reilly took aim and cut loose with the Evans.

His first shot took off a man's bowler hat as he wheeled around a buckskin. The man dived into the water trough, and the horse galloped down the street.

His second shot kicked up dust at the feet of another bay a man in a Mexican sombrero was trying to mount, sending the man rolling over and flattening horse apples, and the horse loping after the buckskin.

Shouts and curses erupted from the crowd. The man emerged from the water trough, clawing for a revolver, and falling to the other side. Reilly drilled the trough with a .44 slug.

Off to Reilly's left, someone turned up a lantern in a second-story room and opened a window. Reilly spun, aimed, and broke a pane of glass, heard a curse. After that, he turned back toward the saloon. A bullet thudded into the wood frame near his head, but, unfazed, Reilly pulled the trigger. He saw the Yavapai cocking a Winchester, silhouetted in front of the door. Reilly's bullet clipped the doorway behind him. His next shot carved a furrow across the warped plank at the Indian's feet. His third chased the Indian as he dived through the batwing doors. His fourth, fifth, and sixth shots punched holes in the swinging doors.

His eyes burned from the gunshots. A shout came behind him, and Reilly turned and sent two rounds after a man waving, of all things, a broom. The man took off running down an alley. He left the broom in the street.

The stink of sulfur filled the air. Reilly dropped to a knee.

The roan horse stood patiently waiting.

Reilly jacked another round into the Evans and kept firing, shattering the saloon's window, throwing up dust at the throwing feet of the tethered horses, and slamming into ends of the hitching rails. A couple of shots came flying, but by now the drunks were leaping through the busted glass or diving to the ground. Two managed to crawl underneath the saloon's doors. One of those, the man who had taken a bath in the water trough, left a trail of water behind him.

Horses screamed. Reilly kept firing.

He thought of Ruby Pardo. The woman sure knew how to fix a rifle. He'd give her that much. The Evans had never fired truer, and this time, it didn't jam.

The string of horses to his left pulled the hitching rail off its posts, and the horses thundered away from Reilly's gunshots. Another horse, a big dun, jerked free, rearing, and somersaulted in the dust, gathered its feet, stumbled, regained its feet, and took off.

"Hey!"

Reilly spun around, jacked another round into the Evans, fired from his hips at a man on the other side of the street. The man managed one shot, which busted a pane of glass to Reilly's left; then he dived inside a door. Reilly took careful aim and fired two more rounds into the café.

Lights began appearing in various windows. Somewhere, a bell tolled.

He looked back at the saloon. All of the horses had scattered. A few men chanced potshots, without really aiming, and Reilly figured he had bought enough time. He fired twice more at the saloon, once at the second-story window, and a final shot in the open doorway, then grabbed the reins—the one the bullet had clipped had shortened it only four inches, could have taken off some of Reilly's fingers—leaped into the saddle, pounding the roan's flanks with the hot rifle barrel, and galloped down the street.

He rode east out of town, following the road, hoping he was following Jim Pardo. A couple of miles out of town, he saw the faint glow of a cigarette and slowed the roan to a trot, reining up when he spotted Pardo, sitting in the saddle, grinning, a Colt in his hand.

"Sounded like a war back there," he said as Reilly reined in. Swede Iverson and Gene Peck sat nervously behind Pardo, eager to run.

"Thanks for your help," Reilly said sarcastically. He realized he still held the Evans, and now took time to shove it into the scabbard.

Pardo took a final drag on his smoke and flicked the cigarette into the darkness. "I never got the habit of risking my neck, Mac."

"At least you waited for me," Reilly said.

"'Cause I've taken a liking to you."

"We'd best raise dust," Reilly said. "I ran off their horses, but they'll have a posse on our trail *muy pronto*." He glanced skyward. "And that moon'll rise in an hour or so. Be light as day out here."

With a nod, Pardo holstered his Colt, and gestured at Peck and Iverson. "Let's *vamanos*," he said, and raked the sides of the blood bay he had stolen with his spurs.

They galloped on east for two or three more miles, then turned south, not stopping, barely slowing, until they reached Smith's Mill on the eastern banks of the Hassayampa, where they traded in their winded mounts for fresh horses, all brown, almost a matched set. There Reilly reloaded the Evans, finding he had only five rounds left, plus the one bullet he'd stuck in his vest pocket. He started to fetch that round, but something inside told him to save it, so he did. The Scotsman at the mill didn't bother asking for bills of sale for the horses he was getting, and didn't offer any for the ones he was trading, but he did warn them: "Best take it easy with *these* horses. Nearest settlement's Phoenix."

An hour south, they picked their way east into the rocky hills, letting the full moon light their saguaro- and boulder-lined path. Peck and Iverson rode point, and Reilly rode alongside Pardo.

Exhausted, Reilly had almost let the clopping of hoofs on the hard stones lull him into sleep, when Pardo's voice suddenly jerked him awake.

"I heard a good story at Miguel's Saloon," Pardo was saying.

After he stifled a yawn, and rubbed his eyes, Reilly asked, "What was it?"

"The town law, McCutcheon . . . I forgets his first name."

"Thaddeus," Reilly said.

Pardo turned and stared. "You got a good memory, Mac."

Reilly shrugged.

Pardo looked ahead. "Anyway, Marshal Thaddeus McCutcheon says a lot of folks in Wickenburg say the Hassayampa flows backward. That's cause it's underground." He snorted. "If it ain't just dry."

"That's a fine story," Reilly said.

"No, Mac. That ain't all of it. Because the river flows backward, them Wickenburg folks say that if you drink from it, you'll never tell the truth again." He cackled, and slapped his thigh.

"Reckon you've partook of water from the Hassayampa," Reilly said.

"Now, Mac," Pardo said, "that ain't very polite of you." He laughed again, though, and pushed back his hat. "Can't wait to tell Ma that one. She'll love it."

Reilly felt a wry smile cut across his face. "I need to thank your mother, too, for fixing—" He stopped himself. He had almost said *my* Evans. "Fixing your rifle. That Evans is a good-shooting weapon."

"Well, why don't you draw it, and put a round between that gent's shoulder blades?" Pardo jutted his jaw in the general direction of the gambler-turned-stagecoach bandit, Gene Peck.

A knot formed deep in Reilly's gut. His throat felt dry.

"I'm not in the habit of shooting a man in the back," he said.

"Call his name," Pardo said, "and when he turns around, you can shoot him in his head." He tapped a finger above his nose. "Right about there."

"I don't think so, Jim."

"Why not?"

Reilly shrugged. "You could have left him back chained to that mesquite tree."

"Yeah, but he might have sang out. Not that it mattered, not how things turned out. But he might have been irked at us, what with him getting left behind on two jailbreaks." He shook his head, and pointed again at Peck. "I don't think I have no need of that fellow. Kill him."

"No." Firmly.

Pardo turned again, studying Reilly. "You're soft, Mac. And me, being so kindhearted, letting you carry that fast-shooting Evans, and them two other guns you taken off them Wickenburg laws."

"We might have need of those guns," Reilly said.

Pardo snorted and shook his head. "I don't think that posse is gonna catch up with us. Ain't heard a sound behind us since we left town."

"They spoke highly of that Yavapai tracker," Reilly informed him.

Another snort. "Injun."

"Indians make good trackers," Reilly said casually. "The way they talk in Wickenburg, he might be able to trail us all the way back to the Dragoons."

"Yeah." Pardo sounded irritated. "Maybe I should have rode back when you held off them boys. Maybe I could have put a bullet in that injun's head." He tapped his forehead again. "Right there."

Silence. They crested a hill, picked their way down a rocky slope. Somewhere to the north, coyotes sang out their melodious yips.

"I miss Ma," Pardo said softly after a while. "Worried about her."

"She's tough," Reilly said. "She can take care of herself."

Pardo, however, was shaking his head. "She said something before we left, Mac. I said something about me having to kill Wade Chaucer, eventually, and she said, 'Not if I kill him first.'"

Reilly shot Pardo a quizzical look. "You planning on killing Chaucer?"

He answered first with a shrug, then looked over at Reilly. "I'll have to, one of these days. Or Chaucer'll kill me, though that ain't likely. Now Wade Chaucer, he wouldn't have no . . . um . . . no . . . revulsion . . ." He nodded with satisfaction at the word he had chosen. "No, sir, he wouldn't have no revulsion at the thought of shooting that Peck fellow in his back. Why, if I'd turn my back on Chaucer long enough . . ." He grinned, but his face saddened.

"Ma's all I got," he said after they had ridden another thirty yards. He wet his lips, sniffled, and his whole body suddenly trembled.

"You all right, Jim?" Reilly asked.

Nothing for another twenty yards; then Pardo's head bobbed slightly. "Just worried. You see, I made Ma promise that she'd stay clear of Chaucer. She done it. Swore she wouldn't try nothing."

"Then there's no need to worry," Reilly assured him.

Pardo chuckled. "Well, maybe you're right, Mac, but, see, I know Ma. Knowed her all my life. Sure, she promised me, but, well, I reckon Ma has drunk her share of water from that backward-flowing Hassa-yampa River. That woman's a born liar."

The levity died in his voice. "Ma's all I got," he said again, his eyes narrowing into mere slits.

For the next hour, there was no sound except the creaking of leather, the jingling of spurs, the clopping of hoofs, until Gene Peck reined in and turned around.

"Where are we going?" Peck asked.

"You ain't going to Yuma," Pardo said, and rode past the gambler. "Ain't that what you wanted?"

A short while later, they descended into a dry riverbed, and Pardo reined up, looking upstream, downstream, running a tongue across his lips. "This'll be it," he muttered.

"What?" Reilly asked.

"The Agua Fria. There's a fork up this way, I think. They was talking about it back at Miguel's. This Mex-ican named Gonzales has a place just up this riverbed. Raises horses. Good horses. We can replace these nags and get us some real horseflesh that'll get us maybe to Florence, where we can steal some more that'll take us back to Ma and that Dagmar woman."

Reilly stood in his stirrups, looking upstream. "That man raises horses . . . *here*?"

"Got himself an artesian well. A veritable oasis, I was told." Pardo grinned, pleased with his vocabulary.

He said it again. "Yes, sir, a veritable oasis. Let's ride."
Directing Peck to ride ahead, he kicked his horse into
a walk alongside Swede Iverson's.

"Swede," Pardo said, "I been meaning to have a bit
of a parley with you."

"All right."

"I got a job I'm undertaking, one that would need
a good dynamiter like you."

"A bank?" Iverson asked.

Pardo shook his head. "Not exactly." His smile
faded quickly. "And it ain't no mine, and it ain't no
railroad tracks, for you to kill people." Suddenly, he
reined up, and the Colt leaped into his hands.

"Mac," he said, dropping his voice into a whisper.
"Did you hear that?"

Reilly had pulled up short. He shook his head.
Ahead of them rode Gene Peck. The sky was lighten-
ing to a dim gray in the east.

"Peck!" Pardo called out in an urgent whisper.
"Peck!"

Gene Peck kept riding, turning at a bend in the
riverbed.

Reilly heard it. "A horse," he said, "whinnying."

"Must be Gonzales's place," Pardo said. "Well, looks
like them boys at Miguel's hadn't drunk none from
the Hassayampa. They musta been telling us the
gospel truth." He shot a glance eastward. "Be daylight
directly."

"I bet Señor Gonzales is already awake," Reilly said.

"Then let's do us some horse-trading." Pardo
kicked his horse into a trot, with Reilly and Swede
Iverson following a few rods behind. They rounded
the bend, saw Gene Peck ahead of them, then saw the
muzzle flashes as a dozen rifles opened up, cutting
down Peck and the brown horse.

CHAPTER FIFTEEN

Raindrops pounded the tent in the predawn light, cooling the air but soaking through the canvas until water began dripping on Wade Chaucer's face. With a vile oath, he sat up, yanking the Remington from underneath the pillow, and found his pants. Beside him, Three-Fingers Lacy rolled over, muttering something incoherent. Chaucer pulled on his pants, then reached for his boots.

"Is it raining?" Lacy asked sleepily.

"No," Chaucer said, "God's pissing on your tent."

"Don't be sacrilegious, Wade." She sat up, combing her wild hair with her fingers, then stared at the water forming a puddle in the center of her bed. "Must be a monsoon," she said.

"Monsoons strike in the afternoon," he told her as he shoved his pants legs inside the tops of his boots, stood, walked to the folding table, disgusted as his boots slopped through the wet ground, and turned up the lantern. Next, he grabbed his gunbelt, laying the nickel-plated pistol on the table while he buckled on the shell belt.

Lacy sat up. "Where you going, Wade?"

"Find some coffee," he said.

"But it's raining."

"Slacking up," he said, and the storm was, too, just an abnormal morning shower.

"Don't you want to . . . ?" She purred, and Chaucer looked at her, found her tempting. Her breasts surged against the dirty plum-colored camisole she wore. He made himself look away, and his gaze fell upon the uncorked bottle of bourbon on the table. He took a sip, then set it down.

"What would your Jimmy say about that?" he asked. "Or Ruby if she found me leaving your tent this early in the morn?"

When her face froze in fright, Chaucer laughed.

"You . . . you wouldn't tell him, or her, would you, about us?"

"I might," he said. "Just to rile him. To see the look on his face right before I filled his gut with lead."

"Wade," she begged, and thunder rolled across the Dragoons.

"Don't worry," he said, softening, and he walked back to the bed, and sat beside her, kissing her gently on her lips. "Jim, well, he won't be coming back from Wickenburg."

Her eyes widened.

"When I went on a scout," he said, "I rode all the way to Benson."

"Benson?"

He nodded. "Sent a telegraph to Wickenburg law. Told him to be on the lookout for Jim Pardo. Said he planned to break Swede Iverson out of jail."

"Wade!" She pulled away from him. "You set him up. That town law, he'll kill Jimmy."

He shoved her down, rising, feeling the heat rush to his head. "What do you think he'll do to us, woman?"

He looked at his feet, saw his boots covered with grass and mud, standing in a half-inch of water. "I'm sick of living like a cur dog, hiding in this heap. So it's high time you made a choice, Lacy, dear. Jimmy, or me? This camp, or a real town?"

Grabbing his hat, he left her trembling on her bed.

The rain had stopped. It remained dark, except for the glow of the lantern inside Lacy's tent, but he could make out Duke and Phil starting a fire, having set up a canvas cover to keep the fire pit relatively dry. Good, they'd have coffee boiling in a few minutes. He'd announce his plan over breakfast this fine morning, let them know that Pardo wouldn't be returning from Wickenburg.

"What about Ruby?" Lacy called to his back.

He snorted and walked toward the fire, trying to avoid any puddles of water he could see in the darkness. He had taken four or five steps toward the fire when the deadly metallic click of a rifle being cocked stopped him. Phil and Duke heard the noise, too, and stood, staring.

"You're a double-crossing bastard, Wade Chaucer," Ruby Pardo said as Chaucer turned to face her. "You ain't worth giving no chance to, but I wasn't about to shoot you in the back."

She stood beside the tent, so he could see her outline well, though not her face. Rainwater dripped off her waterlogged hat, and she wore a black poncho made of India rubber. How long had she been standing outside Lacy's tent? Chaucer wondered. From the looks of her, she might have been there all night. He wouldn't put it past her.

"Miz Ruby?" Duke called.

"I'm killing a cur dog," Ruby said, and she took four long strides, keeping the Winchester pointed at

Chaucer's gut. "A cur dog that's been hiding in this heap." The light from the lantern inside Lacy's tent turned up, revealing Ruby Pardo's leathery face and the Winchester rifle. Her feet sloshed through the water.

The sky began turning to a gunmetal gray.

Chaucer grinned, and hooked his thumbs on his shell belt, between the holster across his midsection. The Mexican, Soledad, crawled from underneath his sugans, and slowly rose. The only person missing was Harrah, likely up on the ridge on sentry duty.

"Boys," Chaucer said easily, "looks like we've got ourselves a standoff."

An odd grin lightened Ruby Pardo's face.

Behind him, footfalls told him that Duke and Phil were walking over.

"I'm taking over this gang," Chaucer said, never taking his eyes of the woman with the Winchester.

"You got an odd way of doin' it," Phil said casually.

"Jim Pardo won't be coming back from Wickenburg," Chaucer said. "The other day, I sent a wire to the Wickenburg town marshal."

"You done what?" Duke exclaimed.

Chaucer spun. "That's right. I set Pardo up. Sicced the law on him. He and that Mac fellow are dead by now, or locked up in Wickenburg. Serves him right, for doing in The Greek like he done."

"You don't know that Jim killed The Greek," Phil said.

"Don't I?" His smile returning, he turned back to face Ruby. "Tell him, Miz Ruby. Tell him what your boy planned to do with The Greek."

When Ruby Pardo remained still, Chaucer called out to Lacy: "Lacy, tell these boys what Jim Pardo had in store for The Greek!"

Nothing. "Bitch," he mumbled, then forced his smile to return. "Looks like a standoff, Miz Ruby."

"Standoff my ass," she said. "I'm gonna drill you plumb center."

"It's not like I can stop you. But killing me won't get your boy back. Your boy's dead. Dead, dead, dead." He was waiting for the old woman to blink, to look away, but damned if she didn't keep her eyes locked on Chaucer and her finger on the rifle's trigger.

Bracing the stock against her hip, she let go of the grip and reached into the split of the rubber poncho. Chaucer's eyes narrowed, wondering what she was doing. She withdrew a piece of paper, yellow paper, flapped it open, then let it fall. He couldn't see what was written on the paper, but he knew it was the wire he had sent. Or had thought he had.

"This the wire you mean, Wade?" she said, her voice mocking. "Seems this telegraph never got sent."

He felt as if he'd been kicked by a mule in the chest. "H-how?"

"You must think I'm an idiot. When you took your little ride, I asked Soledad to follow you, see what you was really up to. Saying you was going on a scout. Hell, you ain't done a lick of work since my son brought you into this gang."

He looked past Ruby, found the ignorant Mexican just standing, smoothing his mustache, off to Ruby Pardo's left.

"Why?" Chaucer asked involuntarily. Then angrily: "You enjoy living like this? I've told you boys a million times we'll never get rich riding with Pardo. Why, man, why would you do that . . . to me?"

The Mexican shrugged. "Pardo treat me right," he said.

Chaucer's head turned, finding no help in the

faces of Duke, the fool, or Phil, the old man. He let out a heavy sigh, and turned back to the smiling Ruby Pardo.

"I wanted to see that look on your face." Her smile had widened, and she gripped the rifle with both hands. "Wanted you to know that you ain't got a lick of sense, to think you could outsmart my boy, my Jimmy, to think you could outsmart me." A cruel frown replaced the smile, and Ruby raised the Winchester to her shoulder. "I'll see you in hell, Wade Chaucer," she said, and Wade dived to his right, drawing the gun, knowing he didn't stand a chance as the Winchester barrel followed him to the ground.

A shot punched the water-soaked tent flap behind Ruby Pardo, and she staggered forward, jerking the rifle's trigger prematurely—the bullet kicking up mud into Chaucer's face. Another gunshot popped from inside the tent, and this one dropped Ruby to her knees.

By then, Chaucer had drawn the Remington, and he fired twice. Water flew off the poncho as the bullets struck her, sending Ruby Pardo onto her back. Almost the instant she hit the mud, the rain started again in a soft drizzle.

As Chaucer rose to his feet, he trained the muzzle of the Remington on Soledad, who held both arms out to his sides. Then Chaucer spun around, saw Phil and Duke shaking their heads. Movement behind him turned him around, and he thumbed back the hammer as Lacy bolted out of the tent still dressed only in her dingy camisole, holding a smoking .32 Triumph, the little four-barreled hideaway gun they had taken off that catamount of a girl back when they had wrecked the Southern Pacific. Lacy's face was ashen, and she dropped the .32 in the mud and covered her face at the sight of Ruby Pardo, who lay on her back, still clawing at the Winchester on her chest, trying to work the lever.

More footsteps sounded, splashing across the yard, and Chaucer spotted the woman captive and her child running to the camp. The woman, Dagmar, stopped, and shielded the ten-year-old punk behind her. Next came the pounding of a horse's hoofs. That would be Harrah, riding down to see what the hell was going on. Well, Chaucer would show him.

He walked over to Ruby, and kicked the rifle out of her hands. Next, he studied Lacy, who lowered her trembling hands, and said, "She . . . she . . . I . . ." She whirled toward Soledad. "She had the drop on Wade!" Then looking at Phil. "I couldn't—I had to." To the woman Dagmar. "Don't you see? She . . ."

Her eyes fell to Ruby, and she dropped to her knees and pressed both hands on the old woman's bleeding chest. She looked up. "Help me. Help her! We got to help Ruby."

With surprising strength, Ruby Pardo pried Lacy's hands, lifted them, and flung them aside. Lacy broke into hysterical sobs and covered her face with hands stained by Ruby Pardo's blood.

By then, Harrah had galloped into camp, blurting out a lame, "What's going on?" and dropping from the saddle.

Chaucer stared at Soledad for a moment, then at the other three men, then looked down at Ruby Pardo. Blood seeped from the corners of her mouth. Rain bounced off her hard face. Grinning down at her, Chaucer aimed the Remington at her forehead, and started to squeeze the trigger, only to realize he'd just be wasting lead. Raindrops bounced off her unseeing eyes, and Chaucer turned, and eased down the hammer, but didn't holster the gun.

"She's dead," he announced.

The rain began falling harder, but the darkness began receding. Now, he could see everyone clearly.

"Oh, no!" Lacy curled into a ball. "Oh, no, no, no, no . . ."

Harrah shuffled his feet. The others just stared. Chaucer looked over at Dagmar, back at Phil and Duke, and turned savagely toward Soledad.

"You're nothing but a spy, you damned greaser. I ought to plug you right now. Trailing me, going into that telegraph office after I left. How much did you have to pay that telegrapher not to send my wire?"

Soledad just stared, not at Chaucer, but at Ruby Pardo's lifeless body.

"All right!" Chaucer turned back toward the three white men. "There's still a chance. I can send that wire to Wickenburg. We can be rid of Pardo once and for all. We can run this gang."

Phil was shaking his head. Duke backed away. Harrah's mouth hung open like a panting hound.

"What's the matter with you men?" He gestured wildly around camp. "You call this living?"

"You shouldn't have done it, Wade," Duke muttered. "You shouldn't have kilt poor Miz Ruby."

"Jim'll track you down," Phil said. "There ain't no place you can hide."

"We can ambush Pardo when he rides back here." Realizing that he was begging, he tried to steady his voice. "Hell, there's a pretty good chance Pardo and Mac are dead already. Propped up in their Sunday best at the Wickenburg undertaker's. Dead, and I had nothing to do with it." Trying to sound hopeful. Failing. Failing miserably.

"Where are you going?" he demanded. Phil was walking toward the lean-to.

"Fetch a shovel," Phil announced, never slowing his stride. "I'll bury Ruby."

Harrah had removed his hat, started taking tentative steps toward Ruby Pardo.

The fire Duke and Phil had started had gone out.

Chaucer looked behind him, saw Soledad had sank to his knees, was bowing his head, muttering a silent prayer, then crossing himself.

"You fools!" Chaucer yelled. "What's the matter with you?" He tried something else, something desperate. "What do you think Jim Pardo will do to you all when he finds out you let his mother get shot dead?"

"I ain't runnin'," Duke said.

Dagmar led her fidgeting daughter away.

Phil came out of the lean-to carrying two shovels, and a pick, tossing one shovel to Duke, who caught it, and followed the old Missouri bushwhacker. Harrah had knelt over Ruby's body.

"She looks peaceful," he said, and reached to her face and closed the dead woman's eyes.

"Listen . . ." Chaucer tried, but Phil stopped him.

"No, Wade, you listen. We ain't gonna stop you. Way I see it, it was a fair fight. Well, would have been . . ." He gave the wailing Lacy a hard look, after which he tossed the pick to the rising Soledad's hands. "But we're Pardo's men, and I reckon we'll wait for Jim. But you, you best light out of here." He took two steps, stopped, and pointed the blade of the shovel at Three-Fingers Lacy.

"And take her with you."

CHAPTER SIXTEEN

When the gunfire erupted, Jim Pardo did the damnedest thing.

He stood in the stirrups and dived, wrapping both arms around Swede Iverson, knocking the big man off his horse. Reilly was kicking his own boots out of the stirrups while drawing the Evans from the scabbard, feeling the brown gelding he was riding begin to stagger. A bullet tore off his hat as he dropped behind the falling horse. He hit the ground, knees bending, catapulting himself to the rocky slope of the dry riverbed. A bullet kicked dust into his eyes, but Reilly was running, diving to the top, rolling over, coming to rest, rifle ready, behind the toppled remains of an old saguaro.

Right behind him came Swede Iverson, being pushed by Pardo, who urged the explosives man in a comically kind voice. "Hurry up there, Swede. Don't want you to get shot dead before my little job." The two dived over Reilly.

Bullets sliced over their heads, thudded into the dead cactus, whined off rocks, before a shout down below yelled that they were just wasting lead. A long silence followed as the skies began to brighten.

"How's Peck?" Swede Iverson panted.

Pardo laughed. "Dead. Them boys saved me a bullet. They ain't soft like you, Mac." He laughed harder, then began cursing. Reilly looked over at him, saw him turning, laying his Colt on the ground, gripping his nose. Blood gushed between the fingers. Swede Iverson stared, then reached over Pardo's waist for the Colt, but Pardo's right hand shot away from his bleeding nose, and gripped Iverson's wrist like a vise.

"The hell you think you're doing?" Pardo asked, spitting specks of blood that ran over his lips.

"I'm . . . trying to help," Iverson whined.

"Nobody takes Jim Pardo's gun." He shoved Iverson's hand away from his chest. "Nobody!"

Reilly pulled the Bulldog from his waistband, said, "Here," and tossed the big .44 to Iverson, who caught it and rolled to his side, then crawled toward the unearthed roots of the old cactus. He wondered about what he had just done, giving a murderer a weapon, but, hell, he had broken so many laws since the Krafts had left him locked inside that prison wagon, what did one more matter?

"Smith!" a voice called from down below. A voice vaguely familiar. "Deputy Jim Smith! Or whoever the hell you are!"

Pinching his nose, Pardo yelled back, "Why Marshal Thaddeus McCutcheon, what brings you so far into Maricopa County?" He turned toward Reilly. "Guess now I know why I never felt the hairs rise on the back of my neck, why we wasn't followed. Looks like the posse made a beeline for Gonzales's spread."

"You likely asked too many questions at Miguel's Saloon," Reilly said.

"Yeah." He let go of his nose and tilted his head back. "Figured them boys for nothing but a bunch of drunken hayseeds." His head shook. "This damned nose. Picked a fine time to start bleeding again."

"Don't worry about it," Reilly said. "You'll be bleeding elsewhere once the sun's fully up." He thought a moment, before adding, "Unless you want to surrender."

Pardo grabbed his gun, and rolled onto his stomach, letting the blood drop in the dust between his elbows. "Bloody Jim Pardo don't surrender, Mac. No time. Not ever." He lifted his head a bit, and yelled, "What you want, Marshal?"

"I want you to throw down your guns and walk down here. You, your so-called prisoner, and Swede Iverson. Do that, and I promise you, nobody will get killed."

Pardo cackled. "What about Peck?"

"Peck?" The marshal sounded bewildered.

"Yeah, Peck. You promise me he won't get killed?" He slapped his left palm against the dirt.

"Peck's done for. I can't . . . nobody *else*'ll get killed. That's what I mean."

"No, no, Marshal," Pardo said, chiding. "You don't mean that. Why, the Territory of Arizona means to hang Swede Iverson." He looked quickly at Reilly and said, "I love playing with them fool laws like this."

"I'm talking about you, Smith," McCutcheon thundered. "You won't have to get killed. You haven't done nothing but help bust out some of my prisoners out of jail."

"Well, hell, Marshal McCutcheon, it ain't like you

got a real jail in Wickenburg. I just freed them from that tree you got growing."

"I ain't fooling around no more, Smith. You come on down here now. Come on down, and you'll get to live."

"Nah, Marshal, you see the Territory of Arizona wants to see me swing, too. Along with the states of Missouri and Kansas. Don't think they'd kill me in California for robbing that bank over in Julian, or in Denton County, Texas, but they damn sure have a rope for me over in New Mexico Territory. You see, my name ain't Smith, but Pardo. Bloody Jim Pardo." He looked again at Reilly, and winked. "That'll put the fear of God in all of them."

A lengthy quiet followed, and Pardo rolled over and crawled toward Reilly. "You figure out where he is? From his voice?"

Reilly ran his fingers through his hair. "Maybe," he said.

Pardo pointed his gun barrel downstream. "You and me can sneak down to that bend, cut across, come back, sneak up on that fool law dog. Way I figure it, we get him, capture him—I mean, keep him alive, use him as a hostage—then them others'll quit."

Reilly shook his head. "McCutcheon's no fool. He's likely already posted two or three men down yonder."

"Unlucky for them." He crawled over Reilly's legs, turned back, and shouted in a dry whisper, "You stay put, Swede. Give us ten minutes, then fire two shots into this dead saguaro. Then you yell out that you just killed me, Pardo, and him, Mac, and that you're coming down. Pitch your *pistola* into the riverbed, and walk on down, hands high in the air. That's all you got to do. Oh, yeah, don't get killed."

A muffled curse exploded out of Reilly's mouth,

and he turned and frantically crawled after Pardo, catching up with him a few yards away. "We don't know how many men McCutcheon has with him," he said.

"Enough to go around." Pardo kept crawling.

"He's likely sent men all around us."

"It's what I'd do."

"Then this is a fool's play."

"Un-uh. Means there'll be fewer of them hayseeds hanging around Marshal McCutcheon. Should reduce our taking him to child's play."

"He could have moved by the time we get over there."

"He won't." Pardo stopped, listened, wiped his nose, began crawling again. Reluctantly, Reilly followed.

They moved slowly. Pardo was like an Apache. The marshal kept shouting, but got no answer. As soon as they rounded the bend, Pardo stopped and dropped his head closer to the dirt. Immediately, Reilly did the same, until Pardo turned slowly and motioned Reilly to come alongside him. Once he had, Pardo pointed the Colt's barrel to a spindly mesquite on the dry bank. A second later, Reilly detected the glow of a tip of a cigarette, then movement.

"Now what?" Reilly whispered. Something flashed on the far bank, and Reilly studied it for several seconds, then told Pardo, "There's another man in those rocks over there."

"Makes things a mite ticklish, wouldn't you say, Mac?" Pardo said, before, catching Reilly completely off guard, he slid down the slope, and started running in a crouch across the dried bed, hoarsely calling out, "Hey, hey, guys, I got a message from Marshal McCutcheon."

To Reilly's dismay, the man in the rocks on the other side, stood and took a few steps into the river-bed. "What's up?" he asked. The fellow on this side of the bank also rose, pitching his smoke into the rocks.

"That man," Pardo said, stopping in front of the posse member, and pointing his gun barrel widely in the general direction of where they'd left Swede Iverson by the cactus. "He says he's Jim Pardo. Bloody Jim Pardo!"

"Yeah," said the man. "We heard."

The man on Reilly's side of the bank took a step down, and Reilly started crawling, rapidly, sensing the urgency. "Hey!" the man said, and reached for his holstered revolver.

Pardo turned back, swinging his gun viciously, clob-bering the posse man's head, dropping him like a rock. The other man was drawing his revolver, had it halfway out of the holster, when Reilly stood and dived. He must have caused quite a racket, because the man spun, his mouth opening to let out a scream that never came, because Reilly's Evans smashed him in the chest, and both men crashed into the dirt. Reilly lifted himself up and brought the stock of the Evans squarely on the man's forehead. Slowly catch-ing his breath, he scrambled across the bed toward a smiling Pardo, waiting for a cannonade of rifle fire to cut him down.

Only . . . nothing happened.

"I told you," Pardo said. "They's stupid hayseeds."

"What's going on down there?" a voice called from maybe twenty-five feet upstream, around the bend.

Pardo, still grinning, called out, "Who's that?"

"It's me, Matthew."

"Matt, it's me. Get your ass down here on the double. I think Pardo and them two other outlaws is up to something. Hurry, damn it." He winked at Reilly and lifted the Colt over his head as spurs chimed out a tune. A man cursed as he ducked underneath the arm of a saguaro, and Pardo slammed the Colt across his skull.

"Hayseeds," Pardo said, as he climbed up the path. "Nothing but stupid hayseeds."

Reilly couldn't argue.

They had gone only thirty yards when two gunshots cracked the brightening morning. Pardo slid to a stop, ducking, and cursed, "Hell, I should have left Swede an Illinois watch. Ain't no ten minutes passed!"

"Marshal McCutcheon!" Swede Iverson's voice called out from across the riverbed. "It's me, Swede Iverson. I just killed Pardo and the other man, Mac, I think that was his name. I shot them. Shot both of them. They're dead. I'm coming out. Is that all right with you?"

"You sure you killed them?" Marshal McCutcheon's voice, maybe another thirty yards ahead.

"Yeah, I'm sure. I practically blew the back of Pardo's head off."

Pardo sniggered. "That Iverson, he's a born thespian. I didn't know he had it in him."

"Throw down your weapon, Swede," McCutcheon called out.

"Do I get the reward? For Pardo, I mean."

Pardo laughed harder.

"Throw down your weapon! Then climb down, with your hands up high. Don't try nothing funny."

Pardo straightened. He turned toward Reilly. His nose had stopped bleeding, but his lips and beard stubble on his chin were stained, as was the front of his shirt. "You wait here. Cover me with that Evans. I'll go down and fetch the good marshal." He slid down the embankment, and Reilly crawled until he had found a clearing.

The sun was rising above the mountains now, and Reilly could see clearly. A gun whirled over the brush, landing with a thud in the center of the riverbed. Gene Peck's body lay pinned underneath his dead horse. Another dead horse lay a few rods away. Coming out of the brush on this side of the bank, Wickenburg Town Marshal Thaddeus McCutcheon appeared, placing a boot on the withers of the horse Peck had been riding. From a few yards downstream came Swede Iverson, hands stretched high. Other men came out of the brush, weapons held loosely in their hands.

"That's far enough, Swede!" McCutcheon called when Iverson stood between the two dead horses. "Charley, you, Pedro, and Lewallen climb up the other side, make sure Pardo, if it was Pardo, and that other gent are dead."

"No need, Marshal," Pardo said, and he covered the twenty feet separating him and McCutcheon in an instant, shoving the short barrel of the Colt into the marshal's belly.

"All right!" he yelled. "Every mother's son of you pitch his iron. Do it! Do it now, or I open up Marshal McCutcheon's stomach. Do it, you damned hayseeds! Do it, I say. Tell them, Marshal. Tell them to obey, or so help me you and I go to hell right here and now." His finger tightened on the trigger.

"Do it!" Thaddeus McCutcheon screamed. "For God's sake, do like he says. All of you. Charley, Pedro!" His eyes, wide, looked behind him. "Gonzales. Do it."

Another figure slid down the embankment, and Reilly instinctively drew a bead on the Yavapai's chest.

Weapons dropped. The sun rose. Swede Iverson shrieked, "Hell, you did it," and ran to rip a Henry rifle from one old man's trembling arms. Only the Indian refused to move, his left hand on the hilt of the machete.

The lawman noticed that. "Joe," he begged, "don't do nothing, Joe. This is Jim Pardo, man."

"That's Bloody Jim Pardo to you, law dog. But he's right, injun, if you try something your pal here'll be dying, only slow." He drug out the last word. "Then I'll gun down as many of you sons of bitches as I can. Oh, yeah, you'll kill me, but before you think about collecting any reward on my head, you best know that you're all covered. Ain't that right, Mac?"

Reilly pulled the trigger. The bullet clipped a spine off a saguaro over the Yavapai's right shoulder. Damn, if the Indian didn't even flinch.

"Joe," the marshal pleaded. "For God's sake, Joe, just do as Pardo says."

Slowly, the Indian moved, unfastened the cover of an Army-issue holster on his left hip, drew out an old Colt, and dropped it at his feet. Then he walked across the riverbed.

"The big knife," Pardo said. "Tell him to drop the big knife."

"Machete," Yavapai Joe said, "stays."

Pardo let out a chuckle. "All right, injun. You can keep that blade. Now, you damned hayseeds, I want you all to mount up and ride back to town. Oh, and pick up them three *hombres* that got their heads rattled around the bend. Don't stop till you're at Miguel's Saloon. Then you can finish your celebration. And bill it to the town council. Ain't that right, Marshal McCutcheon?"

"That's right!"

The posse, about fifteen or so, started shuffling off. "Not you, Gonzales," Pardo called out to a dark-skinned man in buckskin britches and a yellow shirt. "You and me, we got us some horse-trading to do."

CHAPTER SEVENTEEN

The artesian well at Gonzales's ranch turned this patch of desert into a verdant oasis, and the water looked like paradise. While Pardo picked out six mounts, Reilly cupped his hands in the pond near the large corral to drink, but his reflection stopped him. Gunpowder and dirt blackened the beard stubble on his face, except for around his eyes. He looked like a raccoon in reverse. His hair resembled a bird's nest. Reilly ran the back of his right hand across his beard, dipped his hands into the water, and began to scrub his face.

He thought of Pontius Pilate, washing his hands, remembered a preacher back in Indiana when he was a kid saying that Pilate was in hell now, washing his hands for all of eternity. Reilly pictured himself beside Pilate, at some washbasin, trying to wash off their sins, but the vision was quickly shattered by Pardo's voice.

Pardo had the horses—two blacks, a bay, a roan, and two pintos—ready and had mounted one of the blacks and held a rope in his left hand to pull the roan behind him. Looking up, finally slaking his thirst with the cool, sweet water, Reilly saw Gonzales and Marshal McCutcheon standing in front of the revolver Pardo held in his right hand. When Pardo thumbed back the hammer, Gonzales dropped to his knees, clasped his hands, and began begging for his life in Spanish. McCutcheon tried to stand up straight, but his knees began to tremble.

"I wouldn't do that, Jim," Reilly said calmly, patting his face dry with his dirty shirtsleeve, then putting on the bullet-riddled hat he had picked up in the dry riverbed.

"You ain't me," Pardo said.

"Yeah, but those posse members will hear your shots. A gunshot'll carry a long way in the desert, in the morning. They hear that, they'll know what's happened, and they'll come charging back."

Pardo looked skeptical.

"He's right," Swede Iverson said.

The skepticism transformed into irritation as Pardo glared at the dynamite man. "Who the hell invited you into this conversation?"

"I don't want that Yavapai on our trail," Reilly said.

Pardo turned back toward him. Gonzales had buried his face into his hands and was bawling like a newborn kid.

"You think that injun's heading back to Wickenburg with them others?" With a mirthless chuckle, Pardo waved his gun barrel toward the hills across the dry riverbed. "That injun's out yonder. Waiting, likely watching us."

"You shoot those two men," Reilly said, "and the Yavapai won't be alone."

"I ain't afraid of that injun," Pardo said.

"I am." Reilly stared hard at Pardo, and let out a

short breath as the gunman shook his head and slowly holstered his revolver.

"You're soft, Mac," Pardo said. "I don't know why I like you. All right, you take care of these two hombres. But just for that, you ride the two pintos."

"That's all right," Reilly said. "I like paint horses."

Pardo shook his head. "No self-respecting white man likes a paint horse. Mount up, Swede. Mount the bay. Lead the black."

As Iverson went toward the horses, Reilly drew the Smith & Wesson—Iverson still had the American Bulldog—and motioned McCutcheon toward the adobe house beyond the corrals. The marshal helped Gonzales to his feet and walked steadily toward the open door. It was a nice building, solidly built, but inside, Reilly found the furnishings spartan. He took a rope hanging off a peg and tied Gonzales's hands behind his back, not too tight, and next bound his feet together. After securing the horse trader, he motioned for McCutcheon to put his hands behind his back, and Reilly took another rope from another peg—that's about all Gonzales had in the place, a table, a chair, and plenty of lariats, saddles, and bridles—and worked on tying the marshal's hands.

While he tied, he spoke, "Marshal McCutcheon, just be quiet for a minute and let me talk. My name's Reilly McGivern. I'm a deputy United States marshal."

"You're a damned crook."

"Shut up." Reilly pulled the rope tight, burning the marshal's wrists. "Let me talk."

"I know who you are. I got the telegraph after you helped break the Kraft brothers out of—"

He jerked harder, and this time McCutcheon grunted in pain.

"That jailbreak was K.C. Kraft's doing, and Deputy

Marshal Gus Henderson's. Not mine. W.W. Kraft locked me in the back of the prison wagon to bake to death, and the next day Bloody Jim Pardo happened along. They'd robbed, or tried to rob, a Southern Pacific train."

"I heard about that, too."

"Yeah, well, Pardo took a woman and her ten-year-old daughter hostage. You hear about that?"

The lawman didn't answer. Reilly took that as a "no."

"He's got them back in his camp in the Dragoon Mountains. With Wade Chaucer and his other men. Oh, yeah, if you ride down the Hassayampa to the Gila, then turn east and south for about five miles, you'll come to a series of buttes. There you'll find what's left of one of Pardo's men, a sharpshooter they called The Greek. Pardo killed him."

"Killed his own man? What on earth for?"

Reilly eased the marshal to a seated position, then started tying his feet. "They don't call him 'Bloody' for nothing." He looped the rope around the marshal's ankles. "Listen—"

"Hurry up in there, Mac!" Pardo yelled. Reilly heard the horses' hoofs pacing outside.

"When you get back to Wickenburg, I want you to wire Marshal Cobb, Kenneth Cobb, in Tombstone. Tell him what I told you. Tell him . . . hell, I don't know what to tell him. Tell him I'm working on it."

"If you're on the level, give me a gun," McCutcheon said. "We can take Pardo and Iverson down now. While they ain't expecting it."

Reilly shook his head. "I can't leave that woman and her kid. Not in that camp. Not with those cutthroats. They saved my hide. I have to get back to the Dragoons, and I need Pardo alive. I go back there alone, or with a dozen posse members, you know what they'll do to that woman and her kid."

The town marshal frowned. Reilly tied a final knot and stood, staring down. "You do this for me, Marshal?"

McCutcheon looked up, studying Reilly's face.

"Mac!" called Pardo.

The lawman nodded.

"Shouldn't take you too long to get out of that," Reilly said. "I appreciate this, Marshal." He looked at the scabbed line across McCutcheon's forehead. "Sorry about what happened back at the Jail Tree. I'd left a note on a cigarette paper. Pardo was picking it up. I had to do something, or he'd have started gunning you, Dunlap, and me down."

That seemed to satisfy McCutcheon. Likely, the lawman remembered the Mexican handing him the paper.

Reilly touched the brim of his hat, and turned, leaving the door open behind him. He swung into the saddle, and took the rope pulling another saddled paint horse.

"What took you so long?" Pardo snapped.

"Wanted to make sure they were comfortable," Reilly said. "On account that I'm soft. Remember?"

They rode back to the pond, where Pardo reined in and let the black drink. As Iverson and Reilly let their own horses slake their thirsts, Pardo handed the lead rope to Reilly and turned the black around. "I forgot something," he said, and spurred the horse into a gallop, riding back toward the adobe house. He pulled up and swung down, then was swallowed by a cloud of dust.

Reilly's stomach knotted. He touched the butt of the Smith & Wesson, but stopped when he heard

Swede Iverson mutter something. Slowly, Reilly turned to stare down the barrel of the Bulldog .44 Iverson pointed at his head. "You aren't thinking of doing nothing, are you?" Iverson asked, with a wicked smile.

Big Swede Iverson had developed a great deal of confidence since he was free, no longer chained to that mesquite tree back in Wickenburg, no longer facing a hangman's noose.

"What's Pardo doing?" Reilly asked.

"He ain't making no noise to alert that posse," Iverson said, and Reilly's heart sank as Pardo emerged from the doorway, wiping blood off the blade of his knife. He closed the door, sheathed the big bowie, and swung into the saddle, loping back toward the pond. He let the black drink some more.

"Did you have to do that?" Reilly asked.

"Not really," Pardo answered as he took the lead rope from Reilly, "but it made me feel better."

"We'll see how you feel when the posse comes back here and finds those two," Reilly said, trying to keep control, but his temper was flaring. "They'll alert every county sheriff, every town marshal, the U.S. marshal, and the United States Army. The whole territory will be looking for Bloody Jim Pardo."

Pardo cackled. "The whole *country* has been looking for me for better than twenty years, Mac. They ain't caught up to me yet." He pointed north. "That Yavapai, I'm betting he'll be waiting for us downstream. We'll ride north a ways, then cut over to the Verde River, follow it a spell, pick our way into the high country. Be cooler up there. We'll ride down to Globe, and follow the Arizona Narrow Gauge tracks to Mesaville, pick up the San Pedro River and ride down to Redington, where I got me a date. Then we'll

head back to camp. See Ma. Make sure Ma's all right."
He spurred the black into a lope.

They made their way through a deepening canyon,
out of the heat, the clopping of the shod horses am-
plified. A raven's *kaw* sounded overhead, and Pardo
reined up, drew his gun, pushed back the brim off his
hat. He looked up the walls, pinched his nose, and
frowned. For five minutes, he stared, then tugged his
hat down, and turned, suddenly smiling, and gestured with the gun at Reilly.

"Too tight a spot," he said. "We'll have to ride single
file. You go first, Mac."

Reilly drew the Evans from the scabbard, laid it
across the pommel, and nudged the little piebald
mustang into a walk. Pardo gave him a good lead
before he kicked the black and started to follow.

The canyon's rocks were black lava, lined here and
there with twisted juniper. Ahead, part of the canyon
had caved in, leaving behind a rocky slope. He looked
over the pinto's head and gave the mustang more
rein to pick its own path over the fallen rocks and
prickly pear. When the horse's ears pricked forward
in interest, then flattened against its head, Reilly
eared back the hammer on the Evans.

He spotted the white bandage encasing the top of
Henry Dunlap's head and leaped from the saddle as
the deputy jerked a rifle to his shoulder and fired.
The bullet whined off a rock, and the echo bounced
across the black rocks. The two paint horses took off
down the canyon, and Dunlap cocked the rifle, but
didn't duck. *Damned fool*, Reilly thought, watching
Dunlap's bandaged head explode as Pardo's Winchester roared. Another figure appeared on the top

of the canyon, and another ran out to try to catch the two runaway paint horses.

Suddenly, Reilly saw a flash above him, and rolled over, raising the Evans to fend off the Yavapai's slicing machete. The blade nicked the barrel, glancing off with a whine. The Yavapai grunted, and Reilly kicked up, flipping the Indian over his head. Bullets ricocheted all around him, and his ears rang from the fusillade. The Yavapai was on his feet, machete still in his hand, but Reilly had rolled to his own feet, and now the Yavapai approached cautiously, black, malevolent eyes boring a hole into Reilly's soul, both men ignoring the chaos around them.

The Yavapai feinted to the left, but Reilly didn't fall for it. They circled each other. A bullet pulled at the shirt hanging loosely under Reilly's right armpit, and the Yavapai charged, grunting, swinging. Reilly ducked as the blade whooshed over his head, and shoved the barrel of the Evans as if thrusting a sword. Easily, he could have pulled the trigger, killed the Indian, but he didn't want to do that.

"Listen—" he began, but had to duck again.

This time the Yavapai grabbed the rifle barrel with his left hand, jerked it forward, pulled Reilly close. He had to drop the rifle and grip the right wrist of the Indian, then fell backward, the lava rocks ripping the back of his vest and shirt, cutting his shoulders. The Evans clattered on the rocks. The Yavapai's left hand found Reilly's throat, squeezing.

Reilly kept his own right hand locked on the hand that held the machete but moved his left and grabbed the Yavapai's throat. His lungs burned for air, yet he tightened his grip. His hands were slippery with sweat, but the Yavapai's eyes began bulging.

A riderless horse leaped over them, the hoofs just

missing both the Yavapai's and Reilly's heads, and the men broke free, rolled over, came up. The Yavapai was quick, and Reilly had to leap backward to avoid the blade of the machete, which ripped through his shirt just above the waistband, catching the Smith & Wesson, jerking it free, sending it bouncing across the rocks.

The Yavapai charged, thrusting the machete, pulling back as Reilly stumbled and fell. He rolled to his right, heard the blade strike the dirt, then gripped a small chunk of rock and flung it at the Indian's head. The Indian tilted his head, let the rock fly past his ear, then moved the machete to his left hand, nodding in respect at Reilly.

"Listen," Reilly tried again, but jumped back as the blade swept up, down, and across. Reilly backed up until he pressed against the canyon wall. The sounds of battle were slowly receding, the echoes dying down. Reilly held up his right hand but jerked it from the menacing blade to keep all of his fingers.

The Indian charged, and Reilly ducked, spun, stepped away from the wall. The Yavapai fell against the wall, and Reilly stumbled again, looked up, saw the blade rising over the Indian's head, saw the Yavapai step closer, start to bring the machete down, saw a purple hole appear above the nose of the Yavapai and a pink mist spray the canyon side.

Reilly never heard the gunshot.

The Indian dropped the machete and sank into a seated position, then slumped to his side, eyes staring at the raven circling overhead, but not seeing a thing.

When Reilly turned, trying to catch his breath, he saw Pardo, still seated on the black, levering a fresh round into the Winchester before shoving the rifle into the scabbard.

"Right here," Pardo said, staring at the dead Indian as he tapped the spot between his eyes.

Reilly grabbed the Smith & Wesson and the Evans, and looked down the canyon, frowning at Henry Dunlap's body hanging over the rocks, and two other dead men, the whiteness of their bodies in stark contrast to the darkness of the canyon.

"Best catch up your horses, Mac," Pardo said. "You, too, Swede."

Reilly looked over to his left, saw Swede Iverson rising from behind a giant boulder. He looked down the canyon again, finding the two paint horses about fifty yards beyond the slide area. Slowly, he started walking.

"Hey, Mac!" Pardo called out, and Reilly turned.

The outlaw was grinning. "I reckon I saved your life."

CHAPTER EIGHTEEN

Nobody much came to Redington, which is why Jim Pardo went there.

Maybe eight or ten years earlier, a couple of Yankee brothers had founded the little settlement on the eastern banks of the San Pedro River. The streets were quiet, but the aroma of green chile stew tore at Pardo's stomach. Redington existed for the farmers and ranchers in the area, but there was another reason it had a post office, two saloons, and three mercantiles. Riding the roan now, having left the black a few miles on the other side of Globe, Pardo motioned Mac and Iverson, who were trailing him, to ride up alongside him. When they did, he gestured toward a well-traveled road that intersected the dusty street they were riding down.

"Know what that is?" he asked.

Iverson shook his head, but Mac replied, "Military supply road. Heads down to Tucson."

"That's right, smart guy," Pardo said. "That's why we're here. You know what day it is?"

Both men shrugged.

"I guess you ain't so smart after all." Pardo grinned

at himself. "But that's all right, Mac, because I know." He fished out a gold piece from his vest pocket and flipped it, watching it catch the sunlight as it arced its way to Mac, who caught it.

"It's not my birthday," Mac said.

"Pretend that it is." He jutted his jaw at the mercantile catty-corner from where they were. It was a two-story brick building, rare for this part of the territory, with big letters painted black across the whitewashed top story and some fancy lettering between the windows. "What's them words say?"

Mac turned and looked, then replied, "H. and L. Redfield and Company. Dealers in Every Thing."

"That's good." Pardo nodded. "Why don't you go in and buy you some clothes? You're a filthy man, shirt all ripped to pieces, vest not much better. See if they got shells for that Evans rifle you shoot so well. Get some .44-40s for my Winchester and a couple of boxes extra for my revolver. A sack of Arbuckle's coffee and some salt pork. And something for Ma." His eyes lit up at the thought of his mother.

"Ain't that a grocery right next door?"

Mac looked, and nodded.

"Maybe they'll have some strawberries. Ma's partial to strawberries. Maybe they'll have some. Be nice to bring Ma a present."

"Wouldn't she prefer a gun?" Mac asked.

Pardo glared. "Strawberries," he said. "See if they have strawberries."

His head bobbed, and he forgot Mac's sarcasm. Yeah, that would be a really nice treat. He could see his mother's face. "Then you see that place over yonder." He hooked his thumb at the barber's pole across the street. "Get a haircut. Get a shave. You, too, Swede."

"Do I get new duds, too?" Iverson asked.

"It ain't your birthday, Swede. You just get a haircut and a shave. When you're finished, meet me in that saloon." He pointed out the place, and kicked his horse into a walk, leaving Mac and Iverson behind.

Half a block past the intersection, he stopped the roan. A dun horse was hobbled by the hitching rail in front of a stone building. The horse was branded US, with a McClellan saddle on its back. Pardo dug out his pocket watch, opened the case, and checked the time. Major Ritcher was early.

He swung to the ground, wrapped the reins around the hitching rail, tested the Colt in its holster, and stepped onto the porch, peering into the darkness before entering the cantina. The Mexican barkeep looked up without much interest, but straightened as Pardo approached him.

"Tequila," Pardo announced, and slapped a coin on the bar.

Lazily, the bartender filled a tumbler, and started to take the bottle away, but Pardo grabbed its neck, and gave the Mexican an icy stare. Shrugging, the Mexican released the bottle and turned back to doing nothing.

"Vy don't you join me, stranger?" a voice called out, and Pardo turned, finding Major Ritcher seated at a table by the window. The Yankee son of a bitch raised a stein of beer in salute. Pardo walked over to him and stared.

"I'll take that seat," he said.

Ritcher lowered the stein, his eyes slow to focus. Then his head bobbed, and he rose and took the chair next to the one Pardo was settling into. As Pardo sipped the tequila, Ritcher began talking.

"The Army train is coming from Fort Bliss in Texas.

It vill be coming down the old Overland Mail route."
He wiped the froth of beer from his lips with the back
of his hand. "They're taking the Gatlings all the vay
to Fort Lowell."

"Not Bowie?" Pardo asked in surprise. "I thought
you said your boss at Bowie wanted them Gatlings for
hisself."

"He did," Ritcher said. "but the commanding officer at Fort Lowell pulled rank. Seems he vants first
crack at those Gatlings."

Pardo topped off his tumbler with more tequila.

"That Army train?" Pardo said. "It'll follow the
Overland route all the way to Fort Lowell?"

Ritcher nodded slightly.

"When's it due at Lowell?"

"Two weeks," Ritcher answered, "from yesterday."

Pardo killed the tequila. "How many guards?"

"Two companies of infantry left Bliss. My C.O. ordered Lieutenant Talley to take I Troop east and meet
the train, then lead it back to Fort Lowell. And, naturally, bring Colonel Livingston his Gatlings and his
howitzer. Dat's a lot of armed men, Pardo, although
Mr. Talley's a little green. Plus the teamsters and
muleskinners."

Pardo stared into his empty glass.

"I said dat's a lot of firepower, Pardo. Two companies of infantry and a cavalry troop."

"I heard you." He still stared at the empty glass.

Silence.

Outside, a rooster crowed, though it was well past
one o'clock in the afternoon.

"So in about eleven days, that train should be
making its way through Texas Canyon."

"Texas Canyon?" Ritcher blurted out.

"Not so loud, you damned fool." Pardo slid the tumbler across the roughhewn table.

"Sorry. Let's see." Ritcher did some mental ciphering, and finally nodded. "*Ja*, eleven, maybe ten." He finished the beer, and carefully set the stein down. "So, do you have my thousand dollars?"

"No."

Ritcher's shoulders tightened. He leaned back in his chair. "You said—"

"Shut up. You'll get your money. I been busy." He grinned. "Maybe you heard. I busted Swede Iverson out of jail in Wickenburg."

"I heard. It's been in every newspaper in the territory. You killed the town marshal. Slit his throat vile he vas hogtied. You killed a Mexican horse trader on the Agua Fria River. You ambushed a posse near the Bradshaw Mountains."

Pardo laughed. "I ambushed a posse? That's funny. They tried to bushwhack us. They just wasn't worth a damn."

"Ven do I get paid?" Ritcher asked.

"I told you. A thousand when you give me the route. Four after we pull the job."

"I just gave you the route."

"Then send me a bill." He jerked the bottle off the table and poured tequila into his tumbler. A horse whinnied, and hoofs sounded outside. Quickly, Pardo set the bottle down and rested his hand on the butt of his Colt, listening to the jingling of spurs. Too soon to be Mac or Iverson. He saw a lone figure through the window. A tall man in beaten clothes. The figure disappeared from the window and entered the saloon. Pardo's left hand gripped the bottle so tightly his knuckles whitened as the man strode up to the bar and ordered a whiskey.

"Duke!" Pardo roared, and the thin, loose-jointed man spun around.

"Boss man," he said, his eyes wide in terror. "You's here."

"Yeah, I'm here, Duke. What the hell are you doing here? Why ain't you in camp?" Pardo was shaking, couldn't stop it, as he kicked the chair behind him when he stood, strode over to the bar. The Mexican beer-jerker backed into a corner.

Duke stood trembling. He reached for the whiskey the barkeep had poured, but Pardo's left hand shot out and knocked the shot glass across the bar.

"Tell me, Duke. What brings you to Redington? This is Chaucer's idea, ain't it? Well, Duke, what's the matter? Cat got your tongue?"

Duke's head shook violently. "It was Phil, boss man. Phil told me to come."

"Phil?"

Pardo stepped back.

"Yeah, boss man, Phil. He sent Harrah to Dos Cabezas. Told me to ride up here. He figured you'd first show up in either Dos Cabezas or here in Redington."

Out of the corner of his eye, Pardo spotted another figure, a tall man with dirty blond hair dismounting a black horse, holding a bucket in his left hand. Pardo turned, halfway drawing the Colt from its holster, before stopping. It was a freshly shaven Swede Iverson, filling the doorway with his giant frame, a grin stretching from ear to ear.

"Hey, Pardo," the man called out, just like a dumb Swede, letting everyone in the saloon know who he was, although the only one here who didn't know him was the Mexican. "I got them strawberries. Mac told me to bring them on over to you."

Pardo felt his heart skip. Shoving the Colt back into

the holster, he reached up and grabbed Duke's shirt-front, jerked the spindly man toward him. "Where's Ma?" he asked.

Duke's eyes bulged. His Adam's apple bobbed. His face went pale. His mouth moved, but no sound escaped his lips, just his rancid breath.

"Where is she?" He shook the tall man savagely.

"B-b-boss," Duke pleaded.

"Where is she?" He jerked the .44-40 from the holster, thumbed back the hammer, jammed the barrel into Duke's stomach. "Answer me, you bastard, or I'll gut you with this Colt. Answer me. What's happened to Ma?"

Duke's trembling mouth shot out the word in a primal scream. At first, Pardo didn't hear him. Couldn't have heard those words. Swede Iverson was saying something about strawberries, picking up one of the fruit in his fingers, revealing it like he was showing off a four-pound trout he had just hooked. Major Ritcher was ducking through the door, practically knocking Swede Iverson out of the way. The bartender was exiting through a back door. Pardo shoved Duke against the bar, the tall man's flailing arms knocking pewter steins and glasses to the earthen floor. The room began spinning, and he heard Duke's words over and over and over again.

She's dead.

She's dead.

She's dead.

She's dead.

She's dead.

She's dead . . . dead . . . dead . . . dead . . . dead. . . .

The Colt fell to the floor, and Pardo knocked off his hat, grabbing his hair, pulling and pulling. No, somebody was screaming, the voice coming from some deep well.

No.

No.

No.

It took a few minutes before Pardo realized it was he who was yelling.

He steeled himself, stopped yelling, quit yanking on his hair. Tears blurred his vision, but he found Duke standing by the bar, dumbly staring down at Pardo. Slowly, Pardo rose, wiped his eyes, and asked, "What happened?" His voice, surprisingly, sounded calm.

Duke made the mistake of hesitating, and Pardo leaped on him, slapping his face repeatedly, ignoring the stupid fool's pleas. "Who killed her? Who? Who done it, damn you? Who did it? It was Chaucer, wasn't it? Wasn't it? Wasn't it?"

"Yeah. Yeah. Chaucer. But . . ."

Pardo shoved Duke away, turned, found his gun, holstered it, started for the door. He should have known. Should have gunned down that son of a bitch before he left camp. He had felt this for some time, knew Ma would try to get that bastard, but . . .

Chaucer.

Something stopped him, and he turned savagely, eyes drilling into Duke.

"Y'all let him go?" His hands tightened into balls. "After he gunned down my mother?"

Duke backed against the bar, gripping it for support.

"Phil said it was a fair fight."

"Phil? Phil let him go?"

Duke's head bobbed slightly. "Only . . ."

"Only what?"

"Well . . ."

"Go on, damn it. Out with it. Tell me everything."

"She, your ma, Miz Ruby, she caught Wade—she had the drop on him. Out in front of Lacy's tent."

"Lacy?"

Duke nodded. Pardo felt his hands turn clammy. He was sweating profusely.

"Your ma had Chaucer covered with the Winchester, said she was gonna kill him. And then . . ." Duke looked around for whiskey, a bottle, a glass, but he had knocked everything to the floor or behind the bar, out of his reach.

"It happened so fast, boss man. Me and Phil, we was tryin' to get a fire goin', get the coffee boilin', and then Wade was divin' and palmin' his Remington. And then . . . well . . . it was Lacy, inside that tent. She had that hideaway gun we taken off the girl."

"The girl?" Pardo's eyes squinted.

"Yeah, boss man. The girl. The girl we taken off the train. Blanche. The one with the potty mouth."

Oh, yeah. He had forgotten about the kid. He pictured the ten-year-old's mother, but then a vision of Lacy replaced the blond-haired German.

"What about Lacy?" he asked, trying to get the bitter taste out of his mouth.

"She shot . . . she shot Miz Ruby twice in the back."

"In the back." Calm. His voice sounded calm. As if he had expected this.

"Yeah. Mind you, she didn't kill her. Lacy, I mean. Lacy didn't kill your mother. But them slugs caught her in the small of her back, like they knocked the breath out of her, and that give Wade all the chance he needed. He had his gun drawn, and put two bullets through Miz Ruby's lungs. I'm . . . I'm . . . I'm plumb sorry, boss man. Phil, he sent me here. To find you when you come in, if you come in. Figured you'd want to know pronto."

He turned, headed for the door.

He saw the bucket at Swede Iverson's side, saw the strawberries, and the madness struck again, savage, blinding him with rage, tormenting his soul. He jerked the bucket from Iverson's hand, threw it across the street, then pulled the Colt from the leather. He emptied the Colt into the overturning bucket, which rained strawberries on the street. People came out of the doors, opened windows, peered up or down the street, staring.

Pardo didn't care. He watched the bucket hit the dirt, and he kept pulling the trigger, even though the hammer kept clicking on empty chambers.

"Ma," he cried, and fell to his knees, dropping the Colt in the dirt, staring down at those red strawberries, staring until he couldn't see anything for his tears.

CHAPTER NINETEEN

Reilly dropped to his knees, pried the Colt out of Pardo's hand, and let it fall. Like a child, that brutal killer buried his face against Reilly's shoulder and bawled.

"Easy, Jim," Reilly whispered, confused. "What happened?"

"It's . . . Ma . . ." Pardo choked out the words. "Chaucer . . . killed . . . her." He punctuated the statement with a mournful wail that even caused Reilly to shudder.

A million thoughts raced through Reilly's mind. He had Pardo now, unarmed, broken. Duke stood in the door of the saloon, next to Swede Iverson, staring, mouths open. He could take them, and Pardo, take them all so damned easily. The major, Ritcher, he had mounted his horse and was loping out of town by the time Reilly ran out of the mercantile, leaving the bag of supplies Pardo had ordered on the boardwalk. He hadn't had time to visit the barber. All Reilly had to do was draw his gun. Arrest them. Yet he couldn't forget Dagmar and Blanche. Chaucer had killed Ruby Pardo, but what had he done with the two hostages?

Was he still in camp in the Dragoons? Why was Duke here? Where were the others? Where were Dagmar and Blanche? No, he couldn't risk pulling a gun on Pardo. It was like he had told the Wickenburg marshal. He had to get back to the Dragoons, had to find Dagmar.

He put his lips close to Pardo's ear, and whispered, "Jim, you got to pull yourself together. Don't let them see you like this, not Duke, not Iverson." He looked at the people milling in the streets. "Not these Redington . . ." He thought of the word. "Hayseeds."

Pardo's breath caught. He was trying to dam those tears soaking the blue chambray shirt Reilly had just bought, which had set him—or, rather, Pardo—back fifty-five cents.

"Come on, Jim. We need to light a shuck out of town. Jim, listen to me. Since I was a just a young colt, I always wanted to be like Jim Pardo. Bloody Jim. The man the law couldn't catch. You were better than Quantrill or Bloody Bill, better than Jesse James, Sam Bass. Better than Bill Longley or John Wesley Hardin. But you can't let these people see you like this. We'll get Chaucer. You'll see. Now stand up, Jim. Come on. We need to get out of town. In a hurry."

There wasn't any law in Redington, but a few merchants were pointing, and those mercantiles had a lot of shotguns, rifles, and revolvers in the cases. If one of them happened to recognize Pardo, or even Reilly, for that matter, these streets could be running red with blood.

Pardo lifted his head, pinched his nose, and forced a weak smile. "Figured my nose would start to gushing," he said. "But it didn't. Never can figure that out." His hand found the Colt, and he was standing, nodding, plunging the empty casings into the dirt, and filling the cylinder with fresh rounds.

Most men, including Reilly, kept the chamber under the revolver's hammer empty, as a safety precaution, to keep from accidentally shooting off a toe, but not Jim Pardo. He kept six beans in the wheel, as the saying went.

"Thanks, Mac." Pardo's eyes were red-rimmed, and snot hung from his nose, yet his voice was firm now. He holstered the revolver, and stared across the street until the people started going back to their businesses. "You get the supplies?" he asked without looking at Reilly.

"Yeah. Back at the store."

When Pardo turned, he almost started to cry again once he saw the strawberries littering the ground near him, but steeled himself and pointed a stubby finger at Duke and Iverson, still standing in the doorway of the saloon. "Mount up, boys. We're through here. We got work to do."

They drifted south to the Southern Pacific tracks and turned east, following the old Overland road. Back in the late 1850s, John Butterfield had created a route for Overland Mail Company, a passenger- and mail-carrying stagecoach road from Tipton, Missouri, to San Francisco, California. When the Civil War broke out, U.S. officials moved the route out of the South and across the Great Plains, but Butterfield's trail still got travelers, from the Jackass Mail to settlers, and the Army. It still got fairly heavy traffic, although the three riders met only a white-haired Mexican hauling firewood on a burro, and that had been ten miles earlier, as they rode east.

Instead of turning south for the Dragoons, Pardo rode ahead, and Reilly, Iverson, and Duke followed in silence. At the edge of Texas Canyon, he reined in the roan, allowing the three riders to catch up.

"What do you think?" Pardo asked no one in particular.

Swede and Duke looked at Reilly for an answer.

As he swung a leg over the saddle horn and stretched, Reilly asked in a casual voice, "You mean as a place to hit that Army wagon train?"

"That's what I mean."

Reilly scratched his beard.

The canyon was fairly wide, yet the road hugged the mounds of twisted rocks and boulders on the northern side. The sky was a brilliant blue, which accented the rocky ledges, the closest ones the color of desert sand, but farther up the canyon they turned a deep red, spotted with growths of juniper, the occasional Spanish yucca, and a bunch of dead mesquite trees whose empty, spindly branches reached out like tentacles of some great sea monster.

Reilly glanced at Swede Iverson, then looked into Pardo's eyes, trying to read that man's thinking, but he couldn't.

"You busted Swede Iverson," Reilly began, then decided to correct himself. "We busted Iverson out of Wickenburg because you wanted a good man with explosives. So you're thinking about blowing up these rocks."

Pardo grinned, until Reilly shook his head.

"You cause an avalanche, you'll not only bury the soldiers escorting that train, you'll bust up your Gatling guns. And the howitzer."

"You ain't so bright after all, Mac," Pardo said, and

hooked his thumb toward the highest peak. "Can you bring down them rocks?" he asked Iverson.

It took Swede Iverson only a glance. "With ease."

"Block this road?"

This time, Iverson had to examine both sides of the canyon with more care. "Sure," he said after a while, nodding with less exuberance.

Pardo's head bobbed with satisfaction. "Now, here's where it gets ticklish. According to Major Ritcher, two companies of infantry'll be guarding that train, been with them since they left Fort Bliss. There'll also be a cavalry troop out of Fort Bowie riding with it, but it'll be commanded by a green lieutenant named Talley."

Reilly's eyebrows arched, although he tried to disguise any recognition. It didn't matter. Pardo was looking at the towering rocks, and Iverson and Duke were staring at Pardo. *Talley?* Reilly thought. *Jeremiah Talley?* But Jerry was supposed to have been off to California. He wouldn't be back yet, unless his orders had changed.

"The cavalry patrol, green or not, will take off first, ahead of the wagons," Pardo continued. "Make sure passage's safe, and once they get here"—he gesturing with his thumb—"they get buried with them big old rocks. And then there's no place for the wagons to go."

"Except out of the canyon," Duke said, "due east."

"How about if I blow up the other side, too?" Swede Iverson rubbed his hands together, excited about the prospects. "I can do that, Pardo. Blow up both entrances to this canyon."

Pardo blinked. "So we got the Army patrol trapped, eh? No way in, no way out?"

"Yeah," Iverson said.

"Then we can just pick 'em off," Duke said and,

slapping his thigh, raised his voice excitedly. "Be like a hawg killin'."

Pardo, saying nothing, looked at Reilly, who grinned.

"Boys," Reilly said, "if you do that, how do we get the Gatlings out of this canyon?"

Frowns quickly clouded their once-excited faces.

"We could haul them up," Pardo said, and Reilly's face froze. "With ropes. Have some wagons waiting on the other side, load them, and raise hell for the Mexican border. I like it."

Reilly didn't. "That'll take a long time, Jim. Too long. Plus, you're likely to run into more than a few patrols out of Fort Huachuca. You bring down these canyon walls, that noise will be heard for miles. Word will be out about what happened here long before you ever reach the border. And it won't just be Army patrols." He pointed south. "You'll have the posses out of Tombstone, Contention, Charleston, Bisbee, maybe as far west as Nogales."

"Uh-huh." Pardo's blue eyes shined. "Give us a chance to test out my new Gatling guns."

Reilly tried to swallow, found his throat parched, and reached for his canteen.

"What about it, Swede?" Pardo asked. "Can you do that? Bury them blue-belly horse soldiers, then bring down the wall and block any escape that train would have?"

This time, Iverson wasn't so confident. "Let me ride through this canyon," he said, and the four men did just that, silently, looking at the palisade of red and white rocks, some of them hanging ever so precipitously, as if a strong wind would blow them over. When they had reached the eastern edge of the canyon, Iverson nodded.

"It could be done, but timing will be important. Real important."

"Can you do it?" Pardo asked irritably.

Iverson's head bobbed again.

"How much dynamite would you need?"

Now, Iverson shook his head. "Not dynamite. Fuses ain't that dependable, and the powder can be temperamental. No, sir, for this job, I'd need nitro-glycerine."

"Nitro?" Duke exclaimed.

"That's right." It was Pardo who answered. "That's how I figured it, boys. Wanted to see if Swede here figured it the same. You done good, Iverson. Had you said dynamite, I would have pegged you for a fool and left you dying here with a bullet in your gut. Nitro it'll be."

Reilly cleared his throat. "Even if you pin down those soldier boys," he said, "that's two companies of infantry that'll be here, plus muleskinners and drivers. And any horse troopers that survive the avalanche. Trained professionals, and more than one hundred twenty men. You'll need more men than what you have now."

"You forget, Mac," Pardo said, "that I've seen how you handle that Evans repeating rifle. Like Duke said, it'll be a hog killing. But I plan to get a few extra men for this job. Just to make you feel better, cut down on the number of Yanks you'll need to kill."

"What if the cavalry troop doesn't separate from the main branch?" Reilly asked. "Or what happens if the wagon train waits until the troopers are all the way through the canyon?"

"Good questions," Pardo said.

"You got any good answers?" Reilly challenged.

Pardo shook his head before a toothy smile

exploded across his face. "Them boys'll be just a few days from Fort Lowell. They ain't gonna be waiting around none. They'll be in a hurry to get to some good whiskey and bad women. They'll be right behind them horse soldiers. I got a feeling. A good feeling."

Reilly ran his tongue across his chapped lips, tried to think of something else to say, some type of argument, then decided against it. The wind moaned through the trees and rocks, rustling the blades of tall, sunburned grass on the edge of the road.

"What's next?" Duke asked.

Pardo pointed east. "Duke, you take Swede back to camp. Tell the boys what we got cooking." He scratched his palm against the hammer of his Colt. "How's that woman, the German woman, Dagmar, and her kid?"

"They was fine, boss man. Fine when I left the Dragoons."

"That's good. That's a fine woman. Yes, sir, a real fine woman. Ten times the woman Three-Fingers Lacy ever was." His face clouded in anger, but only briefly.

"Where you gonna get my nitro?" Iverson asked.

Pardo cackled. "I'm gonna steal it. There are plenty of mines out here."

"That stuff's deadly," Iverson warned. "Slightest touch could set it off."

"They say the same about Bloody Jim Pardo," Pardo said. "All right, Duke. You got your orders. Have the boys wait for me in camp. Me and Reilly got us a chore to do." He drew the Colt, flipped open the loading gate, and spun the cylinder on his arm, checking the loads, then holstering the revolver. "Which way did Chaucer go when he left camp?"

Duke was slow to answer.

"Which way?"

"He just left, boss man," Duke said. "We didn't follow him or nothin'."

"But Lacy went with him?"

"Yeah. That was Phil's doin', boss man. He told Wade to take her with him, and they vamoosed. That's what Phil told him. On account that it was Lacy who shot—"

"Shut up," Pardo barked.

The wind kicked up a dust devil a few yards away.

"Nobody leaves camp till me and Mac get back," Pardo ordered. "Come on, Mac. Let's go pay a call on Wade Chaucer. And Three-Fingers Lacy."

They rode out of Texas Canyon, Swede Iverson and Duke heading east, where they'd soon cut their way south and ride for the Dragoon Mountains, Pardo and Reilly heading west, riding in silence, in the heat of the day, on the trail to Benson until they turned south.

Reilly knew this country, knew it well. Off to the west, he heard the chugging of a locomotive, the train to Benson on the Southern Pacific's spur.

"You ever been to Contention City, Mac?"

"A few times," Reilly answered honestly.

They rode a few miles south before Reilly chanced a question. "What makes you think Chaucer will be in Contention?"

Pardo waited maybe a quarter mile before answering. "I ain't rightly sure he will be."

The horses covered another thirty yards.

"But I'm certain we'll find Lacy there."

CHAPTER TWENTY

Friday afternoon, and the streets of Contention City were filled with people. Spotting a lawman crossing the street just ahead of them, Reilly pulled his hat down low, and was thankful he hadn't had time to shave off that rough beard back in Redington. Pardo didn't seem to give a damn, but the lawman never gave either rider a moment's consideration, and disappeared inside The Western Hotel.

South of town, well beyond the train depot, stood the three stamp mills—the Contention, the Head Center, and the Grand Central—that processed the silver ore from the Tombstone mines for smelting. It wasn't a big town, maybe between one hundred fifty and two hundred people, but it was crowded today. An empty ore wagon rumbled past them, the driver giving them a polite nod, and almost every hitching rail was full. Music banged out of John McDermott's saloon as they rode past, and a woman hurried in front of them, carrying a basket of bread. Out on the field at the edge of town, before the stamp mills, a baseball game was being played, but they didn't ride that far. Pardo turned down an alley, and Reilly followed.

Pardo, Reilly observed, knew Contention better than he did.

They rode past a Chinese laundry and headed into the red-light district near the banks of the San Pedro River. Reilly frowned when Pardo stopped and swung down in front of an adobe building. There was no sign, but everybody in Contention—hell, everyone in southern Arizona—knew this place was Maggie Fairplay's brothel. He knew it pretty well himself.

The door opened as Reilly swung down off the paint horse, and a burly black man flung an overweight gringo through the threshold, then disappeared for a moment before sending a derby hat after the man he had just thrown out. Reilly adjusted the saddle girth while the black man stared briefly at the two men, although he couldn't see Reilly well, then pointed a large finger at the man in the sack suit, who was standing on wobbly legs near the well, brushing the dirt and dung off his pants and coat.

"Don't come back here, bub," the black man said.

"You don't have to worry about that, sir," Sack Suit said, and, fetching his derby, he staggered past Reilly and Pardo. The black man spit over a hitching rail and stepped back through the door, but he stopped when Pardo called out to him.

"Hey, *boy.*"

Taking in a deep breath, Reilly peered over the saddle.

Little Rick Dixon, who weighed two hundred and forty pounds and stood six-four in his stocking feet, filled the doorway, angry eyes drilled on Pardo, who had tethered his horse to the hitching rail.

"I'm looking for a whore," he said.

"You come to the right place," Little Rick said, adding, "*boy.*"

Pardo smiled, respecting the bouncer's spunk.

"I got a specific whore in mind. She's bony, rail-thin, but she's got tits the size of cantaloupes." Jiggling both hands in front of his chest to show the bouncer, who wasn't amused. "Hair the color of a raven's wing, kinda messy, needing a curry comb and brush, like it'd take a groomer a month to comb out the tangles. Talks through her nose half the time. And drinks like a sieve. When I had her last, she went by the name Lacy, but, well, you know whores. They change names as quick as they change customers. But I thought she might be here."

"She's here. Same name. Last room down the hall to the left."

"Thanks."

"Want me to announce you?"

Pardo's head shook no, and he hooked his thumbs in his gunbelt. "I'd like to surprise her."

"Suit yourself. But you gotta pay a dollar. In advance."

Pardo's left hand left the gunbelt, and fished out a couple of coins, which he flipped across the yard. The two dollars landed at the bouncer's feet. Then Pardo pulled out another dollar, and sent it sailing, too.

"There's three bucks," Pardo said, his voice filled with amusement, a forced friendliness. "One for my pard here." He hooked a thumb toward Reilly, who ducked to work on the latigo. "One for you. To make yourself scarce."

From underneath the pinto's belly, Reilly saw Little Rick's massive hands collect the three coins. As the big man disappeared, Reilly led his horse to the hitching rail.

"I told you she'd be here," Pardo said, but the friendliness had left his face. "She just couldn't stay away, damn her soul." His fists clenched, and he stood there, shaking, staring through the entrance. "Let's go," he said hollowly, and walked inside.

The inside smelled of sweat and stale beer. The back door was open, and Reilly saw no sign of Little Rick. No sign of anybody. Pardo turned down to his left, his spurs jingling as he walked down the narrow hallway, his hand resting on the holstered Colt. Reilly shot quick glances down the other hall and across the parlor, before following.

Pardo reached the end of the hall and put his left hand on the brass doorknob, half turning, watching the door with one eye and Reilly with another. A door opened, and a woman stepped out. She wore a gathered skirt of blue calico, black hose and no shoes, and a corset cover, trimmed with lace, with the ribbon drawstrings loose, revealing ample cleavage. Her auburn hair hung loosely, and the bruise that had blackened her eye had faded away. She recognized Reilly immediately, and started to call out his name, when Reilly grabbed her, pulled her to him, and kissed her.

He looked up over her shoulders, and pushed her gently back into her room, staring at Pardo while he asked, "You need me for anything?"

Laughing, Pardo shook his head and opened the door.

Reilly quickly stepped inside, shut the door behind him. He wanted to kiss Gwendolyn Morgan again, but he hadn't enough time.

"Reilly!" she shouted, and leaped into his arms, kissing him again. He decided he'd make time.

Gently, he pushed her away. She looked confused, but happy to see him.

"Reilly, what's going on?" she asked. "They say you

teamed up with the Kraft brothers, say you busted them out of the prison wagon. There's a wanted poster of you tacked up at the town marshal's office."

He was out of breath. "Yeah, well, it's a long story. Have you seen Ken Cobb?"

She frowned. "Reilly, he don't come here till the end of the month, when he says he's working. *Working.* Yeah, he's working to get away from his wife. And when he comes here, he don't see me. He prefers our resident Celestial."

Laughing, he walked to her bed, found a bottle of Jameson Irish whiskey, three-fourths full, and thumbed out the cork.

"I need you to get a message to him," he said. "Can you do that for me, Gwen?"

"Of course, Reilly. But what's going on?"

He filled a tumbler, held the bottle toward her, and when she nodded, he handed her the glass, then poured a shot for himself. The whiskey warmed him, calmed him, and Gwen sat on the bed, holding the glass in both hands, but not drinking, just staring.

"Busting the Krafts free was Gus Henderson's doing," Reilly said. "We got ambushed by K.C. and his men. They killed Frank Denton and Slim Chisum. Then W.W. Kraft blew Henderson out of the saddle with a shotgun. K.C. didn't like that, but it was too late to do anything about it. They had captured me—my rifle jammed, and Henderson got the drop on me— threw me inside that prison wagon, left me there to bake to death. And I would have, had not Jim Pardo and his gang happened by."

"Pardo?" Gwen drank half the tumbler, coughed slightly. "Bloody Jim Pardo."

Reilly nodded. He thought about pouring another

drink, but instead, set the bottle and glass on the table. "You got paper and pencil?"

"Sure, Reilly." She finished her whiskey, and fetched a notebook and pencil, and Reilly began writing.

Ken:

Haven't much time. I'm with Bloody Jim Pardo, who freed me from the prison wagon in the Sulfur Spring Valley. Gus Henderson set us up for the ambush, paid for his sins with his life. Will explain later. If I'm still alive.

Pardo plans to attack an Army wagon train bound for Ft. Lowell at Texas Canyon. Train's bringing Gatlings & a howitzer. Get word to the Army. ~~We~~ *You can hit Pardo there in ten days or so.*

Pardo has a woman and child held captive, taken from raid on the S.P. That's the main reason I haven't tried to capture Pardo myself.

That, he thought, *and because I don't want to get killed.* He signed his name, then added a postscript:

Please trust me. You've know me long enough to know I didn't have anything to do with the Krafts' escape.

Then, he thought of something else.

Swede Iverson with Pardo. Plans to use nitro in Texas Canyon ambush.

And something else:

*Get word to 2nd Lt. Jeremiah Talley,
escorting the Army train with his cavalry
troop. Talley can also explain why I took
the Krafts toward Ft. Bowie.*

He folded the note, wrote on the paper, *Ken Cobb,
Marshal, Tombstone,* and handed it to Gwen, who stuck
it between her breasts. Their eyes locked, and Reilly
reached for her, but pulled short when something
banged on the door.

"Come on, Mac!" Pardo's voice.

"I'll explain everything later," he said, and kissed
her. He turned to the door, opened it, and saw Pardo
standing in the hallway, holding the big bowie, the
handle of which he had slammed against the door.

"You don't give a man much time," Reilly started,
but stopped, staring at first at the bloody blade,
before taking a tentative look down the hallway. The
door to Three-Fingers Lacy's room remained opened,
and from inside came a low yet agonizing moan. He
watched Pardo wipe the blood on his pants, then
sheathe the knife.

The Irish whiskey soured in the pit of his stomach. The low moan became a sniffling, then a piercing wail.

"I didn't kill her," Pardo said. "But from now on,
she won't have to explain why she's called Three-
Fingers Lacy." He laughed, and headed down the
hallway. Other doors opened, but no one dared enter
the hall as Pardo's and Reilly's boots thudded on
the earthen floor. Suddenly, Little Rick blocked their
way, and as Pardo drew his pistol, Reilly shoved him
aside, moved hurriedly toward the bouncer. Little

Rick's eyes flickered in recognition. Then the big black man tried to bring up a baseball bat-stick, but Reilly had pulled the Smith & Wesson and slammed it against Little Rick's head. The bat-stick bounced along the floor, and Reilly tried to catch the giant, but couldn't, and the bouncer crashed against the wall, slid down, fell over on his side.

"I'm sorry," Reilly whispered. Little Rick wasn't out, but his eyes wouldn't focus, and blood rolled down his close-cropped hair, pooling behind his left ear. His eyes fluttered, his fingers tightened into balled fists, and he let out a low groan.

A door down the hallway swung open. A woman gasped. The door closed.

"You're soft, Mac," Pardo said. "Should have let me plug the black bastard."

"Didn't want to risk a shot," Reilly said, as he rose. "Bring the law down on us."

"Yeah, well, don't make the mistake of shoving me when I'm drawing a gun, Mac. Next time, I might shoot you. Just to teach you some manners."

Maggie Fairplay, the madam of the establishment, came charging out of one of the rooms down the right hallway, and Pardo and Reilly quickly stepped outside, into the bright light of the afternoon.

As they swung into their saddles, Wade Chaucer rode into the yard.

"Damn!" Chaucer yelled, and palmed the Remington.

Pardo dived, drawing his pistol, landing and rolling as Chaucer's first shot thudded in the adobe wall of the whorehouse. Reilly was trying to draw the Evans, but the pinto started bucking, and he dived off. Chaucer ignored him, shot again at Pardo. A bullet dug into the soft dirt by Reilly's leg, and he rolled over, jerking the Smith & Wesson from the waistband, putting a bullet in the door frame, knocking Maggie Fairplay onto her ample backside. Reilly gathered his legs, leaped behind the well.

The pinto kept bucking, stirring up a thick cloud of dust. Pardo's Colt roared twice. The door to the brothel slammed shut. The Remington barked again. Reilly tried to find Chaucer, but couldn't see him for the dust. Pardo emptied the Colt, reloaded. Chaucer's gun spoke once more. The gunman cursed. Suddenly, he turned the blood bay gelding and galloped down the alley, almost running over a Chinese woman who had stepped out of the laundry to see what was going on.

Pardo leaped into the saddle, kicking the roan's sides, shoving the Colt into the holster, yanking the Winchester from the scabbard. "Keep the law off me, Mac!" he yelled, and was swallowed by the dust as he galloped after Chaucer.

Reilly leaped to his feet, ran into the cloud, broke free, saw the bucking pinto, and he lunged for the reins dragging on the ground. He missed. Damn near got his right hand smashed by a hoof. Tried again. Missed. The pinto bucked and squealed, but on his next try, Reilly's hand gripped the rein. The leather burned his palm, his fingers, as the horse reared, but Reilly, grimacing, held tight. His knees dragged across the dirt. He saw the Chinese woman staring at him. Heard Maggie Fairplay cursing behind him. Heard gunshots on Contention's main street. Thought he heard the sound of breaking glass. And people screaming.

He had pulled himself to his feet now. He had dropped the Smith & Wesson. Didn't know where. Didn't care. He cursed the bucking horse, then put his right hand on the saddle horn. A moment later, he was in the saddle, holding on for dear life. The Chinese woman screamed and dived back into the laundry, as Reilly and the pinto bucked past. Finally, the horse finished its bucking and settled into a high lope, cutting down the alley, into the main street.

Reilly pulled on the reins, the pinto sliding to a stop. He jerked the Evans carbine out, eared back the hammer. The town marshal had appeared in front of The Western Hotel, and Reilly shot his hat off, the bullet smashing the plate-glass window behind the lawman, who dived back inside with an oath and a grunt.

He saw the dust, leading south, and he spurred the pinto, galloped past the butcher's shop and a couple of mercantiles, hitting the pinto's side with the rifle barrel, chasing Pardo, chasing Chaucer. On past the stamp mills. Thundering over the railroad tracks, riding east into the desert, toward the Dragoons.

Chapter Twenty-one

A quarter mile out of town, Reilly pulled hard on the reins. He stood in the stirrups, looked ahead, left, right. Nothing. The pinto snorted, pawed the dirt with its front hoofs, wanting to run, but Reilly tugged on the reins again, saying, "Easy, boy."

Seconds later, he heard the shots.

He turned in the saddle, swearing, looking back toward Contention City. Chaucer wouldn't have doubled back, would he? Even if he had, would Pardo be mad enough to ride back there, as busy as town had been? More shots rang out.

"Hell," Reilly said, and turned the pinto around, raked its sides with his spurs, galloped back toward Contention, holding the Evans in his right hand, feeling the wind blast his face until he reached town.

The paint horse slid to a stop, and Reilly leaped from the saddle, levering a fresh round in the Evans. A woman screamed. Then, Reilly saw her. The same woman he had seen earlier, carrying the freshly baked bread in a basket. She rounded the corner, her face ashen, eyes wide, mouth open but no sound escaping it now. She plowed into a column, spilling four loaves of bread and dropping a newspaper, then hurried across the street and through a side door, which slammed behind her and was bolted shut.

Across the street, horses bucked at their hitching rails. Reilly secured the pinto to the wooden column the woman had hit, pushed himself to the back of the adobe wall. Curses rang out. More shots. Dogs barked.

Reilly peered around the corner. A man drove a buckboard, whipping the mules furiously, turned the corner on the other side of the street, the wagon leaning on two wheels, almost flipping over, almost spilling the driver, then righted itself.

The marshal stood again in front of The Western Hotel, long-barreled Colt in his left hand, waving his black hat—the one Reilly had shot off just a few minutes earlier—over his head with his right, yelling, "Get off the streets! Everybody, get off the streets!"

It seemed that everybody was listening. Except for Bloody Jim Pardo and Wade Chaucer.

They remained mounted, about a block apart. Pardo stood in his stirrups, fired the Winchester. Chaucer leaned over in the saddle, snapped a shot from his Remington. Then both men spurred their mounts into the alley. The marshal spun around in the street, set his hat back on his head, pointed the pistol first at Chaucer, then toward the disappearing Pardo, unsure who to shoot at.

Reilly wet his lips. Stared down at the Evans.

Tried to remember how many rounds he had left. Four? Maybe? The Redington mercantile hadn't had any cartridges for an Evans .44, but that hadn't surprised Reilly. That was one of the drawbacks of shooting an Evans repeating rifle. Few merchants carried that ammunition. He remembered the extra cartridge, the one he had stuck in his new vest pocket. Patted the pocket, felt the bullet, decided to leave it there. Reached for the Smith & Wesson, then remembered he had dropped it, lost it, back outside of Maggie Fairplay's brothel.

Pardo and Chaucer emerged, still on horseback, riding down the boardwalks, crouched, firing. A bullet splintered a wooden column. Pardo's head knocked a lantern swinging. Horses at the hitching rails bucked, screamed, kicked. One broke free, took off toward the Contention Mill. A cowboy ran out of McDermott's saloon, grabbed the reins to his buckskin gelding, swung up, rode out of town. Another cowhand started, then dived back through the saloon doors.

The marshal spun, aimed at Chaucer, ducked as Chaucer's Remington roared. Answered by Pardo's Winchester. Windows broke. Then horses kept moving across the boardwalk. Reilly watched the marshal decide to let those two fools kill each other. The lawman dived through the busted front window of the hotel.

A horse went down, tripped the big dun by its side, which ripped free of its tether, rolled across the bay horse, gathered its legs, tripped once, then rebounded, loped toward the San Pedro River.

Reilly had to marvel at both men, Pardo and Chaucer, as their horses stepped off the boardwalks, and both men kicked their mounts into lopes across the street, back around a corner. He could see Pardo rein up, turn around, spin the Winchester's stock forward, then jerk it back, levering a fresh round into the chamber, and spur his horse again.

He smelled bread. Looked down, saw a loaf, squatted,

picked it up, his teeth tearing savagely into the bread. He was starving.

Pardo wheeled the roan, kicked it into a gallop, charged down the street. Like a jousting knight out of that Walter Scott book—what was the name? *Ivanhoe*, Reilly remembered, yes, *Ivanhoe*—Chaucer came out on his blood bay, rode to meet the challenge.

"Jesus!" came a shout from The Western Hotel. "Would you look at them two fools!"

Flame and smoke leaped from the barrels of Remington revolver and Winchester carbine as both men fired simultaneously. Pardo's hat went sailing over the horse's back. Chaucer flinched, fired again as Pardo charged past him. A horse across the street dropped dead. The others tied to the hitching rail, pulled out the post—a scene much like the one Reilly had caused in Wickenburg—and they galloped toward the railroad tracks.

The air smelled heavy with dust and gun smoke. Reilly took another bite of bread, chewed, shoved the loaf inside his vest, wiped the sweat from his forehead, and raised the Evans again. Down the alley on the other side of the street, he spotted Gwendolyn Morgan, Maggie Fairplay, Little Rick, and the Chinese laundress. Little Rick pressed his left hand against his bleeding head, held his right hand to keep the ladies back, out of danger. Maggie and the laundress were trying to get past the big man's oak-sized arm. Gwendolyn had spotted Reilly, and she just stared.

He looked back up the street.

"Fifty dollars!" came a voice inside McDermott's saloon. "Fifty dollars says the man in black comes out alive!"

"I'll take that!" a Scottish voice shouted from the mercantile.

Oddly enough, music started again inside the saloon. Reilly groaned. "Oh, My Darling, Clementine." He hated that damned song.

Pardo and Chaucer turned their horses, charged again, leaning forward, low, Chaucer holding the reins in his left hand, Remington in his right, Pardo using both hands on his Winchester, reins in his teeth. Both guns spoke again. This time, Chaucer lost his hat. They thundered past each other, wheeling their horses, Pardo's rearing, Chaucer's kicking, bucking, then galloping back down the street.

He could see the grim determination on Chaucer's face, see the bloodstain on his left shoulder. The Remington roared, and Pardo's roan went down hard on its forefeet, throwing Pardo over its head, into the dirt, the Winchester rifle arcing stock over barrel through the air, landing in the street twenty feet away, bouncing another thirty.

Pardo came up, his face and hands bleeding, clawing for the Colt. Chaucer jerked the blood bay to a stop, turned, fired. Dust flew up at Pardo's side, but now Pardo was rising, shooting, and the bay horse was screaming, falling on its side, kicking, while Chaucer kicked free of the stirrups, leaped off, landing on his feet, staggering. Pardo shot again. The bullet sliced across Chaucer's right leg, and he went down. Came up. Snapped a shot.

Pardo had to roll out of the way of his horse, struggling to get to its feet. The roan staggered off toward Reilly. Pardo went the other way.

They ran, shooting, heading to the same side of the street, Pardo dove and fired, flying into the alley next door to McDermott's saloon; Chaucer took cover behind a water trough. The horses there had long ago pulled free from the rail and taken off to parts unknown, leaving behind broken reins dangling from the rails in front of The Western Hotel.

Chaucer lifted his head, aimed, snapped a shot. Ducked as Pardo's bullet sent water splashing in the trough.

Thankfully, the piano player inside the saloon ceased "Oh, My Darling, Clementine," the noise replaced by the barking dogs, all of them keeping a respectful distance from the two gunmen. The front of the Contention Mill overflowed with spectators, too. A window slid open on the second story of the hotel, and a buxom redhead hung out, looking up and down the street.

"Marshal!" a man yelled down the boardwalk. Reilly turned, saw it was a preacher. "Why don't you stop this violence?"

"Why don't you, parson?" came the lawman's reply. "Or get the hell off the street!"

The preacher stiffened at the rebuke, then, clutching his Bible, went back inside the café.

Reilly had a good view of Pardo, saw his back pressed against the saloon's wall, wiping his bloody hands, torn up from the sand and gravel on the road, on his pants, then reloading his pistol. As soon as he had snapped the loading gate shut, he spun, fired, hitting the water trough low. Water sprayed out of the hole. Chaucer returned fire, blasting off a chunk of adobe brick that showered Pardo's hair.

Then Pardo turned, sprinted down the alley, disappeared around the rear corner of the saloon. Reilly looked down the street. Almost immediately, Chaucer rose, dived, fired, landed on the boardwalk, and rolled onto the other side of the hotel.

"Hell." Reilly frowned. He couldn't see either man.

Above the din of the barking dogs, a train whistle blew.

Reilly looked across the street, saw Gwen still staring at him. Maggie Fairplay had dropped to her knees, and crawled under Little Rick's big arms, and now was looking up, asking the big bouncer a question. The Chinese woman stood twisting her hair around a finger, letting it fall, then twisting it again.

The roan horse limped past Reilly and kept going. Reilly didn't bother trying to stop it, knew it would never carry Pardo out of Contention City. If Pardo survived.

Reilly turned, collected a few other loaves of bread and the rolled-up newspaper, and moved to the pinto. He opened the saddlebag, and stuffed the bread and paper in it, gathered the reins, and swung into the saddle. He nodded at Gwen, and at the bouncer, Maggie, and the laundress, who had turned their attention toward him, and rode down the side street, turned behind the assayer's office, rode along the eastern edge for two blocks, cut down the alley. He stopped across from The Western Hotel, saw Chaucer climbing the stairs, taking the steps easily, softly, coming up, eyes focused below, not seeing Bloody Jim Pardo appear at the other corner of the hotel.

Slowly, almost casually, Pardo raised the Colt's barrel, but he kept walking, keeping time with Chaucer as he climbed the steps. When Chaucer reached the top, he looked over the balustrade, and started for the side door. That's when he saw Pardo.

That's when Pardo fired.

The bullet caught Chaucer in the small of his back, slammed him against the door. Almost as a reflex, he pulled the trigger on the Remington, his left hand still gripping the doorknob. Then as his left arm slammed into his right arm, the Remington flew out of his hand, over the balustrade, bouncing off the corner of the water trough, splashing into the water.

Chaucer spun, left hand still holding onto the knob, as Pardo's second bullet caught him in the shoulder, pushed him into the corner. He grunted, and his left hand released the knob and hung limply at his side.

The white shirt above his empty holster exploded red, and Chaucer almost folded in half, somehow straightened, staggered forward a few steps, dragging his feet. Both arms dangled at his side. His head was bent, chin against his shirt.

Another bullet drilled him over his left breast pocket, and Chaucer sank to his knees, right hand stretching, reaching, grasping for the railing to the stairs, missing. Then Chaucer was tumbling down the stairs, tearing down a section a few feet from the bottom, landing on his back at Pardo's feet.

Reilly had seen enough. He dismounted, led the pinto into the street, gathered the reins to a dun horse in front of Avery's Mercantile, and, pointing the Evans toward the hotel window, walked across the street.

"What's happening?" came a question from the butcher's shop.

"Hell if I know," a man answered from the saloon.

The dogs stopped barking.

The redhead on the second story of the hotel yelled, "The little runt killed the gent in black!"

"Hell's fires!" a voice called from the saloon. "That bastard cost me fifty bucks!"

The Scotsman in the mercantile cheered.

Reilly stopped in front of Pardo, who looked down at the dying Wade Chaucer, calmly ejected the empties from the Colt, and just as casually reloaded.

The locomotive chugged toward the depot, coughing thick, acrid black smoke, steam hissing.

"We best light a shuck out of here," Reilly said.

"In a minute," Pardo said. He thumbed back the hammer and pulled the trigger. Chaucer's body jerked. Kept jerking as Pardo emptied the cylinder.

Reilly looked across the street, saw the face of the railroad engineer and firemen, their mouths hanging open, then looked back at Pardo, who plunged the empty casings, letting them fall on Chaucer's lifeless, bloody body, and reloaded again. This time, he holstered the Colt and knelt over the dead man.

Pardo reached into his vest, pulled out something. Reilly felt sick, tried to swallow, couldn't, and turned away as Pardo pried open Chaucer's mouth and shoved inside the fingers Pardo had cut off Three-Fingers Lacy's hand.

"That's for Ma," Pardo said, and he stood, nodding in satisfaction. "That's for Ma, you miserable son of a bitch." He nodded at Reilly, took the proffered reins, and mounted the dun. "Thanks for keeping the law off me, Mac. I'm hungry. You got anything to eat?"

The dogs started barking again. The train whistle blew, and the engine belched out steam as it reached the depot.

"I rounded up some bread," Reilly said.

"Good. Hope it's sourdough. Ma always liked good sourdough bread." He jerked out the Colt, put a final bullet in Wade Chaucer's brain, and spurred the dun. Only he didn't ride out of town. He rode down the main street, leaped over Chaucer's dead horse, and dismounted, picked up his hat, slapped the dust off his thigh, and yelled at The Western Hotel.

"The man I killed shot down my ma. Don't y'all

give him no Christian burial. Wade Chaucer don't deserve that."

He swung into the saddle, and spurred the dun north out of town. Reilly didn't look back. He just followed Pardo out of Contention City.

CHAPTER TWENTY-TWO

"If you steal nitro from some local miner, you might tip your hand," Swede Iverson told Pardo. He pointed a cigar for emphasis. "Laws might start wondering what's going on, because it's gonna take maybe two crates of nitro to bring down them canyon walls. Besides, lots of mines these days, they don't use nitro anymore. Not even dynamite. They been using gelignite, on account that gelignite don't sweat, don't leak nitro the way dynamite will." He stuck the cigar back in his mouth, leaned back, and stretched.

They were back in the Dragoon Mountain stronghold, gathered around a campfire, everyone: Pardo, Iverson, Phil, Harrah, Duke, Soledad, Reilly, Blanche, and Dagmar. Thunder rolled in the distance, and the skies kept darkening. It was monsoon season, and Reilly expected an afternoon downpour within the hour.

"What do you suggest?" Pardo asked. He took a long pull from a bottle of mescal, and passed it to Phil.

"We could make it ourselves," Iverson said.

"Make it?" Duke exclaimed. "Make nitroglycerine?"

"Ain't it dangerous?" Harrah asked.

Pardo looked irritated, but said nothing.

"Oh, it's a handful, nitro, making it, carrying it, doing anything with it. My daddy was in California in the spring of sixty-six when they was shipping three crates of nitro for the Central Pacific to use while they was building the Transcontinental Railroad. One of the crates blew up. Tore apart a Wells Fargo office in San Francisco, killed fifteen people. My daddy said you could find bits of brains and other organs, plus people's various appendages, all over the block." He laughed, and flicked ash from the tip of the cigar. "After that incident, the state of California outlawed any transportation of liquid nitro."

"It explodes on contact, right?" Phil asked.

Iverson shrugged. "Contact, sure. But it's so volatile, temperamental, like a woman." He winked at Dagmar. Pardo's eyes turned to slits. "But it could blow up if the temperature dropped or rose just one or two degrees. Blow up whenever it's a mind to."

"That's a problem," Reilly said. "It's going to cool down significantly in an hour when this monsoon hits."

"Yeah," Duke said, "and how do we transport this nitro out of these mountains? That could blow us all to hell."

"Possibly," Iverson said. He accepted the bottle of mescal from Harrah's hand. "Downright probable."

"What would you need, Swede?" Pardo asked. "To make us some nitro?"

He removed the cigar. "Nitric acid. Sulfuric acid. Glycerin. Bicarbonate of soda. Some beakers. Ice."

"What the hell do I look like to you, Swede?" Pardo said. "An apothecary?"

Iverson grinned. "Well, there's another way. Probably a little easier, but just as dangerous. We could sweat some dynamite."

"Steal the dynamite," Reilly said, "and, like you said, you might tip Jim's hand."

"We ain't got to steal it, Mac," Iverson said. "I got a couple boxes hidden over by Total Wreck. And as hot as it's been, it should be leaking out that liquid beauty by now. Should have enough to pack four or five crates of the juice."

Pardo said, "Then why the hell did you suggest we make some if you already got some?"

With a shrug, Iverson returned the cigar back to his mouth. "Well, I was hoping to save that nitro to blow up something else, but that's all right. It'll wait. You can use mine."

"All right," Pardo said. "It's settled. We all go. But not until Dagmar reads me the newspaper Mac fetched for us while I was filling Wade Chaucer's body with some holes. Grab that paper, Mac. Miss Dagmar, if you'd be so kind . . ."

Reilly rose, went to the corral, and took the newspaper out of the saddlebag. It was the *Tombstone Epitaph*, and, after knocking off the bread crumbs left from the loaves he and Pardo had eaten after they'd left Contention, he scanned the front pages for any items about him, saw nothing, then looked at the back cover, finding only advertisements. He flipped open the page, looked at the headlines, again, finding nothing that interested him, that was about him, and closed the paper, and handed it to Dagmar before taking his seat by the fire.

Thunder rolled. Closer now.

Dagmar Wilhelm began reading. Beside her, Blanche leaned forward and poked the fire with a walnut stick, just to give her something to do. Still smoking his long nine cigar, Swede Iverson stared at the young mother. Pardo stared, too, scratching the palm of his hand against the hammer of his holstered Colt.

She read about a flood at one of the mines, about a performance at the Birdcage Theater, about the weather, about a Mexican matron giving birth to triplets. She turned the page. She read more about the weather, an editorial about the town council's lack of action about removing the myriad beer barrels from the streets, a story about the Apache outbreak, something about the delicious cream soda available at Yaple's, and a piece about a wagon accident on Toughnut Street that left a miner paralyzed. She read about how the Cochise County baseball team fell, 42–28, to the Pima County baseball team in Tucson, but how the boys from Cochise had led after the sixth inning and did our county proud.

Under the headline NEWS FROM THE SOUTH, she read about a gunfight in Nogales that left Special Deputy Marshal Kenneth Cobb dead.

Reilly sat up. "What?" he asked.

Everyone was staring at him. Blanche stopped playing with a stick in the fire. Dagmar swallowed, and repeated: "'Reports from Nogales, A.T., inform us of the tragic death of Kenneth Cobb, special deputy for United States Marshal Zan Tidball, who has resided in Tombstone for the past thirteen months, at the hands of K.C. Kraft.'"

Reilly sank back, mouth open. Stunned, he quickly recovered, putting up a facade, and laughed. "Old Cobb, eh, took a bullet. That's a shame." He looked past Dagmar at hard-eyed Jim Pardo. "Cobb's the lawman who arrested me." He tried to think of where he told Pardo he had been arrested, if he had told him anything. Decided it didn't matter. "Well, I guess

I owe Mister K.C. Kraft a beer next time we meet. He saved me the trouble of tracking down that lawman and killing him myself."

His stomach almost heaved. His mouth went dry. He reached for the bottle of mescal Harrah was offering him. Tried to think while Pardo apologized for Reilly's interruption and asked Dagmar to continue with her story.

"'A prompt reply from our telegraph to the Nogales Town Marshal confirmed the earlier wire, we are sad to report. Marshal Cobb had walked into The Silver Lode Saloon at noon, Friday instant, and happened to see K.C. Kraft standing at the bar. He reached for his Colt's revolver, but Kraft's younger brother, W.W., sitting in the corner and out of Marshal Cobb's view, shouted a warning, rose from his seated position, and grabbed Marshal Cobb's hand, preventing him from finishing his draw.'"

The mescal burned a wicked path down Reilly's throat, exploded in his stomach. *It's all right,* he told himself, thinking about that letter he had written for Cobb, the one he had given Gwendolyn Morgan to deliver to the marshal. Gwen would have read the note. She would get it to somebody. Maybe Tidball in Tucson. Maybe Fort Bowie. He winced in pain, perhaps from the mescal, though more than likely from the fear of what would happen if that note wound up in Major Ritcher's hands.

Damnation, he thought. *Why didn't I say in that note that Ritcher's a traitor, that he's working for Pardo?*

"'At that instant, K.C. Kraft, according to eyewitnesses, spun, and drew a Remington revolver, discharging three shots in quick succession, the second bullet striking Marshal Cobb in his sternum, the other shots missing their marks, but the one that hit the marshal took deadly effect, driving the marshal backward into the street, where he sank to his knees, muttering, "I am killed," and collapsed.'"

If, Reilly thought, *Gwen knows that Ken Cobb is dead, what will she do? If she doesn't know, she'll take the note to Tombstone, learn of what had happened in Nogales, and . . . and what? Give it to the city marshal?* Reilly tried to think. *Who is the city marshal in Tombstone? Can he be trusted?* Or would Gwen take it to the sheriff? He knew Deputy Constable Isaac Roberts there. No, Ike was dead. He had caught a bullet back in March trying to serve papers on a lot jumper.

"'At that time, L.J. Kraft, the third brother of these notorious outlaws, who recently escaped . . .'" Dagmar cleared her throat, wet her lips. Reilly was looking at her now, cursing the newspaper editor at the *Epitaph* for not putting that story on the front page, or putting a headline over it that he would not have scanned over. "I'm sorry," she said, giving Pardo a little smile, and the gunman grinned back. "Where was I? Oh, yes. 'Recently escaped from jail . . .'" The story hadn't said jail. He knew that. It had mentioned him. "'. . . came charging down the street on a black horse, leading the horses for his brothers, firing a pistol in the air, urging Nogales's fair citizens to "GET OFF THE STREETS," and out of the saloon charged K.C. and W.W., who mounted their fearless steeds, and charged out of town, crossing the border.

"'Marshal Cobb was carried back inside the saloon, and laid on a billiard table, while Doctor Ezra Goldman was quickly summoned, but the marshal had expired before the good doctor set foot inside the saloon.

"'We promise to have more details of Tombstone's great loss in our next edition. Our sympathies go out to Ken Cobb's widow, mother, and three children.'"

Dagmar wet her lips again. "Let's see. Here's a story about the price of silver. It says—"

"That's all right," Pardo said. "That's enough reading." He stroked his chin.

"Them Kraft brothers," Soledad said. *"Muy mal."*

"You know them?" Duke asked.

"Sí. They hide out in Nogales. On the Mexico side of the border. That is where *mi madre* lives. That is where I take Rafael. . . ." He cast his eyes downward, lowered his voice. "That is where I bury my brother. The Krafts, they were there."

"Muy mal, you say, eh?" Pardo showed his teeth. "You think you could find this K.C. Kraft in Nogales?"

"Sí."

Reilly's stomach began twisting into knots. "What are you thinking, Jim?" he asked.

"I'm thinking it's like you said, Mac. We'll need some more boys to shoot down them soldier boys when we trap them in Texas Canyon. I'm thinking the Kraft boys—I'd read about them before. Well, I've had some reading done to me before. But I'm thinking they might be good for this here deal I got cooking up with the blue-belly army. Besides, they's family, them brothers. Three of them, sticking out for each other. Family's important." He winked. "Besides, you owe K.C. a beer for gunning down that John Law, don't you?"

"Three men won't be enough," Reilly said.

Pardo laughed. "You don't know them Kraft brothers, Mac." That brought a wry grin to Reilly's face. He knew the Krafts. Knew them too damned well. "They got some friends. Soledad, you tell K.C. to bring as many of his gang as he wants. More the merrier. More blue-bellies to gun down."

The trees began rustling in the moaning wind. The temperature began dropping, and Reilly could smell rain in the air.

"Hand me that paper, woman," Swede Iverson shouted. "I want to read that story again. See if there's something in it about me."

Reilly froze. So did Dagmar. Damn, Reilly thought, he never should have brought that newspaper with him, should have left it on the boardwalk in Contention City. But Jim Pardo yanked the *Epitaph* out of Dagmar's hand, and held it across the fire. "Ask politely, Swede," he demanded.

Once he removed the cigar from his mouth, Swede Iverson forced a smile. "Begging your pardon, both of yours," he said, tipping his Irish cap, "but might I have a chance to read that newspaper?"

"That's better," Pardo said, and he extended the paper. Iverson reached across. Dagmar's lips mouthed, *No.*

Reilly started to rise, gripping the neck of the mescal bottle, ready to swing it, but Blanche whipped out the stick she'd been stirring the coals with, the burned end catching the paper, knocking it from Pardo's grip. The *Epitaph* fell onto the coals and erupted in flames while Pardo and Iverson cut loose with dozens of curses at the ten-year-old girl.

"Sorry," she said, a forced meekness.

Savagely, Iverson reached for her. Blanche fell away, dodging a blow from the explosives expert's backhand. Dagmar shot to her feet, covered her daughter's body with her own. Reilly was up, dropping the mescal bottle while jerking the American Bulldog from Iverson's waistband, shoving the big man over the fallen log he had been using as a chair. He cocked the revolver and aimed at Iverson's forehead.

"Put it away," Pardo said, and he stepped over the

log, helped Iverson to his feet. Slowly, Reilly eased down the hammer and shoved the .44 into his own waistband.

"That's my gun," Iverson said, and pointed.

"Bull," Reilly said. "I loaned it to you back at that horseman's place."

"But I—"

"Shut up," Pardo snapped. "Especially you, Swede. I seen how you was looking at Miss Dagmar, and I don't like it."

He turned around to face the others.

"All right, boys. It's settled. Soledad, mount up, ride to Nogales, tell the Kraft boys that Bloody Jim Pardo wants them to join him in a little job. Tell them that we'll meet at this side of the Dragoons." He pointed north. "Tell them to bring as many boys with them as they want. Tell them we got us a hog killing planned. Ain't that right, Duke?"

Duke slapped his knee. "That's right, boss man. It'll be a regular—"

"Shut up." Pardo pulled his hat down. "But you tell them, Soledad, that they got to be here, at the northern tip of the Dragoons, in six days. Then we'll ride over to Texas Canyon and have ourselves a real party."

"What about us?" Phil asked.

"We ride to Total Wreck first thing tomorrow. To fetch us Swede's dynamite." Looking back at Iverson. "How long will it take to sweat nitro out of them sticks, Swede?"

Iverson kept his eyes on Reilly. "They've probably already sweated. All we have to do is get the nitro loaded and not blow ourselves into oblivion doing it."

"What about the woman? And the kid?" Harrah asked.

"They'll be tagging along. We won't be able to get the nitro up here, and once we're pulled our little job, we'll be raising dust for the border. So everyone leaves camp. It'll be a party."

"How many wagons do you have?" Iverson asked.

"One," Pardo said. "A buckboard. It's hidden down below. We'll fetch it tomorrow. Why?"

"You'll need two more."

"How come?"

Lightning lit up the sky. Four seconds later, thunder crackled.

"Because I'm thinking we'll have three crates of nitro. One for each wagon."

"Can't you just haul that juice in one wagon?"

"Sure." Swede Iverson smiled. "But what happens if one batch decides to blow up? Then you lose all of it. This way, you got a better chance."

Pardo's head bobbed. He slapped Iverson's broad back. "I like the way you think, Swede. Don't worry. We'll get us a couple of extra buckboards before we get to Total Wreck. All right, boys, best take cover before them skies open up. I got to go talk to Ma."

He was walking up the hill when the first sheets of icy rain tore across the camp.

CHAPTER TWENTY-THREE

Reilly stepped inside the tent that had been Three-Fingers Lacy's, which Pardo had said he could use. Pardo had moved into his late mother's tent. He took off his hat, shook off the water, sent the hat sailing to the bed, then sank into the chair at the desk.

The tent flap flew open, and Blanche stepped inside, soaked from the rain. Reilly stared. The ten-year-old stared back.

"How's your mother?" Reilly asked.

"She's fine. They been leaving us alone. I got my gun back." She pulled up her britches, and he saw the handle of the little .32 Triumph sticking out of her brogans. "Got two shots left. That whore who was in this tent shot that old crone with this gun." She pointed at the bullet holes, leaking rain, in the flap.

Blanche smiled. "Nobody saw me pick it up. They was all confused, moping around after that old woman got killed, then burying her, and that Chaucer bastard and this whore had to leave camp in a hurry. Ma led me away, but I sneaked back. Just picked it up out of the mud, cleaned it." She swallowed. "You want it?"

He drew the Bulldog .44 from his waistband, checked the loads, ejected four spent cartridges. "I have a gun," he said, thinking, *With two shots left. Plus maybe three or four in the Evans.* "You best keep it in case . . ." He smiled wearily. "Better get back to your mother, Blanche."

"How you gonna get us out of here?" She pulled down her pants legs.

Reilly sighed. He didn't have a plan, but he'd have to make his play before Soledad returned with the Kraft brothers. "You just follow my lead, kid," he said. "Maybe at Total Wreck. Maybe at Texas Canyon. Then you and your mother keep your heads down."

The girl started to say something, but gunshots, muffled by the wind and rain, stopped her. She turned, pushed open the flap, stepped outside. Shoving the revolver back into his waistband, Reilly grabbed his hat and quickly followed her. They looked up the hill where Jim Pardo had gone. Somewhere in the forest came more shots, followed by a primal scream.

"Get back to your mother," Reilly said, and he ran through the puddles, past Phil and Harrah, climbed up the hill, ducked underneath a branch, and followed the trail. It was hard to see in the rain, but he slid to a stop when he detected the form of Pardo, on his knees, head bent, rain pouring off the brim.

He moved closer, could see Pardo now. Sobbing. Gun in his right hand, the barrel in the mud.

"Jim," Reilly called out, and was answered by thunder. He heard footfalls behind him, turned to find Harrah and Phil, but he waved them back with his gun barrel. He squatted beside Pardo.

"What's the matter, Jim?" he asked.

Pardo shook his head, then slowly pointed at the pit before him.

"They dug her up," he said, releasing his Colt and burying his face in his hands. "Wolves. They dug up Ma!"

Reilly cringed as he looked into the shallow grave. Lightning flashed. He made out ripped bits of an India rubber poncho, parts of Ruby Pardo's boots.

Suddenly, with a animal's ferocity, Pardo turned, staggered to his feet as he grabbed the Colt, and took a few steps back toward camp. "You dumb sons of bitches!" he screamed at Phil and Harrah, aimed the gun, pulled the trigger, the hammer falling on a spent shell. "You don't know no better than to put rocks on a grave! She's gone. Wolves. Coyotes. Cougars. Something dug up my mother and ate her, you dumb bastards!" He kept cocking and firing, but the Colt was empty.

"Easy, Jim." Reilly reached over, took the gun from Pardo's hand, let it slide into the water-slick holster.

"She's gone," Pardo sobbed. "Ma's gone."

"No, Jim, she isn't," Reilly whispered, his arm over Pardo's shoulder, steering him up the path. Briefly, he wondered if he could shoot down Phil and Harrah, but then his gun would be empty, and he still would have to deal with Duke and Swede Iverson, maybe Soledad, if he hadn't left camp. And Pardo. He looked through the falling rain. Didn't appear that either Harrah or Phil had anything other than the shotgun Phil held. He motioned the two gunmen to return to camp, and they obeyed. "Ruby's right here," Reilly said softly. "She's right here with you."

"You . . . think . . . so?"

"I know so."

"I . . ."

"It's all right, Jim. You can talk to your mother anytime. Anywhere. And you know what? She'll listen."

"Ma always listened," Pardo managed. "To me."

"She always will, Jim."

They were coming down the hill now, back into camp.

"I ought to kill Phil. Kill them all. Letting them animals make a meal out of my ma."

That would help things immensely, Reilly thought.

"Guess I can't, though."

He steered Pardo into Three-Fingers Lacy's old tent, let him have the chair, while he found a bottle of bourbon they'd left behind, and he pushed out the cork and put the bottle in Pardo's right hand. "Have a drink, Jim," Reilly said, and sat on the end of the bed.

Pardo switched the bottle to his left hand, and took a long pull, then another. He had stopped crying now, but his eyes were rimmed red. "Thanks, Mac," he said.

Reilly shrugged.

"It's funny, Mac. Ma never liked you. Didn't trust you. Told me I shouldn't trust you."

"Do you?"

"I'm starting to. It's funny. I'm starting to think of you as my kid brother. Remember? I told you about him. The one who didn't live."

He took another pull, and passed the bottle to Reilly. There was just enough for one more drink, and Reilly took it, then dropped the bottle on the wet ground.

"That's fine with me," Reilly said. "I've always thought of you as my big brother. Remember? He was killed during the war."

"Damn Yankees," Pardo said. "Yeah, I remember." He pulled out the Colt, began ramming out the empty shells and refilling the cylinder with fresh loads from his shell belt. "We'll make them damn blue-bellies pay for what they done to our families. They killed my pa. I tell you about that?"

Reilly shook his head.

"Well, they didn't really kill him. Pa died of fever. Actually, he was about to be shot by his own men for breaking some kind of damn-fool rule, but fever got him before they could line him up in front of a firing squad."

He's mad, Reilly thought. *He's a stark, raving lunatic.* Saying, however, "That's all right."

"My nose ain't bleeding." Pardo holstered the Colt.

"That's good."

"Family's important."

Reilly nodded. "The most important."

"It's good to talk like this." Pardo took off his hat, set it on the table. "I'm still half a mind to kill Phil and Harrah. Even Duke."

"I wouldn't stop you."

"Damn right, you wouldn't. I'd kill you if you did, even if I think of you like my brother. I saved your life, you know."

Reilly was rubbing his beard. He stopped, stared deep into Pardo's deadly blue eyes.

"Stopped that Yavapai from splitting your skull. You owe me, Mac."

"What do you want me to do?" He felt uncomfortable now. Wished he had something to drink.

"Oh, I'll think of something. Right now, it's just . . . well, I was thinking of making you my partner. Split everything even. Fifty-fifty. Like brothers should do."

Reilly's head bobbed slightly. "I'd like that, Jim."

"Well, I ain't done it yet, Mac. I want to talk it over. With Ma." He stood, grabbed his hat. Lightning flashed, followed by a deafening burst of thunder. After Pardo had gone, Reilly just sat there, staring at the two bullet holes in the canvas tarp, watching the rainwater seep through, wondering just how in hell he was going to be able to save Dagmar and Blanche, and himself.

The town of Total Wreck lay scattered about the rolling desert hills in Pima County, well south of the Southern Pacific tracks on the eastern slope of the Empire Mountains, just a little due east of the Santa Rita Mountains. It was home of the Total Wreck Mining and Milling Company—earning its name from a man's comment, "This whole damned hill is a total wreck"—a number of houses, a few stores, three hotels, four saloons, some brick, most adobe, but several wood structures, too, a lumberyard, and the seventy-ton mill.

Once it had been populated by as many as two hundred people, but the mine was beginning to play out, and silver prices had dropped, so from where Pardo stood in his stirrups on a barren hill east of town, the whole damned place looked practically deserted.

"I want you, Phil, and you, Harrah, to ride down there and buy us a couple of buckboards," Pardo said.

"Buy?" Duke laughed. "Hell, boss man, I figured we'd just kill a couple of people on the road and take their wagons."

Ignoring Duke, Pardo kept his eyes on Phil. "You think you can do that?"

"Sure," Phil answered.

"Don't go to one of those saloons," Pardo said, and pulled his money purse from his vest pocket, handing a few folded bills to the old Missouri bushwhacker.

"How about horses?" Phil asked.

"Unless you want us to hitch you up, Phil, yeah, I think horses would be in order. Trade your two mounts for a couple of good draft animals. *Good* draft animals, you hear?"

"I hear you."

The sun was directly overhead, blistering the parched ground.

"This place is a total wreck," Pardo said, and laughed. "All right, Swede. How far is it to that sweating dynamite of yours?"

"About a mile south," Iverson said, and wiped his brow with his Irish cap.

"Can these boys find it all right?"

Iverson nodded. "Just drive back up this hill, Phil," he said. "You'll come down on that side, through a bunch of boulders strewn every which way, and follow a little switchback, that you gotta be looking for, else you'll miss it. There's a wooden cabin tucked up against the hill."

"Lead the way," Pardo said.

Phil and Harrah eased their horses down the hill, toward the town, while Swede Iverson nudged his black gelding across the brown, dusty hilltop, followed by Mac, driving the buckboard, with Dagmar and Blanche sitting beside him. Next rode Duke. Pardo brought up the rear.

They rode down the southern side of the hill and through a forest of brown boulders before Pardo saw Iverson's cabin. The Swede dismounted and began working a pump, while Mac set the brake, leaped off the buckboard, and helped Dagmar and the kid down. Pardo looked behind him, then stared at the cabin, cautious, before deciding nobody had been here in months. He eased the roan the last few yards and stopped in front of the sweating, furiously pumping Swede Iverson, who finally gave up and looked up at Pardo with a sheepish grin. "She's dry as a bone."

Without comment, Pardo swung down and tethered his horse to the pump.

"Where's your dynamite?" he asked.

Iverson tilted his head toward the cabin.

"Let's go," Pardo said, and followed Iverson. They passed the buckboard. Pardo heard Mac tell the woman and her kid, "You stay here," and Mac joined the procession.

Iverson stopped at the door, put his hand on the latch, and carefully pulled it open. A tarantula scurried outside, and Pardo stepped inside, only to jump back upon hearing the angry whir of a rattlesnake somewhere inside the dark, dusty, cabin. He quickly drew the Colt, eyes searching for the snake, but Iverson started laughing.

"I wouldn't do that, Bloody Jimmy," he said. He pointed inside.

Pardo stepped back. Sunlight reflected off several gallon-size jars, what looked like canning jars from the Ball Brothers Glass Manufacturing Company, or maybe John L. Mason's fruit jars. The rattler continued its deadly whine, but Pardo cocked his head, studying those jars. At first, he thought somebody had been canning carrots, or something, but then he understood.

"You put dynamite sticks in fruit jars?" he asked Iverson.

"Yep. And unless I miss my guess, they've sweated out a bunch of nitroglycerine." He slapped his thigh, and broke out laughing. "You shoot that rattlesnake, and this whole hill might just blow up." He pointed at the Colt, which Pardo quickly holstered.

"I'll fetch the snake," Swede Iverson said, and grabbed a grubbing hoe from inside the door and stepped inside.

Pardo turned toward Reilly, then heard Iverson yelling, "Out of the way, boys, here she comes."

Both men leaped aside, and a moment later hoe, handle, and rattler came flying outside.

The snake hit the ground first, bounced once, and began crawling toward a rock. When Pardo drew his Colt, a scream came from inside the shack, "No, don't—" but the roar of the revolver drowned out Iverson's warning, and the rattler's head flew off.

"Are you crazy?" Iverson yelled. His face was white when he emerged from the shack. "You could have blown us all to hell."

Pardo holstered the revolver, started to say something, but Iverson gestured inside. "That stuff's touchy. I told you that. Anything can set it off, so . . ." Pointing at the Colt. "Don't shoot that thing again."

He wiped his sweat-soaked face, caught his breath, tried to steady his nerves.

Silence.

Reilly broke it a moment later. "You left jars full of dynamite sticks in a cabin this close to town?"

Iverson managed a weak smile.

"That's mighty risky," Reilly said.

Iverson nodded. "Yeah, but nobody really knows about this cabin, despite how close it is to town. Still, I kinda figured some fool might come inside while I was gone, and then Total Wreck would be Buried Total Wreck when this hill came sliding down on top of her. But, 'twasn't meant to be, I guess." Calmer now, he said "All right, let's get to work," before returning, treading ever so gently, inside.

Pardo looked at Reilly, who smiled. "After you, Jim," he said.

When they entered the cabin, they found Swede Iverson on his knees, staring at a jar on the edge of the table, purring like a kitten, stroking the jar with his hands.

"Look at that," he whispered. "Ain't that a work of beauty?"

Pardo stepped closer. It was stuffy in here, the heat almost unbearable. The jar held two sticks of dynamite, brown, bent. White crystals had formed on the sides of the sticks, and Iverson removed his hand from the glass, extending a finger at the syrupy clear liquid at the bottom of the jar.

Pardo tried to swallow, but his mouth had turned to sand.

"How?" Sweat poured down his face. "How do we get it out of that jar?" he asked in a low whisper.

With a snort, Iverson answered, "Very carefully."

CHAPTER TWENTY-FOUR

Sweat matted Reilly's hair, streamed down his face, soaked his shirt. He held his breath as Iverson slowly unscrewed the lid of the jar, and carefully set it on the table.

Iverson had been prepared, stocking the cabin with crates, beakers, blankets, a doctor's black satchel, and plenty of cotton wadding, all of which they had moved outside underneath a mesquite tree. Iverson ran a tongue over his lips, reached inside the jar, and carefully pinched one of the dynamite sticks. Reilly's eyes locked on the bottom, watched it rise as Iverson lifted it, watched the syrup slowly roll off the stick, into the bottom pool of liquid nitro. His heart pounded, echoed in his head. He realized he wasn't breathing, and slowly sucked in a lungful of torrid air. He blinked sweat from his eyes, drew in another deep breath, watched the crooked stick of dynamite come out of the jar.

"All right, Pardo." Swede Iverson's voice was barely audible.

Pardo took a tentative step closer, holding an old saddle blanket in both hands. Carefully, barely even moving, Iverson lowered the dynamite onto the blanket. "Stand still," he whispered, and his fingers reached inside the Ball jar, took hold of the second, and final, stick inside the glass, and began lifting. It came out of the pool, stopped, rose another quarter inch, half inch.

"Stop!" Reilly's warning came out as a hoarse breath. Swede Iverson stopped.

A bead of liquid had sprouted from the dynamite's wrapper, held there for a moment, then slowly rolled to the bottom. Reilly tried to swallow. Couldn't. The bead formed a pear shape, suspended, then let go. Reilly shut his eyes tight. Tried to think of a prayer. He thought he heard a small *plunk* as the drop hit the pool. He opened his eyes. Breathed again. Wiped the sweat off his face.

Sweat dripped off Iverson's cheeks, and he smiled and resumed his removal of the stick. Slowly turning, he placed the second bent stick several inches from the first he had placed on the blanket Pardo held. Now he straightened. Reilly moved over to fold the ends of the saddle blanket over the dynamite, his eyes meeting Pardo's, neither man saying a word.

"All right, Pardo," Iverson said. "Take those babies outside. Behind the cabin. In the shade. Keep them covered with the ends of the blanket ever so gentle, my friend. These sticks are still sweating, so watch your step." Pardo barely seemed to be moving, his eyes focused on the folded blanket in his arms. Reilly and Iverson watched him, balling their fingers into fists as Pardo stepped through the threshold. When he turned around the corner, Iverson reached for the jar, stopped, withdrew his right hand and wiped his slick palms on his trouser leg, then took the jar in his hand and made his way gingerly to the mesquite tree.

He had rigged a beaker inside a bucket of water, the water coming from their canteens since Iverson's well was dry. He set the Ball jar on a smooth rock next to the canteen and backed away until he was at the satchel, sitting on top of a crate. He opened the crate and withdrew a long eyedropper, which shook in his hands.

"I could use a drink," he said, and let out a hollow laugh.

"When the boys get back with the wagons, I'll have them ride back to Total Wreck." Pardo had returned from disposing the dynamite. "Get some whiskey and a couple barrels of water."

"You want me to ride into town now, boss man?" Duke called. He stood by the buckboard, about thirty yards from the cabin, allegedly keeping watch on Dagmar and Blanche.

"I want you to shut the hell up," Pardo said. Looking back at Iverson. "We're fifty miles from Texas Canyon. This is gonna take forever, Swede."

"You can't rush perfection, Mr. Pardo," Iverson said, the eyedropper still jiggling in his hand.

"We've got to be at Texas Canyon before that Army train," Pardo reminded him.

"We will be. We will be."

The eyedropper fell to the dirt, and Iverson turned, smiling at Pardo, shrugging. "My . . . hands." He wiped perspiration off his brow. "I forgot what a . . . thrill . . . this is. Forgot . . ." He wet his lips. "I need somebody, somebody steady, to take the nitro from this jar, and put it in the beaker." He held out his trembling hands. "I . . . I . . . can't."

"Jesus!" Pardo exploded. "I thought you were a nitro expert. You've done this how many times? We ain't never touched the stuff."

"It's real . . ." Iverson swallowed. "Real easy. Just takes . . . more nerve . . . than I got today. Without a little whiskey to steady . . . these hands."

Pardo whipped off his hat, slapped his thigh. "You best buck up, Swede. We've got three crates to fill."

"If I only had some whiskey," Iverson pleaded.

"After Phil and Harrah get back," Pardo said.

Iverson clenched his fists, which shook uncontrollably. He laughed. "Well, I'll do it, Mr. Pardo, but don't blame me when this cabin and all these rocks land on your head." He pried open his fingers, bent, reaching for the eyedropper.

"Hold it," Pardo barked, and put his hat back on. He looked at Reilly, then at Duke, back at Reilly. "How about it, Mac?"

Reilly's Adam's apple bobbed. He rubbed his hands over his trousers.

"I'll do it," Blanche called out, and ran from the buckboard, ignoring her mother's shouts.

"Easy," the lawman whispered.

Blanche smiled crookedly, and eased the eyedropper out of the Ball jar and moved it to the beaker in the bucket of water. She drew a breath, held it, exhaled, and squeezed the liquid nitroglycerine into the beaker. Smoke, or maybe steam, rose from the beaker. Iverson had told them nitro would do that, that there was nothing to worry about. It didn't stop either Blanche or Reilly McGivern from worrying, though. When the last drop had fallen, she carefully removed the eyedropper and tiptoed back toward the jar.

"I thought," she told the lawman in a whisper, "we could blow up Pardo."

Reilly's eyes looked past the girl, over toward the

buckboard, where Pardo, Duke, and Iverson waited with a sobbing Dagmar Wilhelm. His eyes fell again on the kid. "Let's just not blow ourselves up," he said, smiling.

"Maybe we can sneak a little vase of our own."

"No," he said forcefully.

She looked up at him, glaring. "I'm starting to think maybe you don't want me and my mother to go free. Starting to think maybe you like riding with Bloody Jim Pardo. Maybe I should have left you in that jail wagon. Maybe I should tell ol' Jimmy about that deputy marshal's badge I pulled off your vest."

He started to say something, but instead just shook his head, wiped his sweaty forehead, pursed his lips.

She had the eyedropper in the jar, filled it, lifted it, started for the beaker, angry, mad at herself, mad at this so-called lawman, hating the world. She was moving a little too fast, then Reilly was yelling, "Look out."

Her eyes locked on the drop of moisture hanging precariously from the end of the dropper. Then it broke free, and gravity took it toward the rocks.

Blanche's scream was wiped out by a loud pop that kicked up grit and a thick, blinding cloud of dust. Something struck her in the center of the forehead, knocked her backward.

She held her breath. Time stood still. She landed on her backside, still clutching the dropper with both hands, waiting to be blown to bits. But . . . nothing happened, except, over the ringing in her ears, she heard her mother screaming her name. Blood rolled down the bridge of her nose. Swallowing, she looked up, and as the cloud of dust passed, found the marshal standing above her, his eyes wide, his mouth open.

They both let out heavy sighs.

"You all right?" Reilly asked.

She felt as if she might start crying, but quickly stopped that.

"Y'all all right?" Pardo yelled, his shouts echoed by her mother's screams.

"I'm all right!" she yelled back at them. Then, softer: "I'm all right."

The marshal had leaned over, took the eyedropper from her hand, told her that a piece of rock had cut her forehead. She lifted her hand, gingerly felt the nick, wiped the blood away, watching as Reilly McGivern put the eyedropper in the smoking beaker, and let the nitroglycerin fall.

He rose, sweating profusely, and walked toward her, stopping, pointing with his hand that didn't hold the eyedropper. "You get back to your mother," he said, and the tone of his voice told her not to argue.

She climbed over the rocks, and hurried across the yard, falling into her mother's arms. She couldn't stop shaking, couldn't stop the tears no matter how hard she tried while her mother hugged her tightly, almost crushing her spine, rocking back and forth, kissing her hair, telling her everything was going to be fine, that everything would be all right.

Pardo was there, too, muttering something that sounded like an apology, saying he never should have let a little ten-year-old girl do a man's job, that he thought it was a funny joke, but she had done well, especially holding that beaker so steady when she fell. "Hell, you could have blowed us all to kingdom come." Then he backed away, turned hurriedly, unable, Blanche figured, to withstand the look her mother was giving him.

* * *

Now that Phil had returned with two barrels of water and a jug of prime rye whiskey, they worked as a team. At the cabin, Swede Iverson removed the dynamite sticks, which Pardo carried out to the hillside in blankets, covering them before returning to the cabin. Phil and Reilly removed the liquid from the jar and transported it to a beaker, which, when filled and stoppered with a cork, Harrah would set in a crate on one of the three buckboards.

Each beaker was wrapped in wet cotton and put in a crate that was filled with water. Each crate, resting on blankets, its sides wrapped with tarpaulins, would hold only twelve beakers.

Duke kept his distance, guarding Blanche and Dagmar.

At dusk, they took a break, eating salt pork and beans that Dagmar had cooked, washing down the grub with rye and water. Their clothes were soaked from sweat, and the entire camp smelled sour. They ate and drank in silence, while Blanche cleaned the skillets, and Dagmar prepared coffee. The air began to cool.

They had filled only four beakers.

Iverson brought the jug to his mouth, took a long drink, swallowed, and started to lift the jug again.

"That's enough whiskey, Swede," Pardo said.

The explosives man nodded, and set the jug aside.

"We should rest," Iverson said. "Get some sleep. Start up in the morning."

"No." Pardo shook his head. "We work through the night."

"But—"

"No buts, Swede. We got a lot of miles to cover. How's that coffee coming, Dagmar?"

"Be ready in a minute."

"Good. Good." He kept looking at her, liking the way she moved, how her clothes conformed to her body. Even that bratty little kid of hers was earning her keep, scouring the skillets with sand.

He picked up the greasy salt pork with his fingers, tore off a mouthful with his teeth, chewed, washed it down with a cup of water. He watched her bring the coffeepot over, filling each man's mug, saving him for last. He stared at her, unblinking, as she filled his cup, wanting to say something to her, wanting, really, to grab her, and pull her down on him. She was everything Three-Fingers Lacy never could have been. She wouldn't look at him, though, dared not make eye contact. He smiled at her anyway, until she turned back, and asked Mac if he wanted a refill.

Pardo glared, but Mac had the good sense to shake his head.

She headed back to the fire, stopping when Swede Iverson called out, "I'll take a little more, sweetie." He saw her stiffen. Then her shoulders sagged, but she turned, and carried the pot over to that cad.

Pardo set his cup down, scratched his palm against the hammer of his holstered Colt. Maybe, he thought, Swede Iverson could blow himself up once they got the nitro to Texas Canyon, once they had those Gatling guns and that howitzer.

Accidentally, of course.

The last of the beakers was loaded onto the third buckboard shortly after dawn, and Pardo wasn't waiting. He ordered Harrah to drive the first wagon, Mac the second, Phil the third. The girl and the woman would ride with Mac. No. Make that Harrah. He didn't like the way Dagmar had looked at Mac last night when she asked him if he wanted more coffee. Harrah wouldn't try anything, and, hell, Dagmar despised Harrah.

"Duke," he said, "you watch our back trail. Make sure nobody's following us. Swede, you and me, we'll ride point." That sounded right. He'd keep well ahead of all of those wagons, just in case one—or all three—decided to blow up. Yeah, he'd ride point. Keep Swede out of harm's way, too. He still needed Iverson to cause that avalanche and trap those soldier boys at Texas Canyon.

"What about the dynamite in those blankets behind the cabin?" Mac asked.

"What about them?" Pardo was growing a little impatient. He had to be back at Texas Canyon in a matter of days.

"Those sticks are still sweating. They could blow up."

"Not *could*, Mac," Swede Iverson said. "They *will*. At some point, they will go boom." He laughed heartily. Man was fine now, Pardo figured. He'd been almost worthless until he got some rye to settle his nerves.

"Just what the hell do you want to do about them?" Pardo demanded, and swung into the saddle. He turned his horse, saw Mac just standing there, without an answer.

"That's what I figured. The sticks stay all wrapped up in their blankets. Now let's ride."

He spurred his horse, and loped over the hill, getting as far away from the cargo he was escorting as he could.

CHAPTER TWENTY-FIVE

A corporal stopped her when she arrived at the sprawling compound of adobe buildings on a plateau surrounded by the Chiricahua Mountains. She set the brake on the surrey she had rented in Contention City and slid down, almost collapsing into the stunned soldier's arms. A couple of privates whistled. Another clapped. The corporal, a young man maybe twenty-two, blushed.

Exhaustion had overtaken Gwendolyn Morgan. "I'm sorry," she said, and tried to remove the burgundy boat hat that was cocked to her left side.

"That's all right, ma'am," the corporal said. "Here, why don't you sit in the shade." It sounded more like an order than a question or suggestion. He helped her up the steps, eased her onto a bench. A moment later, the corporal was offering her a dipper of water while fanning her flushed face with his slouch hat, the three privates staring over the kneeling noncommissioned officer's shoulders.

Closing her eyes, she drank greedily, cherishing the cool water as it traveled down her throat.

"Ma'am," the corporal said, "what is it that brings you to Fort Bowie?"

She peered into the corporal's brown eyes.

"I came from Contention," she said.

"Contention City?" The corporal slapped his hat on his head, rising. "You came all the way from Contention?"

Her head bobbed. Suddenly, she remembered her purse. She stood, weaving, weak from the heat, stumbled past the three privates, into the sun, found her purse in the seat of the surrey, came back to the bench, and collapsed.

Things had been a blur since Reilly McGivern's last visit. She had read his note—a woman's prerogative, she figured—had rented the surrey, ridden to Tombstone, where she learned that Special Deputy United States Marshal Ken Cobb had been murdered down in Nogales.

Now what? she had wondered, pulled the note from her purse, and reread it. He had mentioned a Lieutenant Talley, and Fort Bowie, so she had climbed back into the surrey, lashed the horse with a whip, and now . . . well, she had made it, despite nothing to eat on the two-day journey, finally climbing through Apache Pass to the military post.

"Is Lieutenant Talley here?" she asked.

The corporal shook his head. "No, ma'am, he's in the field, Missus . . . ?"

"Miss Morgan," she said, and smiled at the corporal. "Gwendolyn Morgan. Call me Gwen."

"Yes, ma'am." He began blushing again, trying to ignore the muffled giggles of the privates behind him. "Well, Miss Morgan, I mean, Gwen, the lieutenant won't be back to Bowie for another week or two."

"That's right." Her head bobbed as she remembered

the note. She clutched her purse tighter. "He's . . . I'd like to see the commanding officer."

"The colonel?" The corporal looked dumbfounded. "I mean, General Crook, he's in the field, too. Colonel's in charge."

"Yes. The colonel then. It's a matter of life of death, sir."

"Don't 'sir' me, ma'am. I am no officer."

"I'm no soldier. Please, take me to the colonel."

"Well, yes, ma'am." He held out his hand, and helped her to her feet.

As they walked across the parade ground to another dreary adobe building, she felt every eye from every soldier marching or riding across the parade ground fall on her. *Like they've never seen a whore before,* she thought. The corporal opened the door, holding it open for Gwen. Inside, a black-mustached man peered up from a pile of papers littering his desk, removed his spectacles, and rose.

"Begging the sergeant major's pardon," the corporal said, "but this is Miss Gwen Morgan, and she wants to see the colonel."

She didn't like the look of the sergeant major, whose eyes covered her body up and down before he spit a mouthful of tobacco juice into a brass cuspidor by the desk. "Colonel's busy," he said.

"Please," Gwen begged, and the sergeant major motioned to another bench.

"Take a seat. Dismissed, Corporal."

She must have waited an hour, and the sergeant major never went to the colonel's door. Gwen began to wonder if the colonel was even there. Maybe she should have just given the note to the corporal. He was a pleasant fellow. He would have helped her.

Another door opened, and a heavyset man stepped

into the office. The sergeant quickly jumped to attention, and fired a salute as a man with close-cropped blond hair and thick eyebrows walked to the desk. "Sergeant Major," he said in a German accent, "you vill deliver dis . . ." He must have caught Gwen out of the corner of his eye, because he turned, lowering the envelope he held in his right hand, and stared, whispering, *"Nicht schlecht."*

"Vell, Vell," he said, and smiled. *"Guten Tag, fräulein. Wie geht es?"*

She didn't understand a word he had said, but she understood that look. She'd certainly seen it enough.

"Major, this is Miss Gwen Morgan," the sergeant major said. "Wants to see the colonel."

The major bowed, turned, and whispered something to the sergeant major, who grinned and shot a quick lecherous look at Gwen, then accepted the envelope and listened attentively as the major gave his instructions. Clicking his heels, the major turned, bowed slightly at Gwen, and walked back to his office.

"Major," Gwen said, rising, "please. This is an urgent matter. It has to do with Bloody Jim Pardo and a planned ambush on one of your wagon trains."

The major stopped in mid-stride, turned. The sergeant major was walking out the door. The major watched the outer door open and close, then walked over toward Gwen.

"Pardon me?" he said.

"Please," she said. "Jim Pardo plans to ambush one of your wagon trains. With Swede Iverson. At Texas Canyon. May we talk?"

"Certainly," he said, and motioned her into his office. He closed the door behind him, pointed out a chair, and she took it, while he sat on his desk. She opened the purse, removed the note, and held it to him.

"This is from Reilly McGivern. He's a deputy U.S. marshal. Usually works out of Charleston."

"Is that vere you vork?"

"No. I'm in Contention City."

"And vat is it dat you do in Contention?"

"I . . ." She shrugged.

"Ah," the major said, and, laughing, reached behind him and opened a cigar box, removed a thick brown one, and struck a match.

Gwen waved the letter Reilly had written.

The major didn't speak until his cigar was going. Afterward, he gestured with one end of the cigar at the note. "You have read it?"

"Yes."

"I see. I know dis name, McGivern. Isn't he the one voo freed the Kraft brothers?"

Her head shook violently. "No, that's all a mistake. He says so in this letter. He told me it was another deputy, Henderson was his name, who set up the ambush." Her mind was swimming with images, mostly of McGivern riding out of Contention with Bloody Jim Pardo, not doing anything to arrest him, after he had killed one of his gang members. Maggie Fairplay had told her, after what had happened in Contention, that, "Reilly McGivern is as crooked as the nights are long," but she didn't believe that. She had known Reilly too long.

The major took the letter in his hand, opened it, and read.

"How many men does Pardo have?"

"*Seis,*" Soledad answered, and lifted the glass of tequila.

Across the table, in a crowded cantina in Nogales,

Mexico, K.C. Kraft laughed over the sound of castanets, a strumming guitar, and laughter. "Six men? He's going to attack an Army wagon train with six men? Yeah, I'd say he does need our help."

Sitting on either side of the tall, leathery gunman, his two brothers laughed. Soledad drained his glass, and placed it on the table.

"You tell your boss that I told him *gracias*, but *no gracias*." He gave Soledad a sharp nod, dismissing him.

As Soledad started to rise, the youngest brother shouted out, "Hold on there, Mex. Let's hear him out, K.C. This job sounds like fun."

K.C. Kraft's eyes hardened, and his fist clenched the bottle of beer he was lifting toward his mouth. He slammed the glass on the wormwood table, and turned toward his brother. "It sounds like suicide, W.W."

"Nah, brother, you're getting soft." He winked, motioned Soledad back into his chair, and asked, "What's Bloody Jim got up his sleeve that makes him think he can pull off this damned robbery?"

Half-standing, Soledad looked at K.C., who let out a weary sigh and gestured with the beer bottle for Soledad to sit down again. Once Soledad was sitting again, he said, "Pardo has a man who knows ka-boom. Dynamite. Only, no, he plans to use, um, how you say, nitro . . ."

"Nitroglycerin?" K.C. asked.

"*Sí*. That is it. Big ka-boom."

W.W. Kraft clapped his hands. "Hot damn. That would be something to see."

"Yeah. It'll probably be the last thing you see." K.C. Kraft took a long pull of beer. The castanets stopped clicking, followed by applause and whistles.

"Pardo, he say, you bring as many men as you got," Soledad informed him.

"I don't have that many," K.C. Kraft said.

"Oh, hell, K.C., you got enough."

On the other side, the third brother, L.J. Kraft sat quietly cleaning his fingernails with a pocketknife, his tumbler of tequila untouched.

K.C. drained his beer. "What's in it for us?"

Soledad shrugged. Pardo hadn't told him what he could offer, other than the glory of riding with Bloody Jim Pardo. "There are many Gatling guns, I think. One cannon."

"And how many men guarding them?"

Another shrug. "*Setenta. Ochenta.*" Actually, he seemed to recall the *gringo* called Mac mentioning a much higher number.

With a comical smile, K.C. Kraft shook his head. "Seventy or eighty. Yeah, against a dozen men I can round up. Plus your boss's six."

"*Siete,*" Soledad said, "*con* Pardo."

"Oh, right. Pardon me. Nineteen, maybe twenty, against seventy or eighty."

"But ka-boom. Swede Iverson, he bring down the walls of Texas Canyon. Like Jericho. On top of *soldados.*"

K.C. kept shaking his head. "Forget it. Tell Pardo no."

Soledad bowed, started to rise, but the youngest brother, W.W., shot to his feet. "I'm going, K.C. This is a haul that'll make us famous. No sense in letting Jim Pardo hog all the glory."

The castanets resumed their clicking. The music and laughter grew louder.

"Go ahead. I won't stop you."

W.W. savagely snatched the bottle of tequila off the table, muttered an oath, and followed Soledad into the dusty streets of Nogales. "Where are we supposed to meet up with Pardo?" W.W. Kraft asked as Soledad gathered the reins to his horse in front of the hitching rail.

"Sierra Dragón," Soledad said. *"Del norte."*

W.W. walked down a few rods and mounted a buckskin. He was waiting for Soledad to tighten the cinch of his saddle when the saloon doors swung open. Soledad looked up over his saddle and saw K.C. and L.J. Kraft standing on the boardwalk.

"Family," K.C. Kraft said underneath his breath. "I hate having a damned family."

She was a handsome woman. Armin Ritcher liked the way Gwendolyn Morgan looked. Liked how that boat hat of hers was cocked, showing off her attitude. She wore a well-fitting dress the color of violet, dusty from her travels, but still mighty fancy for a Contention City prostitute, a full skirt gathered in front and back, and a cloth-topped, high-heeled shoe that must have taken her an hour to lace up. A petite gold pocket watch hung from a chain around her soft, sweet neck. Something told Ritcher that she didn't always dress up so nicely.

He looked at the note she had given him, and read it again.

Ken:

Haven't much time. I'm with Bloody Jim Pardo, who freed me from the prison wagon in the Sulfur Spring Valley. Gus Henderson set us up for the ambush, paid for his sins with his life. Will explain later. If I'm still alive.

Pardo plans to attack an Army wagon

*train bound for Ft. Lowell at Texas Canyon.
Train's bringing Gatlings & a howitzer. Get
word to the Army. ~~We~~ You can hit Pardo
there in ten days or so.*

*Pardo has a woman and child held
captive, taken from raid on the S.P. That's
the main reason I haven't tried to capture
Pardo myself.*

Reilly McGivern

*Please trust me. You've know me long enough
to know I didn't have anything to do with
the Krafts' escape.*

*Swede Iverson with Pardo. Plans to use
nitro in Texas Canyon ambush.*

*Get word to 2nd Lt. Jeremiah Talley,
escorting the Army train with his cavalry
troop. Talley can also explain why I took the
Krafts toward Ft. Bowie.*

Ritcher folded the note, saw it was addressed to Ken Cobb.

"When I found out Marshal Cobb had been murdered," the woman told him. "I didn't know what to do, who I should give this to."

"You've done right, child," he said. "How did you get here?"

"I rented a rig in Contention. God. Maggie's going to be furious at me for missing all this work."

"It's all right."

"You'll get word to Lieutenant Talley? He's a friend of Reilly's."

"I'll send out a galloper. Don't vorry, ve vill stop Bloody Jim Pardo. We vill vindicate your beau."

"Oh, he's not, well, I mean, I'd like, but . . ."

He offered her a cordial of brandy. She drank. He dipped the end of his cigar in his brandy, admiring the auburn-haired beauty. Ritcher grinned.

Jim Pardo was a fool. He had a deputy U.S. marshal riding with him. The tall, dark-haired one he called Mac.

This will be all right, Ritcher thought. *I'll just ride over to the Dragoons, tell Pardo all about his new man. That might be worth a few extra dollars—and that son of a bitch owes me. Might make Pardo think better of me, especially after what happened in Redington.*

He frowned. He hadn't shown much backbone in Redington, riding out of town as fast as he could once Pardo found out his mother had been killed. But what was a fellow supposed to do? Pardo had gone completely mad, shooting in the streets. Ritcher had to run. He put the cigar back in his mouth, saw Gwen Morgan staring at him, and he forced another smile.

"Did you share this note, or its contents, vith anyone else?"

"No, sir. Nobody knows but you, Major."

"Please, call me Armin."

She said nothing, merely looked into her brandy cordial.

He smoked the cigar, then set it on the ashtray on his desk. "Miss Morgan, if you vill vait here, I vill order a trooper to intercept Mr. Talley's command. I vill inform the colonel of vat you have told me. After vich I vill personally escort you back to Contention City."

"You don't have to escort me, Major."

"It's Armin, my dear. Please, call me Armin. And I must certainly escort you back to Contention. Apaches have bolted from San Carlos. It's not safe for anyone to travel alone. You risked your lovely life just riding out here, alone. Besides, I must go to the marshal's office in Tombstone and Tucson and clear your heroic Marshal McGivern's name."

She smiled. Damn, but she had a wonderful smile, for a whore.

CHAPTER TWENTY-SIX

From where the trail crested the ridge, Pardo and Swede Iverson stopped their horses, turned in their saddles, and peered down the winding road. Slowly, the three buckboards crawled up the slope. The path had been carved into the hard, rugged rock, hugging the hillside, barely wide enough for one wagon, the ridge slopping downward from the road, below which sprouted a forest of yucca and ocotillo.

Per Iverson's instructions, the wagons were spaced about one hundred fifty yards apart, creeping up the hill, Duke following the last wagon, the one driven by Phil, about two hundred yards behind on his horse. Pardo looked south, then turned and studied the terrain down the hill, his eyes scanning the desert for signs of anyone. He saw nothing. *Who the hell would travel in this heat?* he wondered, and looked back down the trail.

The first wagon stopped. He could make out Harrah as he set the brake. Dagmar and Blanche eased off the driver's seat next to him, gripping the edge of the wagon, their feet barely on the road, and made their way to the back.

What are they doing? he wondered.

Both grabbed spare blankets, came back, and knelt beside the right front wheel, shoving the blankets into what appeared to be a hole. They started to climb back into the wagon, but Harrah quickly shook his head, pointed ahead, and the girl and her mother hurried up the road maybe fifty yards before they stopped, turned, and watched. Ever the protective mother, Dagmar stepped in front of her daughter, but the girl dropped to her knees, and peered around Dagmar's leg.

Harrah removed his hat, wet his lips, wiped sweat on his thighs, and slowly reached for the brake.

"This," Iverson whispered, "is gonna be a mite ticklish."

Pardo started to say something, then found his hand reaching for the saddlebag, unfastening the buckle, dipping inside, withdrawing a Ball jar of rye. He unscrewed the lid, drank his fill, then offered some of the whiskey to Iverson, who accepted with a nod of thanks.

The big bay horse took a step forward. Pardo's eyes fell on the wheels, watched the wagon dip as it crossed the hole, then rose, moving only inches, then a foot, slowly, easily, Harrah looking to his right, over the edge of the wagon, watching the rear wheel hit the hole, dip, and come up.

Pardo took the jar from Iverson's outstretched hand, finished it, pitched it over the side, hearing the glass smash against a boulder. The woman and her kid turned, started walking up the road, ahead of the wagon. Harrah started to reach for his hat, thought better of it, and kept both hands on the reins, both eyes on the road.

* * *

Reilly pulled hard on the reins as he neared the blanket-lined hole, set the brake, and looked behind him. He removed his hat, waved it over his head, warning Phil to halt, and waited until Phil had stopped his buckboard. Far behind him, keeping a more than respectful distance, Duke swung off his horse and stepped on the other side of the gray animal, using it as a shield, the gutless coward.

Drawing a deep breath, Reilly held it for the longest while, slowly let it out. His head lifted, studied the sky, saw the storm clouds forming to the southeast, other dark clouds scurrying across the sky toward the noonday sun. Wet his lips. Tried to dry his hands on his vest. Pulled his hat down low and reached for the brake.

The big dun horse snorted, and, once he had released the brake, took a step forward as Reilly flicked the reins. He felt the wagon lurch, the right wheel dipping into the hole, measuredly coming out. Flicked the lines again. "Easy, boy," he whispered, blinking the sweat out of his eyes. The wagon moved slowly. The rear wheel hit the hole, came up. Reilly didn't bother stopping, just let the big dun pull the wagon, feeling better now, though he didn't know why. They still had many miles to travel before they reached Texas Canyon.

He shot a quick glance behind him, saw Phil's wagon starting to move. Looked back up the road. Clouds passed over the sun, and the air immediately felt cooler. He filled his lungs again, looked at the Evans repeater leaning against the driver's box.

From behind him came a tremendous roar, and he turned again, almost blinded by a brilliant white flash, heard himself cursing, saw his left arm reaching for the brake, felt the wind rush from his lungs as the whole mountain behind him came down, felt the concussion knock him off the seat, felt himself flying over the side of the wagon.

The surrey wheeled off the main train and headed down the hillside to the shade, where the land flattened briefly before buttressing against a rugged ridge. There, Ritcher tugged on the reins, stopping the wagon, and smiling at Gwendolyn Morgan. "Best vater the horses here," he said pleasantly. "Get out of the sun for a few minutes."

He pulled the brake lever, hopped down, and offered to help Gwen out of the rig. She gave him a pleasing smile, stopped, turned, and picked up her purse. When she turned back, he took her hands, soft, delicate, pleasing underneath his gauntlets—not like the hands of the whores he had known—and eased her out of the buggy. She bumped against him. He liked that, too, but she quickly pulled away.

"Dere's a spring over dere." He pointed at the ruins of an old stone house. "Behind those. Near the big valnut tree."

She looked, nodding favorably. "I wish I had known of this place when I was coming to Fort Bowie." Turned back to him. "It's lovely."

"*Ja,*" he said, eyes fixed on her bosom. "It is. Most definitely." He looked up, saw her hard stare, and forced a grin. "Forgive me, Gwen." He gestured toward the ruins. "This vas an old stagecoach station, but the owners quit. Apaches ran dem off. But the spring should be full of vater after dese latest monsoons. And it's a long vay to Contention. Go ahead. I'll grain the horses. Ve'll vater dem later. Dey are too hot to drink now. Don't vant dem to get colicky."

"Thank you, Major," she said.

He stared at her, shaking his head, saying, "Armin. Please call me Armin."

"Armin," she said, but she spoke his name as if it were a filthy word.

He watched her walk off, watched how her hips swished beneath that violet dress, and made himself turn, find the grain sack. His big black stallion, tethered behind the surrey, snorted. His saber rattled against his side. He looked back as Gwendolyn Morgan disappeared behind the crumbling walls and started walking away from the wagon and two horses, loosening the black silk bandana around his neck until he held it in his right hand. His left hand gripped the saber, to keep down the noise, as he carefully picked a path to the edge of the ruins.

She knelt beside the giant walnut, purse at her side, cupping her hands in the pool of water, splashing her face. She had removed the boat hat, too, and her long auburn hair hung past her shoulders, wet with perspiration.

He looked behind him, up the road, for any signs of travelers, but saw nothing but a bleak expanse of desert. He looked back at Gwen, her back still to him, moaning with pleasure at the coolness of the sweet-tasting water. He imagined her moans and smiled. Ahead of her, behind the spring, cicadas sang, and a bird chirped in the brush.

Running his tongue over his cracked lips, Ritcher stepped down the path, slick with moisture, let go of the saber, and took both ends of the black neckerchief in his hands, twisting the silk cloth tightly, wrapping the ends around his gauntleted hands, trying to control his breathing, feeling his heart pounding against his ribs.

She must have heard him, or felt his presence, because she stopped drinking the water, started to turn, her right hand reaching for the purse that contained the letter Reilly McGivern had written her.

Quickly, he brought the silk bandana over her head and yanked back savagely, dropping her to her buttocks, hearing her muffled shout. Instantly, as the ends of the bandana crossed, he switched hands, pulled tighter, moved around her, jerking her into the shallow pool. She was on the ground, arms splashing, face under the water. He could let her drown. It would be so easy.

But that wouldn't be much fun.

He pressed his knee against the small of her back, pulled her head up, heard her trying to catch her breath, but the black silk was biting into her neck. He let her up. Playing with her. Saw her try to get to her knees. Then he pulled her back down. On her back. He liked the way the black silk cut into her neck. Liked how her hair was plastered across her forehead. He sank onto her stomach. Liked the way she squirmed underneath him.

He looked deeply, longingly into her bulging eyes. Her lip was busted, blood mixing with the water on her face, running down her cheeks, into the spring. Her tongue started to protrude. Her left arm was pinned underneath her back, her right splashing, clawing for the bank. Ritcher's gaze followed the arm. He had wondered why she didn't try for the bandana that was strangling her. Or why she didn't try to claw his face with those wonderful fingernails.

Most women did.

That's what killed them.

But, no, this stupid whore was reaching for her purse. As if that letter she had written Reilly McGivern could save her. He choked back a laugh, and looked again at her, pulled tighter, trying to crush her throat, pressing tight against her stomach, watching the light fade from her eyes, blood began seeping from her nostrils.

Not so fast, he told himself, and loosened his hold on the bandana. He liked the mark it had left on her throat.

She swallowed, filled her lungs, tried to buck him off.

Cackling, he slapped her, picked up the rolled end of the bandana he had dropped, and pulled tighter. She bit her tongue. He leaned forward, wanting to breathe in her last gasp of air, wanted to smell her last breath. Her eyes started to still, yet her right arm still slapped savagely against the water and stones.

He was staring at her, watching her die, savoring the moment.

Again he stopped. Watched her breasts rise as he let her breathe again. Then his eyes fixated on the gold watch, and he reached down, dropping one end of the bandana to snap the watch off its chain, put it into the pocket of his blouse. He always liked trophies, like the scalp of the Apache woman he had taken three years earlier, or the amethyst earrings from that dressmaker in Bisbee.

"Dere, dere," he said, as if soothing a child, his face just inches from hers. "Are you all right, my sweet?"

Her lips met, and she spit in his face.

He jerked up, found the bandana again, pulled harshly, almost pulling her head out of the water, felt himself rising off her. He'd had enough. Needed to kill her now. Get rid of the horse and buggy. Ride off to the Dragoons or Texas Canyon to find Pardo. Warn him.

He sank back on top of her, pulling hard, watching her face and lips pale, watching the eyes begin to still. Her right arm had stopped splashing. Her resistance began to slacken.

She was bringing her right arm up. To attack him.

"Too late, my sweet," he whispered. "You are much too late to fight me now."

He saw her hand rise. She held something in it.

His head turned. His mouth opened.

"Damn!" he screamed, and let go both ends of the bandana. Staring down the barrel of a sawed-off .36-caliber Colt, he started to fall off her torso as he raised both hands in defense, yelling, "Don't—"

The pistol's roar silenced his scream at the same instant he saw a brilliant flash of white light and felt his head explode.

CHAPTER TWENTY-SEVEN

Reilly McGivern tumbled over the side of the wagon, but held tightly to the lines with his right hand. Then both hands. Hearing the big draft horse scream, Reilly ground his teeth. The seventeen-hand dun started to run, but Reilly had, miraculously, managed to set the brake. Yet the buckboard lurched forward, rear wheels digging into the road, dragging Reilly on his knees, until he scrambled to his feet, bounced off the rock wall, almost fell, almost dropped the lines, but righted himself, running along the narrow road, between the rolling wagon and the rugged wall.

"Whoa!" he shouted hoarsely, amid the smoke and choking dust that enveloped him. Furiously, he pulled on the lines, coughing, screaming at the horse to stop. The cloud of dust passed, carrying with it the heat of a furnace, and thick, acrid smoke. A second later, bits of rock and stone began falling like hail, bouncing off the brim of Reilly's hat, which, some-how, remained on his head. He looked at the buck-board, still moving, saw the stones hit the tailgate. Saw debris strike the blankets lashed atop the crate of nitro, bouncing off.

"God," he said. "Come on, horse, stop."

He blinked. Scraped his back against the jagged wall of the rising mesa. Saw the wagon turn, saw the unmoving right wheel, rise on a little mound, and slip off the edge.

Reilly closed his eyes, mouthing a prayer, preparing to die.

The explosion knocked Blanche Gottschalk onto her back. She caught a glimpse of something sailing over her. Blinked. Realized it was her mother. She turned just as her mother struck the rocky edge of the road, bounce off, land hard in the dust.

"Look out!"

She rolled over, saw the big bay draft horse pulling the wagon, its eyes laced with fear. Harrah stood in the driver's box, drawing hard on the leather lines, trying to stop the rig. Beyond that, Blanche saw a mountain of dust, smoke, and flame shooting into the clouds, blocking out the blue sky that stretched below.

Dust, smoke began drifting behind the wagon. She looked at the bay animal's churning hoofs, tried to move, couldn't. Harrah's curses rang out. Her ears were ringing. The horse stopped a yard or two from her, snorting, then lowering and angrily shaking its head. She found her feet now, rising, falling, rising again, weaving.

Instantly, she remembered her mother, and turned, saw her slowly sitting up, leaning against the side of the wall, blood leaking from a gash along her chin. Her mother's mouth kept moving, and she read her lips, knew she was calling Blanche's name. She cried out, "Mother!" and started for her, but stopped when something struck her head. And back. And neck.

"Oh, hell!" screamed Harrah.

Turning, Blanche realized that the sky was raining rocks. Harrah, who had sunk onto the driver's seat after stopping the horse, his left hand squeezing the brake lever for all that it was worth, looking behind him, watching the rocks shower on the crate of nitro in the back of the wagon.

Without thinking, Blanche ran, past the bay horse, to the side of the wagon, her brogans sending rocks and gravel sliding down the rolling slope. Her right hand gripped the side of the buckboard, then her left, and she lifted herself, hurdling over the railing, into the back. A jagged rock struck her ear. She flung herself atop the blankets covering the crate, held her breath, felt sharp stones pound her back, her buttocks, her neck, her head. A heavy rock drove her head into the blankets, and she saw a flash of orange, felt blood trickle down her head.

She groaned, but kept her body on the crate, until the shower of rocks had passed. She tried to open her eyes, but couldn't. Suddenly, she felt her body convulsing, heard someone's terrible cries, realized those strange, savage noises were coming from her. Thought she heard hoofbeats, but couldn't feel the wagon moving.

"Blanche! Blanche! My God, where's my daughter?" Her mother's voice.

Next, Bloody Jim Pardo's: "What the hell is that kid doing?"

"Saving our lives, Jim," came Harrah's frazzled reply.

Major Armin Ritcher landed on his ass, rolled over, dipped his head into the spring water. He rose, screaming at the fire that burned his head. Dazed, he rolled back, saw the woman, Gwen Morgan, staggering to her feet, smoking Colt in her hand. She fell, coughing, pointing the revolver in his direction. Pulled the trigger.

The bullet whistled past his ear.

Blood spurted down his head. The first bullet had carved a furrow, damned near parted his neatly shorn hair.

Pain nearly blinded him, but he knew he had to get that wench. Had to stop her. She stumbled again, making her way to the shore, tripped on a rock, busted her nose.

He stood, slipped. Saw her raise the gun and pull the trigger, but this time the bullet dug into the ground just inches from the water, not even close. He blocked out the pain, found his water-soaked hat, slapped it on his head. Gwen Morgan, still coughing, breathing deeply, bounced off the Arizona walnut tree, tripped over its protruding roots, and crawled a few rods before she regained her feet, staggered up the rock-lined path.

She had left the purse. And dropped the sawed-down Colt.

Ritcher reached for his revolver, stopped. No, he thought, the saber.

Standing, weaving, he drew the saber from its scabbard, and half-ran, half-stumbled after that damned little whore.

He envisioned running her through. Slicing her to bits.

Only first . . . he had to stop her.

"Hell," he swore. "The horses."

With a savage scream, he charged, boots sloshing through the water, slipping on the wet stones. He tripped over the same damned root that had knocked

Gwen Morgan off her feet, but he didn't fall. He clawed and slashed, came up the slope. Gwen had stopped by the adobe ruins, sitting on the sandy edges smoothed by wind and rain, running her fingers over her bruised throat, trying to swallow, chest heaving, gasping for breath.

She saw him, her face paling, and stood, frozen, as he smiled and lifted the saber over his head, slashed downward. At the last moment, she regained her wits, dived backward, falling into the cactus and shrubs that had taken root inside what once had been a way station.

His saber sank into the three-foot high wall, bit deep into the old adobe, and vibrated with such ferocity that he let go, and stumbled into the ground.

"Damn," he said, blinking and wiping the blood out of his eyes with his balled up fists. "Damn you, you stinking trollop." He swore again in German, English. She regained her feet, scrambled over the smaller walls, the back of her dress torn to shreds, revealing her corset, also ripped, staining with blood.

She ran for the surrey. He rose, pulled himself to his feet, grabbed the still-quaking saber, and jerked it free.

She was trying to climb into the rig, sobbing, shaking, but unable to lift herself, as the draft horse pawed the earth, panicking at the noise, the fear in Gwen Morgan's eyes, the smell of blood heavy in the air. Turning, she saw him, and gave up. Ran up the road, then back, returning toward the spring and the mountain that rose behind it.

He stopped, caught his breath, and, after again wiping the blood off his forehead, charged after the screaming whore.

* * *

Gwen Morgan remembered the gun. The one she'd dropped on the banks of the spring. She knew she had to get it, knew she'd never escape Major Ritcher without it. She charged down the slope, felt her right ankle give way, twisting on one of the rocks, throwing her to the ground, busting, maybe breaking, her nose.

Groaning, she dragged herself toward the gun, cursing herself for wearing those high-heeled boots. Then again, she hadn't expected to be assaulted by an officer and a gentleman of the United States Cavalry.

I'll never reach the gun.

She looked up, saw it, but ten feet might as well be a thousand miles. She heard the shouts of the major, his pounding feet, the slapping of the scabbard. Gwen pulled herself to her feet, looked over her shoulder, and let out a piercing scream, as the silver flashed over her head.

It missed. The momentum carried Ritcher into a spin, and he dropped to his knees. Her right ankle was no good. She could barely support her own weight. She glanced at the gun, knew she couldn't reach it because Ritcher was already on his feet, and she clawed her way through the brambles, the thorns tearing the sleeves off her dress, scratching her face. She kept running, climbing, pulling herself up the slope.

Behind her, the saber slashed through the vines, chopped down the trees. Her hand found a grip, pulled herself forward.

The saber bit into her left calf, and blood soaked the tattered remnants of her dress. She rolled onto her back, saw Major Ritcher, eyes wild like some hydrophobic skunk, raising the bloody saber blade over his head with both hands. The blade came arcing downward, and she rolled again. The blade bounced off the granite.

Gave her a chance.

Her lungs burned. Her calf bled. She was bleeding everywhere. She crawled up the hill, toward a clearing, heard the major coming after her. She hurled herself the last few feet. Didn't bother to look behind her. Just ran, as best she could. Stumbled toward a boulder. Staggered until a hardened copper hand wrapped around her mouth, yanked her to a body that smelled of deer-hide and bear grease. The hand clamped hard on her bloody lips, pushed her against the granite.

Her eyes opened, and she saw the face. Round, pockmarked, burned a deep, dark copper. Black hair, long and glistening, falling to the shoulders of a dirty, greasy buckskin shirt. A large nose, broken countless times. A dingy red piece of silk wrapped across the forehead, tied in the back. Staring into her own petrified eyes were the black, malevolent eyes of an Apache.

Reilly's eyes opened. The horse had stopped. The sky no longer rained rocks and debris. The wheel to the buckboard remained on the road.

Another cloud of dust—no, this was smoke—passed over, and the big dun snorted, took a step. Reilly drew the leather lines back toward him, toward the wall, his eyes on the wheel, watching it drag down the mound, back onto the road. The horse stopped, and Reilly walked toward it, whispering in a haggard voice, "Easy, boy. Easy."

He reached the horse's side and began rubbing his left hand on its neck in a circular motion. "Good boy," he said, his eyes welling with tears, maybe from the smoke, maybe not.

A smoking piece of leather lay between Reilly's boots. He looked at it, realized it was a line from Phil's wagon. Reilly eased his way back to wagon, wrapping the lines around the brake lever. He let out a little gasp when he looked over the sides of the buckboard, finding the blankets on the crate covered in rocks and debris. Something was smoking, and Reilly ran to the rear of the wagon, climbed in the back, picked up a chunk of smoldering wood, which burned his finger-tips. Quickly, Reilly threw it over the side, brushed the dust and embers from the wool until he was satisfied it no longer would burn. At last, he hung his legs over the tailgate, and looked behind him.

My God. His mouth moved, but no sound escaped.

Ritcher's mouth fell open. The saber tumbled from his hand. Ahead of him stood an Apache, hold-ing the whore, shoving her against the granite wall, then releasing her, bringing up a Springfield rifle, its stock heavily beaded, to his shoulder, aiming at Ritcher's chest.

Like a woman, Ritcher screamed. Turned, ran. He expected a bullet to slam between his shoulder blades at any moment, but the Apache never fired. Vines and brambles cut his face, knocked off his hat, as he tumbled through the overgrowth, down the rise, until he tripped over another root of the Arizona walnut, and his face splashed into the spring water. He lifted his head, turned, screamed again, but saw nothing.

The Apache. He hadn't followed. Hadn't shot him.

Ritcher pulled himself to his knees. He saw the whore's Colt, her purse, saw the note her lover had written. He grabbed both, pulled himself to his feet, staggered up the hill, running, his chest heaving. Looking over his shoulder, expecting to see the Apache, or dozens of them charging down the mountain, but nothing happened.

He swallowed. Ran now to his black horse, still pawing the earth. He looked at the surrey and horse. The Apache, no doubt, would make a meal of the animal. Or steal it.

Ritcher grinned.

After that buck has his way with that whore.

Gathering the reins to the black, Ritcher laughed. The Apache would give that bitch what Ritcher planned to give her. He'd seen women after Apaches had had them. Worthless. Vegetables. Lunatics. That would show that wench Gwendolyn Morgan.

His plan had gone to hell. Someone would find the surrey, the remains of the woman, unless the Apache took her with him. He couldn't return to Fort Bowie. Or could he? Explain that the Apaches had jumped him, taken the woman? He had pursued before the red savages forced him to turn back.

Maybe. But first, he had to ride to the Dragoons. Warn Jim Pardo. He had to make sure that lawman, Reilly McGivern, was dead. Reilly McGivern knew too much. His testimony could put Ritcher in the federal pen at Leavenworth, Kansas . . . or on the gallows.

What had once been a mountain road defied imagination.

Jim Pardo whipped off his hat and shook his head. The side of the mountain had come down, burying the road, spilling down the slopes of the ridge, still smoking, still dusty. Where the road hadn't been filled with debris lay a crater, maybe fifteen feet deep. A section of road, maybe one hundred yards, was gone. Atop the mound of rubble, rose Duke, waving his hat.

"Boss man," Duke called. "The road . . . it's gone. What am I supposed to do?"

Cupping his hands over his mouth, Pardo shouted. "Go back down the road! You know where the black rocks are, at the northern side of the Dragoons?"

Waiting. Duke's head bobbed.

"All right! You'll have to cut around this mesa, ride to the Dragoons. That's where I told Soledad to bring the Kraft boys and their friends. You'll have to meet them there, Duke. Then take them to Texas Canyon. You think you can do that, boy?"

Duke had to let that chore sink in.

"Yeah, boss man!" His head bobbed like a toy. "I'll do it!"

"Good! Good, Duke. Good man!" His voice dropped. "You better do it. And do it right." Louder: "Get out of here. Ride hard. Ride fast. You got to get to Texas Canyon in three days. Savvy?"

"I savvy, boss man!" Turning, Duke disappeared behind the rubble.

When Pardo turned, he faced the smoke-, blood-, and dirt-stained faces of Harrah, Mac, Dagmar, and Blanche. Swede Iverson whistled at his handiwork.

"Poor Phil," Harrah said, and crossed himself.

"Poor Yankee soldiers," Pardo said excitedly. "When we bring Texas Canyon down on their heads. This stuff's great, Swede. Great!"

Swede Iverson smiled, but Pardo saw no humor in the man's face.

"What . . . what caused the wagon to blow?" Dagmar asked in a measured voice.

Shrugging, Swede Iverson replied, "Who knows? Could have hit a bump. Clouds passed over, could have dropped the temperature. Who the hell knows? It's nitroglycerin."

"What the hell is that over yonder?" Blanche blurted out, and Pardo's eyes followed the line of her pointing finger.

He walked to the rocky, ragged wall, bent over, and picked up something between his thumb and forefinger. Grinning, Pardo returned to the edge of the road, and dug a small hole in the soft sand with his boot heel. Next, he held up the tip of a pinky finger, a shard of bone sticking from the bloodied, burned end, for everyone to see.

Dagmar and Blanche turned their heads. Harrah shut his eyes. Swede Iverson laughed. Mac just shook his head.

Pardo planted the fingertip in the hole, spread the dirt back over it with the foot of his boot, and removed his hat.

"Ashes to ashes, Phil, and dust to dust." The hat went back on his head. "Let's ride."

CHAPTER TWENTY-EIGHT

All right, Reilly McGivern, you've done a lot of crazy things in your life, broken I don't know how many laws—even as a federal peace officer—but this time . . .

He stared at the beaker of nitro in his hands, drew a deep breath, slowly exhaled, and heard Swede Iverson calling him. Reilly looked up at the towering walls of Texas Canyon, saw Iverson waving his cap, standing atop a boulder. "Bring it up, Mac. Just watch where you put your feet. Don't trip, my friend."

He stepped away from the wagon, parked in the shade at the southern side of the canyon, and began picking a path up the slopes toward the explosives expert who stood waiting with twine and cotton padding.

If you don't blow yourself up, he thought, *the Territory of Arizona no doubt will hang you.*

They had arrived at Texas Canyon the night before, without any incident since the explosion that had killed Phil. Luck had been with them. No rain, just clouds dumping their contents to the east and south. Few travelers on the road, just a couple of Mexican laborers, a stagecoach, and a couple of vaqueros searching for cattle they thought had been stolen by Apaches.

Reilly hadn't slept since Phil's death. He had tried to get some shut-eye last night, but kept tossing and turning, trying to figure out how he could get Blanche and Dagmar to safety. He had to hope Gwen had delivered his note to somebody in Tombstone, maybe Fort Lowell, and that—and this might be the hard part—somebody actually believed what he had written.

Twenty-three minutes later, he knelt underneath a rocky outcropping and gently placed the beaker on a bedding of ripped cotton sheets Iverson had crammed into a hole he had dug. Finished, Reilly leaned back and watched Iverson wrap the twine six times around the beaker, after which he wet it down with water from a canteen.

"How do you plan on detonating this?" Reilly asked.

Iverson didn't answer until he had backed out of the outcropping, unspooling the twine as he went. At last he sat down, took a slug of water from the canteen, and wiped the sweat off his brow.

"Needs to go almost simultaneously," he said. "We'll plant three more on this side, have them all looped together with this here twine. When I jerk, they'll all explode. We need to plant two more beakers on the other side. No, better make it three. That'll do the job, for sure. Maybe Harrah or one of them Krafts, if they ever show up, can jerk the twine there."

Reilly considered this for a moment. "And for the eastern entrance to the canyon?"

"Same deal," Iverson said, nodding. "Pardo's over there now, looking at things. Like he knows a damned thing about where to put a bunch of nitro. But . . ."

Iverson grinned. "I ain't gonna argue with that crazy bastard. Anyhow, we'll have three, four batches on both sides of that end."

"And two men pulling the twine to detonate it?"

"Yep."

"Four men altogether."

"You're good at math, Mac. But before you volunteer to be a twine-puller, I got to inform you. Pardo says you're our backup detonator. If something happens to this here twine, like, say, a rat chews it up, and when I yank it nothing happens, that's where you come in. You and that fancy repeating rifle you got. You get to shoot into the rocks, hit one of these little bottles. Chances are, that'll cause all of them to blow."

"That's fine with me. But I can't see the other entrance. If something happens over there—"

"Pardo's got that covered, too. He'll put one of the Krafts on that end. Or do it himself if the Krafts don't show."

"Nice of Jim to let me in on all this, me being his partner and all."

Swede shrugged, offered the canteen to Reilly, who shook his head. "I best water that one down again. Getting hot. You go back down and bring up another batch." He pointed toward a huge, angular boulder that looked as if it might slide down the canyon side on its own accord. "I'll have a hole dug for it by the time you bring it back up. Now—uh-oh." He peered down the canyon, and pursed his lips. "Rider coming."

Reilly turned, kneeling, spotted the dust first, then a hatless rider on a big black horse, heavily lathered with sweat. The man was about to ride that horse to death, whipping its sides with the reins. He pulled harshly on the reins when he saw the wagon, almost toppled from the saddle, practically dragged the horse to the rear wheel, and wrapped the reins around a spoke.

"Christ a'mighty." Iverson seethed. "That damned fool might blow up our cache."

Below, leaning against the wagon, the man cupped his hands and yelled, his voice echoing across the rocks. "Pardo!"

Par-do . . . Par-do . . . Par-do . . .

"Pardo!"

Par-do . . . Par-do . . . Par-do . . .

Then Blanche appeared in front of one of the massive, round boulders over on the southern edge of the canyon. "Shut up you damned fool! And get away from that wagon!" Her voice echoed, too.

The man ran, stumbled, regained his feet, charging toward the camp where Blanche and her mother waited.

Reilly swore softly, and said, "It's Major Ritcher."

"And he looks like hell," Swede Iverson added.

His lips were cracked, tongue swollen. It had hurt like blazes just to shout Pardo's name. Dried blood caked his over-baked head, coated with dust from the trail. He tried to wipe the sweat out of his eyes, peering through the haze, looking into the nest of boulders at someone yelling at him. It looked like . . . no, it *was* . . . a damned kid. A girl. Didn't appear to be even in her teens.

Ritcher remembered. Pardo had taken a girl and her mother captive after derailing the Southern Pacific train. He caught his breath, took a few steps, collapsed, dragged himself to his feet, and staggered. The girl disappeared behind the boulder. Delirious, parched, Ritcher careened his way toward the boulder. He had to warn Pardo.

For a moment, he thought maybe this girl had been a mirage. An apparition. A haunt. No, he told himself, she was real. Had to be flesh and blood. When he reached the boulder, he leaned against it, trying to summon enough energy, felt the coolness of the rock in its shadows, wiped his brow, lurched, using the giant boulder for support. He eased around the edge into a rock-strewn clearing, and saw the girl, her head wrapped in a torn sheet, sitting on a white rock with another girl, an older, adult woman, between two dead mesquite trees and a Spanish yucca.

His worn boots clopped on the stones. The woman whispered something to the girl, and rose, stepping in front of the mesquites. Ritcher staggered toward her, but when he saw the canteen, he forgot all about her and rushed to it, dropping to his knees, the rocks ripping his trousers. He pulled the canteen, uncorked it, sloshed it around and heard the water. Greedily, he drank. Drank until the rocks began spinning around him, and he almost passed out.

"Sir . . ."

The woman's voice revived him. Feeling that he might throw up, he dropped the canteen, now empty, and reached for the smooth boulder in front of him, managed to pull himself up, and looked around. The sky was blue, and beyond this fortress of boulders rose the rocky walls of Texas Canyon's northern side.

"Pardo," he said, his voice barely a whisper.

"You're a soldier," the woman said, a touch of hopefulness in her voice.

He turned toward the voice as the kid said, "Ma, he's a traitor."

Blinking, he stared at the woman. Her face had

been burned by the sun, badly bruised, a scab forming over her chin. Her lips parted, and she took an involuntary step back.

He let out a mirthless chuckle. He must look like some monster, but he looked a lot better than he would had those Apaches caught him at McCoy's Well.

"Vere's Pardo?" he asked, and repeated the question, louder. The water had revived his voice, and he was desperate to warn Pardo.

When she didn't answer, Ritcher charged, grabbed the front of her blouse, pulling her savagely toward him, hearing the cloth rip, hearing his own haggard yet roaring voice: "Vere is Pardo, damn you? I must find him."

The girl, whom he saw shoot to her feet out of the corner of his eye, said, "You leave my ma alone."

Ignoring the kid, he shook the woman again. "Vere's Pardo? I must see him. Tell him about Reilly McGivern. About the Apaches. Vere is he, damn you?"

He saw the woman's eyes, filled with fright, watched the girl reach down and pull up her britches leg. He shook the woman, whose lips quivered, but formed no words.

Holding her by the throat with his left hand, he released his hold with his right, drew it back, slapped her. Blood spurted from her nose. "Pardo. I must find him, damn you, you wretched bitch."

Pardo and Harrah eased out of the shadows as soon as the rider had passed, and rounded the bend in the canyon.

"Hey," Harrah said, "wasn't that . . . ?"

"Yeah," Pardo said. He tested his Colt in the holster before turning back to Harrah. "You stay here. I'll see what Major Ritcher wants." He moved down the canyon, sliding, kicking up dust, feeling his pants rip, looking east, from where Ritcher had ridden, but seeing no signs of any other rider. When he reached the buckboard, parked in the shady edge of the canyon, he heard Ritcher's echo, calling out his name.

With a curse, Pardo found his horse, swung into the saddle, and galloped down Texas Canyon as another echo bounced along the canyon. This time, Pardo managed a guess, it was Blanche's voice:

Wa-gon . . . wa-gon . . . wa-gon . . .

He reined in beside the rocky fortress on the southern side of the canyon, heard Blanche shouting, heard a ruction beyond the rocks. Ritcher's voice boomed, and Pardo swore, swung from the saddle, spotting Mac and Swede Iverson kicking up dust as they came down from the canyon's northern rim.

Pardo didn't wait for them. Drawing the Colt, he ran around the giant boulder, and stopped, taking it all in. The kid, Blanche, was trying to get something out of her boot. Ritcher was shaking beautiful Dagmar savagely, screaming something. He slapped her hard, caused her nose to bleed.

"Pardo," Ritcher was saying. "I must find him, damn you, you wretched bitch."

Pardo cocked the Colt, saying, "Unhand her, you damned dirty, stinking, miserable rat."

Ritcher turned. Damn, he looked like he had been mauled by a mountain lion. He shoved Dagmar aside, forming a crooked smile, and reached inside his tunic. "Pardo," he said. He pulled out a woman's purse. "I must—"

The .44-40 bucked in Pardo's hand. He stepped away from the smoke to see Ritcher be driven backward, purse falling onto the rocks, and spun around, his hands reaching out, grasping a mesquite branch for support.

"Par—" Ritcher said, and Pardo shot him in the back.

The impact of the slug drove him away from the mesquite, and to his knees. As the Colt's roaring echo faded, Ritcher shook his head, muttering, "*Nein. Nein.*" And pitched over, his face falling into the razor-sharp yucca.

Once he holstered the Colt, he rushed to Dagmar, whose knees were beginning to buckle, her eyes locked on the dead form of Major Whatever-his-name-was Ritcher. The kid was quickly pulling down her britches leg, running over to Pardo's side.

"Are you all right, Dagmar?" Pardo kept asking, but the woman just stared at the blood pooling underneath Ritcher's body.

"Don't you worry about him, Dagmar. He won't mistreat another woman ever. He won't never lay a hand on you." He wiped the blood off her nose, eased her into the shade. Footsteps and hoofbeats sounded, and moments later, Iverson, Mac, and Harrah ran into the clearing.

"It's all right," Pardo said. "I took care of Ritcher, the damned rapist." He removed his hat, started fanning Dagmar's face. The woman just stared blankly. Pardo looked up at Mac. Mac would know something. Mac would tell him what to do.

But Mac had squatted by the mesquite, had picked up the purse Ritcher had dropped. He was staring at it, his eyes misting over, lips trembling; then his fingers managed to open the purse, and he pulled out a piece of paper, which he wadded into a ball, and rose.

"Mac . . ." Pardo pleaded.

By then, Iverson and Harrah had dragged Ritcher's body out of the yucca, Harrah was going through the man's pockets. "All right!" Harrah exclaimed, and held up a little watch in his right hand. "This'll fetch us a whiskey or two next time we get to Dos Cabezas." Iverson pulled out a sawed-down, small-caliber Colt, which he shoved into his waistband.

Mac exploded. Pardo had never seen him like this before. "Damn you!" he screamed, and kicked the major's lifeless face, which the yucca had sliced to ribbons. "You son of a bitch!" Another kick, this time to Ritcher's chest. "You son of a bitch!" Kicking and kicking, driving Iverson and Harrah away. The ribs of the dead major began to crack, and Pardo turned quickly to Blanche, saying, "Take care of your ma, kid," and racing, grabbing Mac, pulling him away, telling him everything was all right.

Mac broke away, whipped off his hat, slammed it against the giant boulder, and let out a mournful wail. Sinking to his knees, hands balling into fists, shaking his head, Mac said, "No. No. No. No."

Pardo knelt beside him, perplexed. He didn't know how to comfort a woman. He damn sure didn't know what to do about a crazy partner. He just said, his voice tense, "Easy, Mac. Easy there, pard. It's all right, kid. Everything's all right. I killed the major. He didn't hurt nobody. Won't ever lay a hand on a woman again."

CHAPTER TWENTY-NINE

"Did you love her?"

Reilly looked up slowly from the coffee cup he had been staring at and into Dagmar Wilhelm's eyes.

"I . . ." He couldn't finish, shook his head. "Never really thought about it, I guess." His voice sounded hollow, distant. His eyes again dropped to the thick, black coffee, which remained untouched, cold now, and it wasn't likely that Reilly would get hot coffee anytime soon. Pardo had kicked out the fire after frying up the salt pork and boiling the coffee, saying they couldn't risk campfires after tonight. "Her eyes," he said hollowly, "were like yours. Green. Only hers were . . ." He shook his head again. "I don't know." After setting the coffee cup on a rock, he looked over his shoulder where Iverson, Pardo, and Harrah were devouring the last of the salt pork, while Blanche filled their cups with bitter coffee. He slid closer to Dagmar.

"Listen," he said. "I gave Gwen a note, but Ritcher got it. Killed her for it."

"You don't know—"

"I know," he said. "Her watch, her revolver, her

purse, my note. She's dead. And that means we're not getting any help. Damn!" His hands balled into fists. Why the hell hadn't he mentioned Ritcher in that note? He was to blame for Gwendolyn Morgan's death. Most likely, he would be to blame for all of their deaths. His fists unclenched. "We're on our own. And we have to get out of here before the Krafts show up."

"Maybe they won't. Maybe something happened to Soledad. Maybe they told him no, maybe even killed him. They should have been here by now. Maybe . . ." She stopped suddenly, aware of the desperate tone of her voice.

"They'll be here." He sounded resigned.

He glanced again toward the outlaws, saw Blanche returning with the coffeepot, Pardo's eyes following the kid. Turning back to Dagmar, he pointed over the rocks with his chin. "Top of that canyon, there's a door. Right behind that juniper underneath that twisted chimney-like tower. I saw it when I was helping Swede Iverson plant the nitro. That's how Pardo plans to get the Gatling guns and cannon after he's gunned down all the soldiers. Through that opening. There's an animal trail, kind of tight at places, I think, but you and Blanche can make your way through there easily. Find the S.P. rails, just follow those east. It's twenty miles to Benson, but a few miles before that, right before the rails cross Prospect Creek, there's a station at San Pedro. You might get help there. If not, Benson."

"What about you?" Dagmar asked.

"I'll be busy," he said flatly.

She shook her head. "We won't leave you here, Reilly."

"Yeah." Blanche sat down between her mother and Reilly.

His head shook. "That's our only chance. You—" He stopped, turned, stood as Bloody Jim Pardo walked over, hat in his left hand hanging at his side.

"Evening, Mac," Pardo said, and nodded a greeting at Dagmar. "How y'all two fine folks feeling?"

"I'm fine," Reilly said. Dagmar nodded in agreement.

"Well, that's just jim dandy. Glad to hear it. You was half out of your mind, beating the pure hell out of Major Ritcher, though he was past feeling your kicks. Thanks to me. Mind telling me what it was that pained you so?"

Reilly grinned. "I just don't like Yankees."

With a chortle, Pardo slapped his hat on his head, and put his arm around Reilly's shoulder. "That's my pard. That's my kid brother. Listen, Mac, let's leave these ladies alone. They've had a rough day, too. We got a busy day tomorrow, and it'll be a lot busier if Duke don't get back here with Soledad and the Krafts."

"Maybe we should call it off."

Pardo stiffened, and removed his arm from Reilly. "Jim Pardo don't call of nothing, Mac. If the Krafts don't show, we'll just blow this canyon all to pieces. Bury them blue-bellies, bury them Gatlings, send them all to the depths of hell. Come on. We got to form our little battle plan."

Midmorning found Reilly working with Harrah on the southeastern rim of the canyon. Already, the temperature had reached the nineties, and not a cloud in the sky. The wind had picked up, but it blew a scalding wind that sucked the moisture out of everything. The sun already blistered the ground, so Reilly uncorked his canteen and let the water pour over the beaker of nitroglycerine he had just placed in a cotton-padded hole underneath a series of rocks. He had wrapped the beaker with twine.

"That's the last one, ain't it?" Harrah asked.

Reilly nodded, and carefully slid out from underneath the rocks, unwinding the twine as he went. Out of the shade, he removed his hat, ran his fingers through sweat-soaked hair, and took a drink from the canteen, which he then offered to Harrah.

"We got a lot of nitro left," Harrah said after he wiped his mouth with the back of his hand, and returned the canteen to Reilly.

"Yeah," Reilly said. They had placed three beakers, under Swede Iverson's directions, on this side of the canyon; four just across the road, on the northern edge; three on the southwestern side; four on the northwest. Fourteen in all. Iverson had left with one of the wagons, heading back to camp with the nitro, saying he would transfer the five remaining beakers into the crate in the rear of the wagon parked on the southwestern side. "If you hear a loud boom," he had said with a grin, "it'll be me dying."

There hadn't been an explosion, and by now Swede Iverson had likely transferred the nitro. Ten beakers left.

"He said we'd need at least two crates of this stuff, didn't he?" Harrah asked.

"Yeah."

"Well, we just used barely more than one."

"He lied. Or he thought maybe we'd lose two wagons on the way here."

"Bastard. Likely just wanted us to haul all that extra juice for his own nefarious purposes."

Reilly gave Harrah a moment's study and shook his head. Harrah was one to talk about nefarious purposes.

"Poor Phil," Harrah said, shaking his head. "But better him than us."

"Let's get the twine down to that rock," Reilly said, pointing, "where Swede told us to leave it."

"They're all tied together, right?"

Reilly nodded.

"Good," Harrah grinned. "Pardo says I can yank this end, cause the explosion. I'm looking forward to it."

"Don't yank on it yet," Reilly said, and Harrah sniggered as the two men slowly made their way down the ridge, for the most part sliding on their buttocks, Reilly giving the roll of twine plenty of slack, angling away from the last batch of explosives. He ran out of twine, had to tie the end to another roll, and they continued their descent. When they reached the triangular reddish-brown boulder, maybe two hundred yards to the west and one hundred fifty feet below the last beaker of nitro, Reilly took in some of the slack and draped the twine over a sprouting juniper. At that moment, hoofbeats sounded, and Harrah drew his revolver, pressing his back against the boulder, peering down.

Two riders rounded the bend at a high lope, one of them whipping a large sombrero over his head. They reined up at the base of the canyon, and Harrah stood, holstering his gun. "Hey," he told Reilly, "that's Soledad."

"Yeah." Reilly pulled his hat low, and put his hand on the butt of the Bulldog tucked inside his waistband.

"Don't recognize the fellow with him," Harrah said, and removed his hat and waved down the ridge.

Reilly recognized him, though. He looked over his

shoulder, found the sun, and stepped over a few rods so that Soledad and L.J. Kraft wouldn't be able to see his face. The beard, also, might help.

"Mac!" Soledad called. "Mac! *El patrón*, he want you. At camp." Pointing back down the canyon.

Reilly's head bobbed.

"*Pronto, señor*," Soledad said, and neck-reined the horse, turning it back east.

"The Krafts?" Harrah called down. "They with you?"

"*Sí. Y tres muchachos.*"

Harrah glanced over his shoulder. "What did he say?"

He knew that much Spanish. "Yes, and thirteen men."

Grinning, Harrah turned back, and asked, "Where are you two off to?"

Soledad pointed out the canyon. "We go. Find *soldados*. Come back. Let *el patrón* know how far away they be."

"Good luck!" Harrah called to the riders as they galloped off, out of the canyon, into the rugged country that stretched on forever.

They watched the dust; then Harrah said, "You best get back to Pardo. Want me to water down them glasses of nitro again?"

"Yeah," Reilly said absently, but quickly changed his mind. "No. Let's not risk accidentally blowing one up. You just stay here. Keep an eye out."

"Suits me," Harrah said. He squatted behind the rock and fished out the makings for a smoke. Reilly ran his tongue over his cracked lips, then made his way down the slope, picked up the Evans carbine he had leaned against a boulder, and slowly walked westward through the canyon.

He had traveled maybe a hundred yards when he heard horses again. Sucking in a deep breath, Reilly thumbed back the hammer of the Evans and stood, waiting. Five horsemen rounded the bend and stopped their horses, kicking up a cloud of dust that swallowed Reilly. When the dust cleared, they saw Reilly pointing the rifle at the center rider. Of course, three of the men, including the man the Evans was trained on, were aiming revolvers at Reilly. The fourth had a shotgun cradled over the pommel; the fifth was too busy trying to control his skittish mare.

Reilly studied their faces and slowly lowered the rifle. He recognized none of the men. "You riding with Kraft?" he asked.

"Uh-huh." The man in the center, a big, burly man with a thick, dust-coated red beard, holstered his big Schofield, and the other riders did the same. "Well, reckon we's ridin' with Pardo and Kraft now."

"Kraft and Pardo," the man with the scattergun said, and a couple of the riders chuckled.

"You must be Mac," Dirty Red Beard said.

"I am. K.C. and W.W. back in the camp?"

"You know 'em?"

Reilly shrugged. "I've run into them a time or two."

"K.C.'s in camp," Dirty Red Beard said. "Gabbin' with Pardo. W.W.'s up on the hillside." He grinned a toothless smile. "Wanted to wet down the nitro his ownself. Duke took him up there."

"Nice-lookin' woman Pardo's got back yonder," a tall man in a linen duster said.

Reilly bit his lower lip. Damn. Dagmar was still in camp, hadn't made for the door over the ridge. He had hoped, prayed, she would, but knew she wouldn't. She just wouldn't leave him behind, damn her. On the other hand, Pardo wouldn't let Dagmar out of his sight, wouldn't give her a chance to make for the opening at the top of the canyon with her daughter.

"Kid with her?" Reilly asked, but he already knew the answer.

"Yeah," Linen Duster said. "She cusses more than Ezra."

Ezra, the man with the dirty red beard, spit out a stream of tobacco juice and made no other comment. Reilly gestured with his head down the canyon. "Soledad and L.J. rode out. What are y'all doing?"

Ezra pointed a gloved finger ahead. "K.C. told us to ride over here. Get into position. Won't be long now till the Army's comin' down here."

"To get massacred," Scattergun said, laughing again at his own joke.

Reilly nodded. "Harrah's on the southern side. Give him a halloo before you ride up there. Don't want one of y'all to get shot down, accidental-like."

"That's what we'll do." Dirty Red Beard tugged on the brim of his slouch hat. "Be seein' you, Mac."

"Good luck," Reilly said, "and stay clear of that nitro. Harrah knows where it's planted." He stepped between the horses as they trotted past. After a few yards, he looked over his shoulder, but saw only dust. He walked to the bend, and leaned against a white, egg-shaped boulder. He couldn't see the two wagons parked in the shade, but a couple of Kraft's men were crossing the road. On the northern rim of the canyon, he found two more of Kraft's men climbing among the rocks, looking for a good spot. Others would be on the southern side, but he couldn't find any. How many would that leave in camp? K.C. and Pardo, certainly. Swede Iverson? Maybe, though Iverson might have followed W.W. and Duke to the nitro. Then what? He looked to the north again, down a little lower, saw a dun-colored hat resting on a yucca. That's where the twine was. The man would jerk that twine to detonate the beakers of nitro on that side. Reilly wiped his brow.

He eased his way around the bend, trying to walk casually, toward the fortress of boulders that surrounded the camp. When he reached the edge, he listened, hearing voices, unable to make out the words. Then a footstep sounded, and he swung around, lifting the rifle to his waist, aiming the barrel at another man in a linen duster, the man pointing a long-barreled Colt at Reilly's head.

Reilly lowered the rifle. "I'm Mac," he said. "You with Kraft?"

The man nodded, and holstered the Colt. "They's waiting for you."

"Thanks," Reilly said, and walked past the man, looked up, saw nothing, then swung quickly and clubbed the man behind his left ear with the Evans' barrel. He caught the man as he fell silently and dragged him into the shade, pulled the Colt from the holster, and started to toss it away. Thought better of it, and shoved it in his waistband near the .44 Bulldog.

He looked again, listening, then wet his lips once more before he stood. Deftly, he untied the bandana hanging from the man's neck, rolled him onto his stomach, and used the piece of silk to tie his hands together. Next, he pulled the man's knife from its sheath, and slit the tails of the duster, tearing off one piece, which he used as a gag, and another, which he used to bind the man's ankles. The knife he pitched into a hole.

Afterward, Reilly picked up the Evans and slowly rose.

"All right, Reilly Francis McGivern," he said in a low whisper. "Let's start the ball."

CHAPTER THIRTY

Jim Pardo sweetened the coffee in K.C. Kraft's cup with a couple of fingers of rye before sitting beside him, and saying, "The coffee's cold, K.C., but I can't risk having no fire." Making sure K.C. Kraft didn't think Pardo was apologizing for anything.

"The whiskey'll help," Kraft said, and took a drink. "So, you haven't exactly told me your plans for after we kill all of those soldiers and muleskinners."

Pointing over the rocks, Pardo said, "We'll haul out the Gatlings and cannon, any other plunder we get, through a gateway in those rocks yonder. Beyond that, there's a smooth animal trail that winds down to the other side. Your boys are unloading the nitro from the back of that one buckboard, and I'll have them take the wagons to the other side of the canyon. We'll haul the Gatlings in those two wagons and pull the cannon behind it."

"Then what?"

"We raise dust for Mexico. Once we get there, we'll auction the guns off. I don't care if they go to the Mexican army or bandits. Whoever brings me—us, I mean—the highest bid gets the guns."

Kraft took another sip. His head shook wearily. "You really think you can pull this off?"

"I know it."

Shrugging, Kraft drained the coffee, and tossed the cup onto the rocks. "Must be nice to be confident."

"Must be nice to have two brothers," Pardo said. He had turned, facing south, looking up the canyon ridge, watching Duke and W.W. move from one beaker to the other, watering the nitro down with their canteens. A few rods below them, Swede Iverson was fingering the twine, moving down from the boulders to the detonation site.

"It isn't."

Pardo pushed back his hat, and gave Kraft a serious study. "What do you mean?"

"I mean having two brothers is a boil on my ass." He reached for the bottle, and took a long pull. "Two boils, come to think of it."

"Family's important," Pardo said.

"Yours, maybe. Not mine." He set the bottle down, and faced Pardo, unsmiling.

"You don't like your brothers?" Pardo reached for the bottle.

"L.J.'s all right. Don't say much. Does what I tell him to do. But my kid brother"—he jerked his thumb toward W.W.—"hell, the only reason I'm here is because of him."

"Well, I'm glad."

"I ain't. W.W.'s an asshole."

"You can't say that about your brother. He's family."

"You got a brother?" K.C. took the bottle from Pardo, and finished it, then tossed the bottle hard against the boulder, shattering the glass.

Pardo stared at K.C. a moment. "Had a kid brother, but he didn't live long. But I've kinda adopted one of my men. He should be along any moment. And I got my ma. She's dead, but I still talk to her."

"My mother was a bitch."

Pardo shot to his feet, began scratching the palm of his hand against the hammer of his Colt. "You shouldn't say that about your ma, Kraft. You shouldn't."

"Don't preach at me, Pardo." K.C. Kraft moved his hand toward his revolver. "And if you want to pull that Colt, you go right ahead. But you best remember this, Pardo: I got two brothers and thirteen men. You got, what? Five men?" He tilted his head toward Blanche and Dagmar. "And two petticoats." He snorted. "Hell, one ain't even in petticoats yet."

"Family's important," Pardo blubbered.

"Like I said, yours maybe. Mine ain't worth a crap."

Their eyes locked, and Pardo wet his lips, considered ending this partnership with a .44-40 slug, but a voice called down his name, and he turned away from Kraft, looked above the boulders, saw Swede Iverson hurrying down the ridge, kicking up dust as he ran.

"Pardo! Pardo!"

"What the hell's the matter with him?" Pardo said, and heard K.C. Kraft rising behind him.

The explosives man ran, cap in his hand, beads of sweat peppering his forehead, into the rock fortress. "Pardo," he said, gasping for breath. "It's the twine!"

"What about it?"

"It was cut." He wiped his brow, found a canteen, drank greedily.

"What do you mean?" Pardo asked.

"I mean it was cut. About fifty yards down from the last batch of nitro. If I hadn't checked it, when I yanked that cord, nothing would have happened. It was cut."

"Chewed by a pack rat likely," Pardo said. "Did you fix it?"

"Yeah." His sweaty head bobbed. "Tied it back together."

"Then there ain't nothing to worry about."

"But it was cut."

"Who the hell would have cut . . . ?" He turned, glaring at Dagmar, before his eyes drilled through the kid.

"Hell, no," Blanche said. "I didn't cut your damned string."

"Nobody else would have reason," Pardo said.

"Well, it ain't like you'd let me or my mother have a knife, is it?" the kid snapped back, causing K.C. Kraft to laugh.

"Feisty little thing, ain't she?" Kraft said.

"Where's Mac?" Iverson said.

"He's coming," Pardo said, and heard the wagons' traces jingling as Kraft's men took them out of the canyon.

Iverson whirled, screaming, "The nitro!"

"Take it easy, Swede," Pardo said. "We took the nitro out, put it in the shade over yonder. K.C.'s men are taking the wagons to the other side of the canyon."

Iverson took another drink of water, then tossed the canteen down. "I best go check the other twine. Make sure they're tight."

"That's a good plan," Pardo said, and shot another hard look at Blanche.

Iverson stood there like a sun-bathing lizard.

"Well?" Pardo demanded.

"Well what?" Iverson asked.

"Get the hell out of here," Pardo barked. "Go check

on those twine riggings. We can't have no mix-up, no mistake. That Army train'll be here before sundown."

He watched Iverson put on his hat, and hurry around the boulders.

Kraft was sitting back down in the shade, and Pardo joined him. "What were we talking about?"

With a grin, Kraft said, "About my fifteen men to your five."

"Five suits me," Pardo said. "I don't need fifteen. Never have. My five could take your fifteen." He snapped a finger. "Like that."

"Maybe. *Vamos a ver.*"

That made Pardo smile. Wade Chaucer had once said something similar, and, well, Wade had seen. Last thing he ever had seen.

"Maybe," Pardo said happily.

The girl was walking out of the camp. Pardo spun, demanding, "Where you off to?"

She glared at him. "To take a piss."

Which caused K.C. Kraft to guffaw.

"All right," Pardo said. "But don't squat over no scorpion."

When she had rounded the boulder, K.C. Kraft said, "I bet that little hellfire could take care of your five men."

"She's got a dirty mouth," Pardo said, and looked over at Dagmar. "You ought to tan that girl's hide, Dagmar. Wash her mouth out with lye soap. My Ma, she'd never tolerate such language from a girl."

Dagmar shrugged.

Pardo looked back at Kraft. "I been talking to my mother."

"I thought she was dead."

"She is, but mothers never really die. And Ruby

Pardo, well, hell, she was too ornery to let death keep her quiet."

"Heard you killed the man who shot her down."

"That's right. In Contention City."

"What did your mother say about that?"

Pardo chuckled. "Ma knew I'd do it." He shook his head. "It was Mac, my brother—well, my partner, the one I was telling you about, the one I've kinda adopted—he was the one who told me I could talk to Ma anytime, anywhere. And he was right."

"Uh-huh. You got any whiskey around here?"

"No. Plumb out."

"That's too bad."

"Anyway, Ma, she was always my partner. God how I loved that woman."

"Like I told you. My mother was a—"

"I know what you said. And you know what I said. Family. That's important. That's why I got Mac now. Mac and Dagmar." He looked over at her, saw her cleaning the plates with sand. He lowered his voice, letting Kraft in on a secret. "I had thought about taking Dagmar down below the border, selling her and that foul-mouthed kid of hers. She'd bring in a right smart of money, to the right slaver."

"She's a handsome woman," K.C. Kraft agreed.

"Yeah, but now I'm of a mind to keep her for myself."

Kraft snorted again, shaking his head.

"She owes me. I saved her hide from Major Ritcher. 'Course, I would have had to kill him before too long."

Kraft was giving Pardo a long, hard look. Finally, he shrugged, and asked, "You sure you don't have any whiskey around here?"

Pardo didn't answer. "Ma, she don't hold truck with that. She says that would be a bad mistake, me taking

Dagmar, keeping her. That's my Ma. Always looking after me. Never no woman good enough for her only living son. Ma, well, she didn't like Mac, neither. Told me I shouldn't trust him, and I didn't at first. Didn't even after he saved my hide from some possum-playing Apache buck. But I tell her, now, that Mac has earned his keep. She says she reckons Mac's all right."

"Where is this Mac?" Kraft said.

"I don't know. Should be here by now." He took off his hat, fanned himself with it. "You'll like Mac, Kraft. Best damned rifle shot I ever seen. Like I said, Ma, she says—now she says, I mean—that if Mac's all right with me, then he's all right with her. Good old Ma. He's all right in my book. It's a damned good thing I come across him, got him out of that prison wagon before he fried."

Kraft's eyes narrowed, and he turned to stare into Pardo's eyes. "What did you say?" He spoke in a measured voice.

"That Mac's all right in my book."

"After that." Kraft stood up, put his hand on the butt of his revolver.

"That I got him out of that prison wagon."

"Where?"

"'Long about Alkali Flat. They was transporting him to Texas. Apaches ambushed the deputies."

"He was in the wagon?" Urgency in Kraft's voice.

Pardo nodded. "About half dead."

"Handcuffed?"

Another nod. *What's bothering Kraft?*

"Big man, say about six feet tall? Broad shouldered? Dark hair and eyes? Three other lawmen lying dead near the wagon? And boots . . . his boots . . . did they have four-leaf clovers inlaid in the tops?"

"Yeah." Pardo wet his lips. "Do you know him?"

A roar of crazy laughter escaped Kraft's throat, and he whipped out the revolver, took a few steps toward the entrance to the fort, and, waving his gun over his head, he shouted up the canyon after spotting W.W. Kraft and Duke walking along the ridge line, "W.W.! W.W.! Get your ass down here on the double! It's Reilly McGivern! Hurry up! It's McGivern!"

His voice echoed across the canyon.

Mc-Giv-ern! Mc-Giv-ern! Mc-Giv-ern!

On the canyon, W.W. stopped, cocked his head, then started down, Duke following him a few rods behind.

"What the hell are you talking about?" Pardo demanded.

Kraft turned. "You damned fool. That man is no outlaw. That's Reilly McGivern. He's a deputy marshal. A federal lawman."

Pardo's face contorted. He rubbed his palm against the Colt's hammer.

"That wagon was hauling my two no-account brothers to Yuma," K.C. Kraft explained. "I busted them out. We gunned down two deputies, caught McGivern thanks to one of the deputies we'd bribed to help us. And W.W. tossed McGivern in the back to bake to death. Hell, I told him. He should have shot him, but you can't tell that stupid-ass brother of mine anything. He killed the deputy I'd paid to help us. Killed him, but not Reilly McGivern. Damned stupid son of a bitch." He swung around, looked up the canyon, but couldn't see his brother or Duke now. He still hollered, "Get your ass down here! Now!"

He took a step toward the opening.

CHAPTER THIRTY-ONE

"Hold it, K.C."

K.C. Kraft stopped, his boots sliding on the white rock, looked up, found Reilly McGivern perched in a deep crack in the top of the boulder. His tired eyes hardened, focused on the barrel of Reilly's repeating rifle aimed at the center of Kraft's chest.

"Don't move, Pardo," Reilly said, trying to keep both men in sight.

Pardo just sat down, knocked his hat off his head, and started guffawing. Pointing at Reilly, he said, "A lawman. A deputy marshal. Deputy *United States* marshal. I was gonna partner with him. My kid brother. Man whose life I saved from that Yavapai injun out of Wickenburg. Fifty-fifty split. With my pard. My adopted brother." He roared with laughter, and looked straight into the blue sky. "You hear that, Ma? Ain't that something, Ma? God, Ma, how could I ever have doubted you? You was right, Ma. You was absolutely right." He looked back at Reilly, still chortling as he pulled himself to his feet, still shaking his head. "You was right, Ma. You're always right. A law dog. A federal son-of-a-bitching law dog."

His right hand dashed for the holstered Colt.

At the same moment, Kraft leaped to his left, drawing his revolver.

Reilly swung the barrel after Kraft, pulled the trigger. Pardo's bullet slammed into the boulder at Reilly's head, spitting dust into his eyes. He couldn't see if his shot had hit Kraft or not. Turned, levering the Evans, he saw Pardo running, for a better position. He aimed. So did Pardo, but then a coffeepot slammed into Pardo's gun hand, knocked the Colt to the rocks. Pardo swore, dived for the gun, and Reilly held his fire as Dagmar Wilhelm leaped, wrapped her arms around Pardo's feet, tackled him to the ground.

Reilly turned. Behind him, out in the canyon, came the sound of horses, of gunfire. Suddenly, a bullet tore through his side, drove him backward. He dropped the Evans, felt himself sliding, desperately clawing, reaching for anything to hold only to continue his descent, and he toppled over the boulder, landed hard on the rocks, cracking a couple of ribs, the Evans crashing into a yucca plant. He forced himself up, saw K.C. Kraft coming at him, heard the crack of the revolver in Kraft's hand, saw a flash of flame and smoke shoot out of the barrel, felt the bullet rip through his left hand.

Crying out in pain, Reilly rolled to his left, toward the yucca, as K.C. Kraft swayed toward him, blood oozing from a hole in his right shoulder. He had to cock the Colt with his left hand. Steadied the barrel. As he rolled, Reilly jerked the Bulldog .44 from his waistband. Kraft's gun roared, but the bullet whined off a rock near Reilly's ear.

Two men dashed around the corner, behind Kraft, who turned, swinging his gun around. "Don't shoot!"

Duke yelled, and raised the Winchester in his hands above his head.

Reilly swore. It was Duke. And W.W. Kraft.

"It's McGivern!" K.C. Kraft said, and turned back, cocking the revolver with his off hand, as the Bulldog bucked in Reilly's, and a sea of crimson exploded from K.C. Kraft's chest. Reilly fired again, driving K.C. Kraft into a spin. Knowing the Bulldog was empty, he dropped it, jerked the long-barreled Colt he had taken from one of Kraft's men, cocked, aimed, fired in one motion. That bullet tore the hat off Duke's head.

"K.C.!" W.W. shouted. Took a step toward his brother, who lay writhing on the ground. Reilly's shot drove him back.

"Boss man!" Duke's voice. He fired a round from the Winchester, the bullet tearing a gash in Dagmar's right side, but the woman refused to let go of Pardo. Scratching. Pounding. Beneath her, Pardo grunted, lifting his hands in defense.

By now Reilly was on his feet, firing again, leaving the Evans in the yucca, running toward Dagmar, who was clawing at Pardo's face. Fired again. Grabbed Dagmar, pulled her behind an egg-shaped boulder as a cannonade of bullets bounced off the rocks.

He caught his breath. Looked up at Dagmar, whose left hand pressed against her side, blood oozing between her fingers. Reilly glanced at his own wounds. A bullet through his left hand. Two cracked ribs, maybe three. Bullet through his side, just above his right hip, that was bleeding profusely, but hadn't hit any vital organs. He checked the Colt.

Two shots left. "Hell," he said.

Beyond the fortress came the sound of gunfire, echoes bouncing across the canyon. Something was happening outside these rocks, but he had enough problems right here.

"Where's Blanche?" he asked.

"She went to answer nature's call," Dagmar said, her head hugging the rocky ground.

Reilly thumbed back the hammer, pulled himself up with a grimace and a curse, braced his back against the boulder. "She better keep her head down," he said, face tight against the pain.

"You all right?" he asked.

"I think so. It hurts, though."

Another four shots from Duke's Winchester sang out, bouncing across the rocks.

"Something's happenin', boss man!" Duke's nasal twang sang out as he levered another round into the Winchester. "Something's gone to hell."

"Shut up!" Pardo snapped. "Get Mac. I want him dead. I want Dagmar dead! Dead. You hear me. Kill them both!"

Suddenly, Dagmar lifted her head. "Did you hear that?" she asked, and Reilly was about to tell her to keep her damned head down, when he heard it, too.

Swede Iverson came up to the burly man with the brown goatee and dusty hat at the juniper, where Pardo and K.C. Kraft had sent him to cover the north-western edge of the canyon. The man spit out a mouthful of tobacco juice and eyed Iverson with suspicion.

"Morning," Iverson said, and the man grunted his reply as Iverson picked up the twine draped over a mesquite limb.

"What you doin'?" the man asked.

"Checking this twine. Making sure it's secure." He

pointed across the canyon. "Somebody cut the twine on that side. I fixed it. Want to make sure this one's all right."

"Well . . ." The man shifted the quid of tobacco to the other cheek. "Don't pull on that too hard."

Iverson ignored the silly comment. He didn't need some rawhider telling him how to handle nitroglycerin. Fingering the twine gently, he made his way up the canyon, leaning forward, fighting for his breath. So far, the twine was perfect. He stopped, mopped the sweat off his face, looked up. Shots suddenly rang out from the camp below, and he lurched to his feet. Thought he heard shots on the eastern side of the canyon, and he turned toward the man at the juniper, who was rising, bringing up his Henry rifle.

Something flashed above him, and Iverson swung around, looked, his mouth dropping open. Out of the crack in the canyon wall came a dark figure, crouching, followed by another. One of them stopped, raised a rifle.

Iverson spun. He screamed down at the Kraft man by the juniper. "Apaches!" he shouted. "Apaches!" He started running, when the breath slammed out of his lungs, and he felt himself driven forward, tumbling, rolling over the rocks and cactus, sliding down a few feet. He looked up, tried to get his legs to work, but they wouldn't. He couldn't even feel them. He felt something roll from his lips, and lifted his head, looked at the blood pumping from his chest, heard the sucking sound each time he drew an agonizing breath.

"I been shot," he said. Blood frothed from his lips. He looked up. Saw the Apaches running down the canyon, firing, reloading, firing. He heard the Kraft man behind him grunt; then came the noise of the man's Henry rifle clattering as it tumbled down the canyon.

More figures came from the doorway through the top of the canyon. A few Apaches, followed by white men. In blue uniforms. Yellow stripes down the seams of their pants.

"Soldiers." Iverson tried to shout a warning, but his lungs burned. Turning his head, he found he lay near the twine. He reached, grabbed it. "I'll show you. . . ." He jerked it hard, sending a spasm of pain through his chest and neck. He still couldn't feel anything below his waist.

Nothing happened.

He jerked again.

Then, the Apache was on him, wielding a knife in his hand, slicing Swede Iverson's throat, and moving on. More moccasins ran past him, followed by boots. Swede Iverson still gripped the twine. The last thing he heard was the sound of a trumpeter blowing the charge.

"Boss man!" Duke shrieked. "It's the cavalry. It's the damned Army."

"It can't be," Pardo said, but he heard the blaring trumpet, the scores of shots, pounding of hoofs. He whirled. "Get up to that nitro. Pull the twine. Pull it, damn you. Blow it up!" He saw Duke spin, crouch, and head around the corner.

It was going to hell. How could it have gone to hell?

"My brother!" W.W. Kraft began screaming. "You son of a bitch. You bastard. You killed my brother."

Finding the youngest Kraft kneeling by his brother, Pardo could see W.W. was right. K.C. lay on his back, spread-eagled, sightless eyes staring into that brilliant blue sky. Then, like a damned fool, W.W. rose, tripped over his dead brother's boots, started a dash for the boulders behind which Dagmar and Mac were hiding, pulling the Colt's trigger as he ran.

"Come back here!" Pardo yelled, but found himself chasing after him, admiring W.W., even if the kid was an idiot, because W.W. was showing the dearly departed K.C. Kraft a thing or two. About family. About blood. About honor.

W.W. Kraft's pistol roared, knocked a chunk of boulder off. Suddenly, Mac rolled out from the side of the boulder, both hands gripping a long-barreled Colt. Flame shot from the barrel, and W.W. staggered. Mac's gun roared again, and W.W. dropped to his knees, sending his gun sailing toward a mesquite. He let out a wild groan, and fell on his back, joining his brother in death.

Pardo saw Mac raise the barrel, pull the trigger, heard, above the echoes and cacophony throughout the canyon, the hammer click as it struck an empty cylinder. With a grin, Pardo aimed his Colt, and pulled the trigger.

It, too, snapped empty.

He stopped, threw his useless gun at Mac, the pistol striking the rocky ground in front of the lawman's face, and bouncing over his head. Pardo kept running, leaning over, sweeping up W.W. Kraft's revolver, cocking it, squeezing the trigger. The bullet knocked the heel off Mac's right boot.

Don't rush your shot, Jimmy, he heard Ma's scolding voice.

Pardo staggered toward them. Dagmar ran around the corner, screaming, her left side drenched in blood, her face wild with anger, like some damned animal. She wasn't a Three-Fingers Lacy, that was for sure. He swung the barrel of Kraft's revolver, heard the crunch, saw the wild woman drop at his feet, unconscious, and he tripped over her. Got up. Saw Mac crawling toward the yucca, where his Evans repeater rested.

With a snigger, Pardo began pushing out the empty casings as he walked, filling the cylinder with fresh loads from his shell belt, praising the late W.W. Kraft for having the good sense to carry a .44-40 Colt, same as Pardo did, and when he reached Mac, he thumbed back the hammer, and grinned.

"Hey, Bloody Jim!" a voice called.

When Pardo spun toward the voice, he felt a bullet rip into his gut. He fired, knowing he had missed, as another slug hit just about the same place the first bullet had. His knees buckled, and he fell to a seated position, looking up in surprise.

Staring at the person who had shot him.

CHAPTER THIRTY-TWO

She dropped the smoking .32 Triumph, now empty, and ran to her mother, falling to her knees, gently rolling her mother on the ground. "Mama?" Blanche Gottschalk said, then more urgently, "Mama! Are you all right?"

Dagmar's eyes fluttered. Blood leaked from the corner of her head, just above the left eye. A vicious bruise was already forming from where Jim Pardo had buffaloed her with the revolver barrel.

"Mama?"

"I'm all right," she said, and forced a smile.

At which point, Bloody Jim Pardo, sitting on the rocky ground, legs out in front of him, both hands clutching his bleeding stomach, started giggling.

"A kid," he said, and coughed up blood. Swallowed, leaned his head back, and laughed savagely. "A kid. Bloody Jim Pardo is killed by a kid."

Outside, beyond this rocky fortress, bullets continued to whine, horses galloped, men screamed.

"A kid. A damned snot-nosed kid." Pardo shuddered.

"And a girl to boot. You hear that Ma? Ain't that something? I'm gut-shot by a ten-year-old girl!"

Reilly McGivern kept crawling toward his rifle in the yucca.

Pardo fell onto his back, still laughing, coughing, bleeding, dying.

Blanche's mother slowly sat up. She leaned against her daughter for support.

"No!"

Both Blanche and her mother looked at Pardo, who was scrambling to his feet. "No, Ma. I ain't dying like this. Don't you worry, Ma. Bloody Jim Pardo ain't being killed by a girl." He fell against the boulder, but didn't fall, and pushed himself forward, weaving his way, the Colt still in his hand. He pointed it at the crawling Reilly McGivern, and fired, but tripped over W.W. Kraft's legs, spoiling his aim, sending him to his knees. Pardo shook his head, coughed again, and rose.

"Duke!" he yelled. "Duke! Pull the twine. Set off the nitro." He was weaving toward the opening. Fired another round at McGivern, but the shot thudded into a mesquite limb. McGivern had reached his Evans, yanked it out of the yucca, brought the stock to his shoulder, and swung the barrel, but by then, Jim Pardo had rounded the boulder, out of sight.

Her mother said something, and started to her feet. She leaned on Blanche for support, and they moved. Reilly McGivern had pulled himself up, using the Evans as a crutch, and staggered hurriedly toward the opening. He slid to his knees, brought the Evans into position, fired. As Blanche and her mother made their way toward the lawman, another figure slid inside the opening. Reilly spun, aimed the rifle, then lowered it and shook his head at the young cavalry soldier who was busy reloading his revolver.

"Hello, Reilly."

"Jerry." McGivern shook his head, tried to clear away the cobwebs, amazed to find Second Lieutenant Jeremiah Talley sitting beside him. "What . . . ?"

"Long story," Talley said, snapped the loading gate shut on his Remington, turned, and fired. Reilly saw one of Kraft's men tumble.

Spinning, Reilly jacked another round in the Evans, but Pardo had dived behind a boulder. He saw the madman's hand grab the twine he had cut earlier this morning—but that Swede Iverson had repaired just minutes earlier—and give it a savage yank.

Reilly cringed, then heard Pardo's laughter.

"I took care of it," Blanche whispered. "Told Pardo I had to take a piss. Cut it with my teeth."

Cackling, Jim Pardo rolled over onto his back, and jerked the twine. Nothing happened. Beside him knelt Duke, Winchester rifle lying in the dirt, the stupid oaf holding both hands against his right ear, too big a coward to have tried to detonate the nitro himself.

"An Apache," he whimpered. "An Apache shot off my ear, boss man."

Pardo laughed, and yanked the twine again. There was no resistance, and, certainly, no deafening explosion.

"What's an Apache doing riding with soldiers, boss man? You don't reckon they teamed up to beat us, do you? Apaches and the Army, riding together?"

"They're scouts, you damned fool." Pardo coughed.

From below, came a shout. "You two men! There's no escape. Give up. Now." Pardo rolled over, pulled himself up, and fired two rounds at the officer demanding their surrender. He laughed again, raised the Colt, pulled the trigger. Empty.

He let the pistol fall into the dirt, and pressed his hands against his blood-soaked shirt. "Oh, Ma. I can't believe this is happening to me."

Beside him, Duke rose, his left hand over his head, right hand still pressing against his bloody ear, and started walking down the hill. "Don't shoot. I quit. Don't shoot."

Pardo chuckled, dragged himself closer to the Winchester. Picked it up, braced the barrel against the boulder, and shot Duke between the shoulder blades. Watched the coward fall and slide a few feet, dead as Pardo soon would be. Cackling, he butted the rifle's stock in the dirt, and forced himself up, leaned against the boulder, and jacked another round into the chamber.

"Give up, Pardo!" a voice called up.

Pardo lifted the rifle, and staggered away from the boulder. He fired, not at Mac, not at that officer demanding his surrender, not at the Apaches and bluebellies gathered in the rocks below. Swayed, stumbled, worked the lever, fired again. Laughing as he did it.

"What the hell's he shooting at?" Jeremiah Talley asked.

Fear tightened Reilly's face. He drew a bead, pulled the trigger, saw a puff of dust fly off Pardo's side, and drive him back, but the son of a bitch didn't fall. His Winchester roared again.

"What the hell?" Reilly said, cocking the Evans, firing again. Worked the lever. Pulled the trigger. The rifle clicked empty.

Pardo's Winchester roared. Ten shots ripped the earth, whined off the rocks around him. The troopers and Apache scouts were doing their best to kill that crazy man, but shooting uphill, at a moving target, with all the dust in the air would challenge the best marksmen. Pardo cocked and fired the Winchester as he swayed down the hill.

Reilly remembered the extra shell, which he quickly fingered out of his vest pocket, began to reload the Evans.

Beside him, Talley's Remington roared, but Pardo was out of range for a six-shooter. Reilly jacked the last round into the Evans, aimed, fired. This time Pardo hit the ground, and slid a few feet down.

Reilly sighed, looked at Talley, and said hoarsely, "He was going for the nitro. Ten beakers of it. Over there."

A grin spread across Talley's face. "I'm glad we had—"

"Oh, hell!" Blanche blurted. She was pointing. Reilly turned, his mouth dropping open. Jim Pardo had risen, worked the Winchester. Another bullet from an Apache's Springfield hit his shoulder, but Pardo kept coming, firing the Winchester from his hip. Disappearing behind the boulders.

"Damn!" Reilly pushed himself to his feet, using the Evans as a crutch. Reached out for Blanche and Dagmar with his free hand.

"Run!" he yelled. "Run!"

From behind the boulders came the shots from Pardo's Winchester.

Jerry Talley had stepped out, waving his revolver over his head, shouting in Spanish, English, and

Apache for everyone to retreat. Reilly staggered, dropped the Evans. Soldiers tried to mount horses. Apaches ran past them. Reilly tried to push Blanche ahead. He stumbled, fell flat on his face. Moaned, "Go on," but heard Dagmar's sobs. Felt himself being dragged up. He draped one arm around Dagmar, the other over Jerry Talley.

"Come on!" Blanche screamed.

Her shout was drowned out by a tremendous explosion that knocked all four of them off their feet.

Jim Pardo fired the Winchester. Saw the bullet kick up dust just inches from the blanket-wrapped crate in the shade. He worked the lever, jerked the trigger, but the Winchester was empty.

"That's all right," he said, falling to his knees, walking on his knees toward the crate. "That's all right, Ma." Blood now poured from both corners of his lips, and he fell forward, dragging the Winchester behind him, until he reached the crate. Pulled himself up.

Hearing the terrified screams of men beyond the rocks.

Laughing, he shoved off some of the blankets.

"Hey, Ma." He raised the rifle by the barrel above his head. "How about this, Ma?" Brought the walnut stock down on the crate.

Then felt the breath of hell.

CHAPTER THIRTY-THREE

The explosion knocked George Crook's mule to its knees and pitched the general into the sand. He landed on his right shoulder, rolled over, and almost immediately felt hands attempting to pull him up, dust him off, anxious voices asking, "Are you all right, sir?"

Crook shoved off the arms, found his pith helmet, set it on his head, and rose on his own volition. He looked at the smoke and dust belching from around the bend. Then, higher up the canyon's southern wall, another explosion rang out, and again, George Crook was knocked onto his rear. This time, before anyone could reach him, a third explosion sounded, followed immediately by a fourth. On the other side of the canyon came another terrific roar, trailed by three more almost simultaneously.

Behind the general, horses screamed, soldiers swore, hoofs stomped. Sitting down, his pith helmet knocked askew, Crook tugged on his forked beard and stared at the smoke and dust up the canyon, smoke stretching like he had never seen, heading for the top of the world, the steady roar of a landslide as the southern walls came tumbling down, and the northern boulders slid down, tearing a wide swath as they descended.

"Lord Jehovah!" an officer shrieked in Crook's ear, and Crook, feeling twice his fifty-six years, pulled himself to his feet. A gust of hot wind took the approaching smoke and grit and dust southward.

"We've got men in there!" a captain screamed, pointing down the canyon that was engulfed by smoke and dust.

"Steady," Crook said, and took a few tentative steps ahead of his command. He bit his bottom lip.

Out of the carnage thundered a riderless horse, which a few troopers tried to stop, but failed. Then . . . nothing . . . for the longest while.

Rocks and boulders continued to tumble down both sides of the canyon, kicking up more dust.

"Talley!" the captain shouted. "Mister Talley!" He turned, faced the general with a face ashen.

"Steady," Crook said again, and took another step forward.

Now came two more horses, one riderless, the other carrying a soldier leaning forward. This time, the troopers managed to stop both mounts, and pulled a corporal from the saddle.

"It's Corporal Cohan, General!" a first sergeant shouted. "Georgie," the sergeant said, softer, patting the sides of Corporal Cohan's face. "Georgie, can you hear me, Georgie? It's me, Rocky."

"Mr. Bourke," Crook called out in a stentorian voice.

"Yes, General," his adjutant said.

"Fetch my ambulance. Also, send a galloper back to the wagon train. Tell them we need anybody who has ever set a broken bone or bandaged a cut up here on the double."

"Yes, sir."

"We might need anybody who can handle a spade or say last rites," a trooper whispered. Crook thought about rebuking the young man, but instead, took another step.

An Apache ran out of the dust, followed by a few other riders, more horses without soldiers, and some staggering soldiers.

Crook turned. "Help them," he barked, and his soldiers raced forward.

Spotting the general, the Apache ran over. *"Nantan Lupan,"* he said, calling Crook by his Apache name, Grey Fox. He pointed into the inferno, and sank to his knees, shaking his head. His black hair was singed, he stank to high heaven, his buckskin shirt was covered with grit, blood.

"Yes," Crook said softly. "I see."

As the rumbling of rocks died down, he heard other noise from inside the smoke and dust. Apaches singing their death songs. Soldiers praying. Horses screaming. More troopers came out, coughing. Others carried their wounded comrades, some dragging them. Crook found a rock, and sat down, took off his helmet, and mopped his thinning, sweat-soaked hair with a handkerchief. He looked into the cloud. Nobody else emerged from the carnage. Still, he waited. One minute . . . two . . . five . . .

"Sir," a lieutenant said. "Requesting permission to ride in there."

"Very good, Mr. Kincaid. But let's wait ten more minutes. I don't want to lose—" He jumped to his feet, stretched out his arm.

From the smoke and dust emerged a short man. No, it was a girl. A young kid. She was followed by a man, supported by a woman on his left and a man— *Mr. Talley, by God!*—on his right.

"Help them!" Crook cried. "Help them, by thunder!"

* * *

Reilly McGivern opened his eyes to find himself shaded by a sea of dusty blue uniforms and a man with a forked salt-and-pepper beard dressed more for Africa than Arizona. He tried to swallow, but the attempt hurt like blazes. His head was resting on something soft, and he turned his neck, despite the pain, and looked into a pair of mesmerizing green eyes.

"Hey," he said, "you're alive."

Gwendolyn Morgan lifted his hand to her lips, kissed it, and blinked away tears. "Yes, my love, and so are you." Her face looked battered, her eyes red from tears, but she looked beautiful.

Something squeezed his other hand, and he looked over, saw Dagmar Wilhelm, her head bandaged, another bandage wrapped tightly just above her waist. She was holding his hand, smiling.

"Hey," she said.

Reilly wet his lips. "Blanche?"

"I'm fine," he heard the kid call out from behind him.

He looked back at Gwen. "How did . . . ?"

"Marshal, perhaps I should ask the questions here," a deep voice said, and Reilly watched the man with the pith helmet drop to a knee beside his chest.

"My surgeon will be here directly, Marshal," the voice said. "I am George Crook."

"Yes, General."

"You are Reilly McGivern?"

"Yes, sir."

"You have quite a lot of explaining to do."

"Yes, sir. Where are the Gatling guns, General?"

Crook frowned. "Fort Bowie," he said at last. He nodded at Gwen. "Miss Morgan ran into one of my Apache scouts at McCoy's Well, Marshal," Crook explained. "He saw Major Ritcher attacking her, but, unfortunately, Major Ritcher escaped. But I'll hang him when I catch him."

"You don't have to worry about that, sir. Ritcher's dead. Pardo killed him."

"And Pardo?"

Reilly smiled faintly. "Ashes to ashes, and dust to dust."

Crook looked at the still-smoking canyon. "He detonated the nitro, then?"

"Yes, sir. Blew himself up in the process."

"Blew this canyon to hell. Mr. Powers tells me it will take engineers six months to perhaps a year to clear this canyon."

"Yes, sir. I'm sorry about that. . . ."

"Don't apologize." Crook looked over his shoulder. In a muffled voice, he said, "You've done well." He spoke louder. "Today, at least. After we heard Miss Morgan's story, I countermanded the orders, and had the Gatling guns and howitzer delivered to Fort Bowie, the rest of the train proceeding on toward Lowell. We hoped to trap Pardo and his men here." He sighed. "I guess we succeeded, despite this bloody mess."

"Sir," Reilly said.

"Yes, Marshal?"

"There's nitro planted all along the sides of the eastern end of the canyon, too. They haven't exploded yet. I can show you. . . ." He bit his lip from pain. "I can . . ."

"You rest." Crook was standing. "Bring me the prisoners!" he barked, and a couple of minutes later, four troopers shoved two men into the center.

Reilly wet his lips. Soledad kept his head down, his right arm in a sling, his shoulder stained with dried blood. Beside him, hands manacled behind his back, stood Harrah, a dirty, bloodstained rag wrapped tightly over his left thigh.

"Can one of these men find the explosives?" Crook asked.

Reilly nodded. "He knows where they are." He lifted a finger at Harrah. "The Mexican wasn't here when Swede Iverson planted them."

"Very well," Crook said. He grabbed the manacles and jerked Harrah toward him. "You filthy piece of murderous trash. You will lead ten of my men to these explosive."

"I ain't doing . . ."

"You'll do what I say, mister, or by grab I will have you executed right here and now by firing squad!"

He shoved Harrah to an awaiting sergeant, who in turn, pushed Harrah through the crowd.

Reilly jutted his chin at Soledad. "There was a man riding with him."

"Draped over the saddle, Marshal," Crook said. "Dead. Sergeant Sullivan recognized the corpse as L.J. Kraft."

"That's right, sir."

"And Kraft's brothers? Were they . . . ?"

Reilly tilted his head westward. "Back there. Buried, most likely. I killed them."

Reilly closed his eyes. He felt one hand being lifted, pressed against Gwen's lips. Felt the other being lifted, too, pressed against Dagmar's lips. He felt himself drifting away. . . .

The surgeon shoved his way through the crowd, dropped to his knees, began fumbling through his black satchel while he felt for Reilly McGivern's pulse.

George Crook held his breath until the major shot him a glance and said, "He's just sleeping, General."

"Good," Crook said. "Will he live?"

The major hooked a thumb at the caldron up the canyon. "If he survived that, General, a couple of bullet holes shan't bury him."

"Good," Crook said again. "But wake him up. I am not finished with my interrogation. Marshal McGivern still has a lot to explain, especially his behavior of late. Wake him up."

A boot slammed into his ankle, hurt like blazes, and Crook turned around, hobbling, half a mind to shoot some soldier for insubordination. Instead, he found himself looking down into the bright green eyes of a filthy, bloody, ten-year-old girl.

"I'd let Reilly get some sleep, General," the girl said, and looked down, grinning at the deputy marshal. "Lord knows, the son of a bitch has earned it."

THE LAST GUNFIGHTER SERIES BY
WILLIAM W. JOHNSTONE

__**The Drifter**
0-8217-6476-4 $4.99US/$6.99CAN

__**Reprisal**
0-7860-1295-1 $5.99US/$7.99CAN

__**Ghost Valley**
0-7860-1324-9 $5.99US/$7.99CAN

__**The Forbidden**
0-7860-1325-7 $5.99US/$7.99CAN

__**Showdown**
0-7860-1326-5 $5.99US/$7.99CAN

__**Imposter**
0-7860-1443-1 $5.99US/$7.99CAN

__**Rescue**
0-7860-1444-X $5.99US/$7.99CAN

__**The Burning**
0-7860-1445-8 $5.99US/$7.99CAN

Available Wherever Books Are Sold!

Visit our website at **www.kensingtonbooks.com**